WHAT OTHERS ... YING G

Brandi creates strong...
will touch readers' hearts.

AUTHOR OF *CHESAPEAKE* ...

...ION)

Brandi ... ...ption
and fo... ...Their
heartw... ...l plot
will ke... ...NLEY
...R OF
...ERIES

Brandi ... ...acters
who w... ...page
is turn...

...OGERS
...S AND
...ERIES

Brand... ...g and
heart...

...NEALY
...SERIES

Not a... ...weaves
an inf... ...The
more ... brave
settlers I became. Truly a rewarding read.

—DONITA K. PAUL
BEST-SELLING AUTHOR OF THE DRAGON KEEPERS CHRONICLES
AND CHRONICLES OF CHIRIL

A Windswept PROMISE

Brides of
Assurance

BOOK TWO

A Windswept PROMISE

BRANDI BODDIE

REALMS

Most CHARISMA HOUSE BOOK GROUP products are available at special quantity discounts for bulk purchase for sales promotions, premiums, fund-raising, and educational needs. For details, write Charisma House Book Group, 600 Rinehart Road, Lake Mary, Florida 32746, or telephone (407) 333-0600.

A WINDSWEPT PROMISE by Brandi Boddie
Published by Realms
Charisma Media/Charisma House Book Group
600 Rinehart Road
Lake Mary, Florida 32746
www.charismahouse.com

Cover design by Bill Johnson
Design Director: Justin Evans

Visit the author's website at www.brandiboddie.com.

Library of Congress Cataloging-in-Publication Data:
Boddie, Brandi.
  A windswept promise / by Brandi Boddie. -- First edition.
      pages cm. -- (Brides of assurance ; book 2)
  Summary: "Book two of the Windswept Promise series
Pampered town belle Sophie Charlton has always secretly
enjoyed the attention of cowboy Dusty Sterling, a hired worker
on her family's farm, even though she'd never tell him so. But
can she go against the will of her family, who insist that she

make a good match in Assurance's most eligible bachelor? Series Description In the 1870s Kansas was a place of new beginnings and hope as people from many classes and cultures arrived looking for a fresh start. Brides of Assurance follows the lives of three different women from three very different cultures, in small-town assurance, Kansas as they fall in love, overcome the adversities of prairie life, and make choices that will affect their faith and relationships forever. Torn between the day's cultural expectations and the plans God has for them, they must rely on their courage, tenacity, and faith to get them through. "-- Provided by publisher.

ISBN 978-1-62136-281-4 (paperback) -- ISBN 978-1-62136-649-2 (e-book)

1. Frontier and pioneer life--Fiction. 2. Kansas--Fiction. I. Title.
PS3602.O32564W56 2014
813'.6--dc23

2014024860

First edition

14 15 16 17 18 — 9 8 7 6 5 4 3 2 1
Printed in the United States of America

In memory of my mother, Patricia,
who taught me to always stand
strong for what I believe in.

Acknowledgments

I OWE EVERYTHING FIRST and foremost to my Lord and Savior Jesus Christ.

Once again, I would like to thank my editor, Lori Vandenbosch, for her continued work in making my manuscript ready for publication.

The team at Charisma House, for their enthusiasm in introducing the Brides of Assurance series.

My agent, Kimberly Shumate, for her knowledge and dedication to helping me grow as an author.

There were so many other people involved during the stages of completing this book, whether that was through the actual writing process or offering advice and words of comfort over Starbucks coffee. I can't possibly list them all here, but their friendship is invaluable.

And last, but certainly not least, my readers, who continue to show their support.

CHAPTER 1

April 1871, Assurance, Kansas

$\mathcal{S}$OPHIE, YOUR JAMBALAYA'S burning!"

As her younger brother David called, Sophie Charlton dashed out of her bedroom and ran down the stairs into the kitchen. A pot gurgled on the step stove, brown bubbles spilling out from under the lid. She grabbed a towel from the table and hoisted the pot by its handles away from the hot surface. Her brother simply stood by the stove and watched.

"David, why did you let the flame get too hot underneath?" She opened the firebox door and inspected the kindling as it burned to ash.

"Ma said not to touch the food. It's for the Founders Day Festival."

"It wouldn't have been for anything if you had let it burn. This is supposed to go into my food basket."

"I called you to come downstairs, didn't I?" He gave her a matter-of-fact look.

"At the very last moment." Sophie shut the door to the stove and went to the pot of jambalaya. Stock trickled down into the grooves of the table. Steam rushed out as she lifted the lid.

"Is it bad?" David craned his neck to see.

"No, the stock boiled a bit too high but I think it'll still be alright." She grabbed a long-handled spoon and prodded the

1

mixture of sausage, peppers, and tomatoes. "Next time you see it boiling over, take it off the stove. Don't call me all the way from upstairs."

"Well, it's your dish. I ain't the one trying to enter some silly town belle contest."

"It's not silly." Sophie glanced at her freshly laundered and starched yellow-striped dress to make sure no stock had spilled on it. A lady's garments should always be pristine. "And 'ain't' isn't a word, David. You're sixteen years old. How often must I tell you that?"

"That I'm sixteen years old?"

"No, that your grammar is—never mind. I don't have time for this. I have to get ready. Go outside and help Dusty with the wagon." She left the pot to cool on the table's surface next to the pie she baked earlier.

"Dusty's already done hitchin' the horses up. See out the window."

Sophie viewed the family's wagon and the team of horses waiting in front of the walkway on the warm April Saturday. The pair of bay geldings stared past the fence at the main road into town, black blinders strapped on their heads. Her father's hired worker was nowhere to be seen. "Where is Dusty?"

"Probably getting cleaned up. You should finish dressing too."

Stating the obvious. She hated how her brother thought that made him sound clever. "Do not touch that pot. I'll be back down in a moment."

Sophie returned upstairs and passed her parents' room, where she could hear her mother and father talking as they got ready for the festival. She grinned to hold back a squeal. Finally, she was allowed to compete for the chance to be crowned Assurance's town belle. Her mother thought she had been too young to compete in prior years, and last year, her family wasn't in town for the festival at all. This was Sophie's chance.

She walked into her bedroom where Linda, her best friend, waited to help with her hair and dress. "Did it burn?"

"The jambalaya? No, but I hope it'll still taste good. Men will bid on that basket."

Linda rolled her eyes. "Sophie, you know most of those men are coming out to see you. They don't care if you stick a brick in that basket with a saucer of hay."

"But the contestants' names won't be on the baskets to let them know which is which."

"I don't think you have anything to worry about. Now, what ribbon do you want to lace your bonnet with, the yellow or the light blue?"

Sophie chose the ribbon in Linda's left hand. "The blue. We need to hurry. The judging starts in less than two hours."

Linda had her hair styled and topped with a bonnet within fifteen minutes. Sophie checked her reflection with the mirror on the vanity table and pinched her cheeks hard until her efforts were rewarded with two pink marks. "I have to pack the food."

"It can't be cool already." Linda fluffed Sophie's bangs out from beneath her bonnet with a comb.

"It'll just have to cool on the way to town then. Go get in the wagon. Mother and Daddy should already be out there. I'm coming." Sophie picked up her skirt and ran on the tip-toes of her cream side-button boots.

She followed mud prints from a pair of larger boots into the kitchen. "Dusty!"

The cowhand stood over her pot of jambalaya, holding the lid in a dirt-stained hand. Bits of grass fell from his canvas shirt to land dangerously close to the rim. "Howdy, Miss Sophie."

"Dustin Sterling, you get your filthy face out of my

jambalaya." She marched up to him and snatched the lid from his hand. "What do you think you're doing?"

"The smell was real good drifting outside. I just wanted to know what you were makin'." His Texas drawl remained calm and unhurried as he stood to his full six feet. Sophie gripped the lid tighter. How would it look on top of his head in place of that ever-present tan Stetson? If only she could reach that high.

"You're worse than David. I'm making this for the festival. And why aren't you cleaned up? We have to leave in minutes."

"It won't take long for me to scrub my face and change shirts. Is that food for lunch or supper?"

"Neither. I'm entering my basket for bid as part of the town belle contest."

He looked over her with hazel eyes. "You sure make a pretty picture with that bonnet."

"Why, thank you." The urge to put the lid on his head receded. "Hopefully, the judges will think so too."

"Can anyone make a bid on the baskets?"

Sophie pulled two bowls from the cupboard and a large porcelain jar. "Any man. Every lady in the contest will have a basket, but they will be unmarked. The winner gets the basket to take on a picnic along with the lady who prepared it."

"So the winner won't know who he gets to take on the picnic?"

"That's right." Sophie scooped the still-steaming jambalaya out of the pot and ladled it into the jar, careful not to spill any of it on her dress. Dusty should know she didn't have time to sit and visit with him. Why did he persist on trying his luck? Cowboys. So brash and overconfident. She sealed the jar with a cork.

"I just might enter a bid, seein' as how I know what will be in your basket."

She paused. "You wouldn't."

His teeth shone white in his tanned face as he grinned.

"Dusty, no. It's my first time entering the contest. Don't spoil it for me."

"How am I spoiling it for you? You should be happy you got at least one guaranteed bid on that—what did you say that rice and sausage was called?"

"Jambalaya."

"Jambalaya," he repeated in sing-song. "Smells almost like what the Chili Queens sell on the river down in San Antonio."

"Hmph." Sophie hunted for a basket on a lower pantry shelf. The more nondescript a container, the less chance he'd have of distinguishing it from the others. "I'll have you know this is a Creole recipe passed down in my family, not some street fare to peddle around on a cart. You wouldn't like it anyway. I made it spicy."

"I'm gonna place a bid on that basket, anyhow."

She huffed. "Why? Picnic or no picnic, I don't want you trying to court me. I told you before."

His dirt-caked boot heels made dull clicks on the floor as he went through the side entrance of the kitchen that led to the bunkhouse out back. "And I told *you* before. One day, Miss Sophie. You'll come around."

"Not today or any day that my feet touch the green earth," she called after him.

He whistled a tune that carried across the field.

CHAPTER 2

SOPHIE DIDN'T MEAN what she said. Dusty had been around her long enough to know when she was mad and when she was just teasing. And today she was nothing but all caught up in trying to win that town belle contest.

Dusty rode his stallion, Gabe, behind the Charlton wagon as it rolled along the hard-packed dirt road. The bright sun overhead had a mind to burn a hole through his white dress shirt. He shifted in the saddle, hating how his waistcoat felt like a wool blanket around his middle. Too hot a day to be gussied up.

He loosened two buttons at the bottom. Was this how women felt wearing those corsets? He stole a glance at Sophie in the wagon. She shielded herself from the sun with a frilly white parasol, twirling the handle one way and another. Must be nervous.

He couldn't see what she had to be so fraught about entering the town belle contest. She was the prettiest girl in seven county seats and he didn't need to see them all to know.

Sophie touched her forehead with a dainty lace-gloved hand. He guessed the heat was starting to get to her.

"You ladies doing alright?" He spoke to Linda and all three members of the Charlton female line: Sophie, her mother, and eight-year-old Rosemarie. "I have some water if you need a drink." He hoped Sophie would be the one to respond.

Mrs. Charlton answered him. "Thank you, Dusty, but we have a jug here on the floorboard."

Dusty took a swig of lukewarm water from his canteen as they reached the heart of Assurance, the town square. It served dual purposes today, decorated with banners for both the festival and posters for the upcoming mayoral election in September. The air buzzed with the excited chatter of the townsfolk—newcomers and longstanding citizens—as they made their way to the center of the street where a stage had been set up and arrayed with flowers. Banners hung from shop storefronts. The main sign stood out on the roof of the town hotel like a flag, with several yards of fabric and the words FOUNDERS DAY painted in blue letters.

"I see Katherine from school." Rosemarie jabbed her little finger in the direction of the stage front. "I want to go stand beside her. Ouch! Bernard, stop it."

The youngest male sibling of the family took to pulling his sister's hair a second time. "I see Katherine from school," he mimicked.

"The contest is about to start." Sophie rose from her seat in the wagon. "I still have to enter my basket for the bidding." To Dusty's amusement, she picked up her basket as though she were going to leap off the wagon with it in one hand, parasol in the other.

"Bernard, don't pull your sister's hair again. And girls, both of you sit down. There's plenty enough time for you to get to the stage after I take the wagon to the livery." Mr. Charlton settled his children.

Sophie remained in her alert stance. "But, Daddy, the other ladies are already lining up on stage. I won't be eligible to enter the contest if I'm late."

"Mr. Charlton, I can escort Miss Sophie to the admission table," Dusty offered. "Won't be a problem."

The patriarch jerked his head to look back at him before focusing on the street again. "I thought you were going to view the new saddles Wes Browman said he was bringing to sell."

"That can wait a few moments. I understand how important this contest is to your daughter." He caught Sophie peeking out at him through her bonnet. He winked when no one else was looking. She huffed and turned away.

Mr. Charlton slowed the wagon to a halt. "Sophie, go with Dusty, then. We'll stand at the front of the stage to see you shortly."

Sophie stood and took two steps toward the back end of the wagon. Dusty dismounted and came to help her down. Her pink cupid's bow of a mouth formed a frown. He raised his arms.

"I'll hold your basket and parasol." Linda reached for the objects to free Sophie's hands.

Dusty allowed himself to savor the brief moment when her hands came to rest on his shoulders. He lifted her at the waist and made sure to set her down where there wasn't a mud puddle or horse offal to dirty the creamy leather of her shoes. With nary a thank you to him, Sophie took her belongings back from Linda.

"What about your horse?" Obviously, Sophie was trying to make him go away but Dusty considered himself a patient man. She'd have to do much better than that to scare him off, especially when the prospect of winning a picnic with her was so close at hand.

He patted Gabe on the nose. "I'll take him to the stable when I get back. He ain't going anywhere."

"That isn't a word." She left him and began walking toward the stage. The closer she got to the admission table, the more swish went into her walk. Dusty didn't mind having to catch up.

"I'm supposed to be escorting you to the table, not running after you."

"Then try to keep up. I would think all that work on the farm would have you fit as a fiddle."

"A cowboy never runs if he doesn't have to."

At the admission table, the blacksmith Taylor Hastings raised his head when their combined shadows fell across the sign-in book. "Well, well, Miss Charlton. You're finally entering the town belle contest after all, huh?"

"Yes, Mr. Hastings. I didn't know you were volunteering today."

"I'd be judging the contest if I could. Sign your name there and put your initials on the next page for the basket bidding."

Sophie handed Dusty her parasol. "Hold that, please." She bent to pick up the fountain pen next to the book. The blacksmith made no secret in eyeing her while she signed. Dusty gave him a warning glance.

The stage filled with Assurance's eligible young ladies. Dusty recognized almost all of them from seeing them around town, although there were a few unfamiliar faces. Ever since the MKT Railroad finished laying the tracks in Assurance last year, new people arrived from the east and west—white, black, European immigrants—all eager to make a fresh start in Assurance as well as the smaller settlements outside town on the wide rolling plains.

"What you doing here, Sterling?" The blacksmith called him to attention. "Don't think you'd have any luck in this contest." He smirked at the parasol Dusty still held.

"I'm here to bid on one of the baskets these pretty ladies put together. Too bad you can't get in on the festivities as a volunteer." He smiled in triumph as Hastings' smirk dissolved.

"Don't mind Dusty." Sophie finished signing. "Do I need to carry my basket on stage?"

"They go on that long table to your right, where Mrs. Euell is waiting to give you a number."

"Thank you." Sophie picked up her basket again and took the parasol from Dusty. "And thank you, too. I don't think I'll need any more assistance today."

"If you say so." Dusty tipped his hat as she went by. He'd have a gander at that table once she left. If he knew the number assigned to her basket, he'd be one step ahead of all the other fellows looking to bid.

Pretending to change focus, he walked up to Wes Browman's stall situated next door to the basket table. "How do you do, Wes?"

"Just fine, Dusty. I got three saddles for you to look at here." The tanner swept his hand over the merchandise on the bench.

They were nice saddles, but Dusty let his gaze wander over to Sophie. He saw Mrs. Euell hand her a piece of paper, likely an assigned number. Sophie's parasol was in the way of his seeing what it was.

"This one here's got wide stirrups." Wes proceeded to highlight the appeal of his work. "And the black saddle's got toe covers in case you run into brush around that farm."

"I don't like toe covers." When was she going to lower that parasol? Dusty saw two more girls come to deposit their baskets, both identical to Sophie's. He tried to remember what color cloth she wrapped the food in.

"Where's your horse? I can let you try the saddle on him."

Dusty flicked his gaze over to the stallion he left on the opposite side of the street. Gabe stood patiently and watched the buggies pass by. "Maybe later."

"Suit yourself. Say, did you hear about the Lubbett Brothers?"

"The who?" Dusty viewed the other table out of the corner of his eye. Sophie and the two girls left. Their three baskets had numbers Fourteen, Two, and Nine in dark ink hanging from the handles.

"The Lubbett Brothers, boys out of Texas. Paper says how they robbed banks in Fort Worth and Denison before crossing into Indian Territory. Said they're wanted for a thousand dollars each."

"I didn't know. I don't read the newspaper too much."

Wes chuckled and leaned back in the wooden chair. "What do you do, Sterling, 'cept for bale Charlton's hay all day and try to get his daughter to notice you?"

He chose not to comment on Sophie, seeing as how Wes and the boys from the livery always got a source of amusement from his fondness of her. "There's plenty of work to do on a farm."

"You know you'd rather be ranching."

Dusty did miss his old days as a cowhand in San Antonio. When he was twenty, his family sold their ranch to pay off debt accumulated during the War Between the States, an action that, while necessary, hurt deeply. For a time he traveled around Texas, taking work where he could as a wrangler or cattle driver for ranchers looking to sell their longhorns in Kansas and back east. Three years ago, after the cattle market went south, he signed on as a farmhand with Mr. Charlton.

Dusty considered the truth in Wes's observation. He was going on twenty-five, about time for a man to start putting down roots. He couldn't see himself being a farmhand forever. "I'm going to tie up my horse before the judging starts."

He passed the bidding table. Finding Sophie's basket was a lost cause. Every girl entering the contest got smart and brought the plainest basket possible in order to have a fair chance of winning. Mrs. Euell would announce the contents of those baskets. He couldn't recall the name of Sophie's recipe but he remembered her saying she made it spicy.

Dusty paid for two hours' boarding at the livery for his horse and returned to the stage. He edged his way to the front where Sophie stood on the stage's left end, still twirling that parasol like a peddler's wheels headed for the next town.

Mayor Hooper stepped up on the platform to begin judging the contest. Dusty figured he was making the appearance to strengthen his chances of reelection this year. As owner of the town bank and its most powerful citizen, he was expected to win, but his opponent Trevor Fillmore also made an appearance in the crowd. "I'd like to welcome the good folks of Assurance to our annual Founders Day Festival. We like to start the event off with the choosing of this year's new town belle."

Applause erupted. The mayor nodded and went on. "Last year it was Miss Juney Tower who held the crown. Who will it be this year?"

People shouted out names of the contestants. Dusty chuckled when several of the girls onstage preened when they heard their names. He considered calling to Sophie, but it didn't matter to him if she became town belle. That picnic with her was all he wanted.

"Let's cast the votes with a show of hands. Starting with Miss Abigail Corgan." Mayor Hooper stood beside the fetching brown-haired girl dressed in robin's egg blue. She received a hearty round of applause. "Miss Gwendolyn McIntyre." The restaurant owner's daughter got a promising ovation as well. And so it went, seven more ladies down the line, until the mayor stopped before Sophie. Before he could get out her full name, the stage area burst with handclaps, whistles, and a few foot stomps. She covered her mouth to hold back a giggle.

"We have us a winner. May I present Miss Sophie Charlton, Assurance's town belle of 1871."

Dusty clapped for Sophie as she received a spring bouquet from last year's winner. The red sash they put around her was a bit too long for her petite torso, but she carried it off with grace as she smiled and blushed fetchingly under her wide brim bonnet.

Mayor Hooper raised his hand for quiet. "Congratulations, Miss Charlton. This year we're doing something a bit different. We're asking the town belle to devote herself to a worthy cause. It can be anything from leading a Sunday school class to bringing meals to the boys and girls in the schoolhouse. Do you have an idea of what you'd like to do?"

Dusty saw Sophie's expression go from delight to a blank stare. The parasol froze in mid-twirl. What was she going to say?

Chapter 3

$\mathcal{S}$OPHIE'S KNEES TREMBLED beneath the layers of her dress as she stared out at the faces of the town. Every pair of eyes met hers. She could not afford to disappoint. Why didn't Mayor Hooper give the contestants advance notice of the new rules?

Her mind raced with ideas of things she could do for the town. She liked studying the latest fashions back east and having tea at McIntyre's, but those pastimes wouldn't be important to Assurance's residents. She thought of other people she knew besides Linda, her friend Margaret, and the ladies from her mother's circle. What did they concern themselves with?

Sophie bit her lower lip and scanned the crowd. She heard snickering toward the back. In front of the stage Dusty stood gawking at her. She didn't want to make eye contact with him. He knew she was stumbling for something to say.

"Do you have an answer, Miss Charlton?" Mayor Hooper asked.

She noticed her little sister Rosemarie in the crowd. Last week, she heard her mother talking with the newspaper editor's wife, Mrs. Euell, about the abhorrent state of the children's school supplies. Mrs. Euell mentioned that if women could vote in the town, things would be much different.

"Miss Charlton?"

"Voting." She blurted the first word that came from her head and landed on her tongue.

Mayor Hooper's salt-and-pepper eyebrows formed a hairy caterpillar across his forehead. "I beg your pardon?"

Sophie locked her knees and steadied her voice. "Voting. That's what my cause will be."

A train whistled off in the distance as it signaled to arrive at the station. No other sound commenced in the streets of Assurance. The mayor turned aside to her while still projecting his voice for the crowd. "What do you mean your cause will be voting?"

She stalled to come up with an answer. "This is an election year."

"Yes, I certainly know that." The mayor gained a laugh from the citizens. "However, women don't have a vote in our town. Or any town in Kansas, except for school elections."

"Well, we don't get to vote for those elections here, and we have two schoolhouses." She received an odd look from the mayor, but she didn't stop to consider what it meant. She had a cause now. "I'm going to work on getting the women of Assurance to vote in school elections."

People shifted in front of the stage and talked in muffled tones. Was that Dusty smirking? Did no one think she could do it?

"Alright, Miss Charlton. We'll see what you can do." Mayor Hooper's tone wasn't friendly anymore. "Now it's time for the basket bidding."

What was it she said to get him upset? It wasn't his office she attacked. No matter. She'd won the town belle contest and saved face by thinking up a good cause. That was what counted.

She went down the steps where her family waited. Linda was missing. She must have gone to her mother's seamstress stall. Sophie clapped her hands with a smile. "I won."

Her siblings remained quiet. Her mother and father did not appear happy at her success.

Dusty let out a low whistle. Sophie was in the hot pan with her folks. The mayor, too, for that matter. She made him look bad onstage when she started on about women voting in school elections. Guess now he would have to address that in his upcoming reelection campaign.

Dusty cast his thoughts on politics aside when two men came onstage toting a table. They were followed by Mrs. Euell carrying the contestants' baskets, aided by three other matrons. Basket number two was placed on the end. Fourteen and nine went toward the middle.

"Alright, gentlemen, the moment you've been waiting for," Mrs. Euell announced. "Let's start the bidding." She lifted the first basket, a light-colored wicker in the shape of a square. "In basket number one we have chicken pot pie, fresh-baked butter rolls, and shortbread cookies. Doesn't that sound good?"

It did sound appetizing, but it wasn't what Sophie prepared. Dusty waited for several men to bid before it came time for basket two.

Mrs. Euell held it up with both hands. "This is a heavy one. The lucky man who buys this will have his belly full for the rest of the day. There's a whole pudding pie inside, and I hear the lady who prepared this made the main course hot and spicy."

Dusty's hand shot up. "Two dollars."

"Two dollars. Do I hear two-fifty? Three dollars?"

"Three dollars." Chad Hooper, Mayor Hooper's son, joined the bidding. He tossed a quick glance at Dusty before raising his hand.

"Three dollars coming from our new young banker. Anyone want to bid higher?"

Dusty raised his hand again. No way was he going to let that rich tenderfoot win a picnic with Sophie. "Four dollars."

Mrs. Euell smiled down at him. "Four dollars from Dusty Sterling. Come on, men. This basket smells good enough to make me enter the bid. Can anybody bid higher?"

"Five-fifty," said Chad.

"Seven dollars," said Dusty. He heard a response from the crowd. Sophie stood off with her family. She turned around and gave him a pleasant enough look. He was encouraged.

"Seven-fifty," Chad persisted.

Mrs. Euell held up three fingers. "Seven-fifty going once. Going twice—"

Dusty shouted for all to hear, "Ten dollars!"

"You going to bid any higher, Mr. Hooper?" Mrs. Euell prompted. Chad shook his head. "Sold. To Dusty Sterling, one basket of plum pudding pie and Hoppin' John."

Hoppin' John? That didn't sound right. Dusty frowned at Sophie in question. She smiled sweetly.

"Come up and get your basket, Mr. Sterling." Mrs. Euell walked to the edge of the stage. "You just bought yourself a picnic with the pretty Margaret Rheins."

Dusty felt his stomach land in his feet. Margaret Rheins, that girl from England? It couldn't be.

He saw Margaret come up to the stage steps, hair bows, brown sausage curls, and all. Her parents were English immigrants, the third wealthiest family in town, after the Hoopers and the Charltons. She never spoke a word to him before.

He walked up the stage after Margaret. She flattened her mouth as he approached, and trudged to hand him her basket. If a dirge were playing, Dusty would be convinced she was taking part in a funeral procession.

Mrs. Euell held out her hand. "The ten dollars, if you would, Mr. Sterling."

Dusty reached into his billfold and gave her his hard-earned pay, more than half a month's wages. Weeks before he even decided to bid on baskets, he planned on getting a saddle. Now that would have to wait, along with a picnic with Sophie. Time and money would have been better spent if he stayed to look at Wes's saddles.

As Mrs. Euell went away to continue the bids, Margaret nudged his arm with the rim of her basket. "Congratulations, sir." She spoke in her clipped British tone. No enthusiasm.

"I guess we'll have us a picnic." He tried to sound chipper. She didn't look up from her feet as she left the stage area for the tables set up in front of the general store.

Hoppin' John and pudding pie in hand, he went toward the back of the crowd and hung around to see who bid on the rest of the baskets. No wonder Sophie had been smiling. She outfoxed him.

Mrs. Euell lifted basket fourteen. "Here we have a Louisiana delicacy. Jambalaya with hot sausage, and for dessert, pecan pie. I wonder who made this."

Everyone knew Sophie's family originated in New Orleans. Dusty was helpless to stop the twenty or so young men that raised their hands to bid.

"Five dollars."

"Six."

"Eight dollars."

"Eight dollars. Do I hear nine?" Mrs. Euell clearly enjoyed playing the auctioneer.

"Twenty dollars." Chad lifted a triumphant hand in the air. Dusty groaned. Few folks had that kind of money to spare, let alone spend on perishable foodstuffs.

No one attempted to best his offer. Mrs. Euell exchanged

the basket with the mayor's son for several neatly folded bills. "Sold, for twenty dollars."

Dusty headed for the tables while Chad was applauded for making a costly investment. What good would it do to watch him eat a bowl of jambalaya with Sophie?

Margaret sat on the far end of the last table. She plopped her cheek in her hand and cast a wistful stare out at the crowd. "Sophie got a twenty-dollar bid on her basket."

"Ten dollars is mighty good too, in my estimation." Dusty seated himself across from her. He said grace before unfolding the basket cloth containing the food and utensils. Might as well focus on the positive. He had lunch and company, even if that company came off a bit prim. "I didn't know they made Hoppin' John in England."

"We don't. I thought I would try an American recipe for the festival. The plum pudding is from England."

Dusty uncovered a curious brown dish that loosely resembled cake left to bake a little too long. "I thought I heard Mrs. Euell calling it pudding pie."

"She was mistaken." Margaret folded her arms when he offered her a portion. "No, thank you."

What did it mean if a woman wouldn't eat her own cooking? Dusty wondered as he plunged a fork into the crumbly mixture and stuck it in his mouth.

Her brown eyes filled with expectation. "Well?"

He chewed. "Doesn't taste like plums at all."

"That's because there are no plums in plum pudding."

He swallowed. "Well, that doesn't make any sense. What is it made of, then?"

She flattened her mouth again and blinked twice. "Currants. Quite similar to raisins, actually. Also, other dried fruit."

"So it's fruitcake?"

"Not exactly. You should have started with the main course."

Confused, Dusty tried his luck with the Hoppin' John. He chewed a portion of ham, rice, and pinto beans, waiting for the kick to hit his tongue.

"Well?" She asked for his opinion before he could finish the first bite.

Hoppin' John, at least what he had growing up in Texas, was known for being peppery. Margaret's version contained not one ounce of heat. "It's a bit different from what I'm used to."

"You don't like it."

"I didn't say that."

"No need. I can tell." She tossed her hair. "I told Mama that I should have prepared a beef stew instead." She pronounced *mama* in such a way that Dusty never heard, putting all the emphasis on the second *ma*. "It is so difficult to assimilate here where everyone prefers food I've never heard of."

Dusty put down his fork. "You're not from these parts. No one expects you to know our way of cooking."

"Ah, but they do, Mr. Sterling. And preparing that basket was my failed attempt."

"You sure are hard on yourself."

"You try entering a town belle contest. No girl can beat Sophie." Margaret gestured behind him.

Dusty turned to find Chad and Sophie making their way to the other table. Chad pulled the bench out for her to sit. While she unpacked her basket, he looked up at Dusty's table with a smug countenance. Dusty suddenly lost what little appetite he possessed.

CHAPTER 4

$\mathcal{S}$OPHIE KEPT A discreet eye on the next table where Dusty and Margaret sat. It tickled her to see the expression on Dusty's face when he realized he bid on the wrong basket. Served him right for trying to buy a picnic with her when she told him she didn't want him to.

She giggled as she watched him take a bite of Hoppin' John. Margaret had said she was going to combine the food of her British culture with that of the southern region of the American states. Hoppin' John and plum pudding. Bless Margaret's heart for trying.

Sophie made conversation with Chad before her lack of speech could be considered rude. "I understand you just finished your studies at college in Missouri. Are you glad to be back home after a year away?"

Chad ran a hand over his lacquered hair. "Yes, and working in a higher position at the bank. We haven't spoken much since the fair in Claywalk last year, have we?"

He had grown out of his gawkiness in a short time. He reminded her of the male lead in a dime novel Linda had let her borrow, with his frock coat, starched white shirt, and silk cravat. The unusually hot spring day did nothing to rumple his handsome, polished appearance.

Sophie offered him her best smile. "That day at the fair seems so long ago."

"Not to me. I remember we danced and traded partners with Reverend Winford and Miss Pierce. Hard to imagine she's his wife now."

Sophie thought of the reformed saloon girl whose reputation and courtship with the new preacher caused quite the scandal last summer. Talk of the Winfords still managed to leave a sour taste in her mouth. She changed the subject by pointing to the food basket. "Are you hungry?"

"A little." Chad smoothed the front of his cravat.

She unearthed the carefully packed jambalaya, still warm, and poured it into the bowls. Little steam curlicues drifted across the table. She wondered if Dusty could smell the cayenne pepper she used.

"Your stance on women voting caused quite the stir today, especially with my father."

She spilled a bit of sauce onto the table. Her stance had caused a stir with her parents too. There would be a discussion once they got home, away from the ears of Assurance's residents. She knew it was coming. "I didn't mean to make Mayor Hooper mad." She reached for a cloth napkin in the basket.

"You didn't, but he wasn't expecting that kind of answer. He thought you'd do something more...I don't know. Light-hearted." Chad speared a piece of chili pepper and sausage on his fork.

Was he calling her frivolous? Sophie lifted her chin in defiance. After a year of doing farm chores as discipline from her father for her past gossiping and frivolity, her muscles had hardened as much as her will. "Other towns in Kansas let women vote on school elections. Why don't we?"

"I meant no offense. I simply didn't peg you for a politician." He ate the forkful of jambalaya. In seconds, his face contorted. "That is too much pepper." He coughed. "Water."

Sophie reached for the pitcher on the table and filled him

a tin mug. He downed it in two gulps. "I'm sorry. I keep forgetting not everyone is used to spicy food."

Chad continued to cough, drawing the attention of other picnickers, including Dusty and Margaret. Dusty appeared to be in good humor over the scene.

Pretending to ignore him, Sophie refilled Chad's mug. "Regarding the women's vote, I don't think I need to be too political to get my point across. I won't walk with a sign or anything."

Her picnic companion consumed another glass before his complexion returned to normal. "If you don't demonstrate, what will you do, then?"

"I'm still thinking about it." She hadn't the slightest idea of where to go with her promises. "I'd be very appreciative to hear your suggestions."

He gave a soft laugh. "My father's the politician. I am capable of giving the new town belle other assistance, however." His gaze lingered on her in a subtle flirtation.

She batted her eyelashes. "Such as?" She noticed he wasn't touching his bowl of jambalaya.

"Being your escort for the remainder of the festival. You should enjoy this day. Worry about your cause later."

Sophie's ears grew warm. Dusty was listening. Out of the corner of her eye, she saw him turn his head. "You won the bid on my basket, Mr. Hooper. Of course you can be my escort." She said it loud enough to carry across the table. That should make Dusty give up. "Provided you finish my jambalaya."

The look on Chad's face was worth the twenty dollars he paid for her basket of food. "Sophie, the dish is, ah, rather hot. You can't expect me to finish all of it."

She loved teasing. If Chad could withstand her humor and spicy cooking, then he was a man worth her company. "I spent all morning making that jambalaya. I couldn't bear for it to go to waste." Innocently, she looked toward the vendor stalls. "Maybe one of the food sellers has some milk to aid you."

Chad stabbed his fork into another chili. "No, I'll be fine with water." He gulped down the food without further comment, sniffling as the heat of the spice burned his nose.

Sophie ate her portion of jambalaya while studying Chad's watering eyes. "So good it makes you want to cry, doesn't it?"

The day continued into evening with music, games, and a skit played onstage by the children of Assurance's east schoolhouse. Sophie maintained company with Chad until it was time to leave. He walked her to her family's wagon at the livery.

"I have to be away on business for the bank. May I call upon you in three weeks' time, say the second Tuesday of next month?" he asked, helping her into the wagon. Such a proper gentleman.

Sophie couldn't help but feel a tinge of triumph at snaring him so quickly. "You may. You can have dinner with my family. It was good becoming reacquainted with you."

"Please don't be formal. Our families have known each other for years."

She settled on the low bench beside her with Bernard and Rosemarie, who played with a newly purchased doll from the festival. "Don't let your work keep you a stranger."

Chad offered a little bow. "Have a good evening. You as well, Mr. and Mrs. Charlton."

Sophie's mother commented on him as they set out on the road back to the farm. "A nice young man. He's matured very much since last year, hasn't he?"

Sophie's father assented. "Going to take right after his

father, from the looks of it. Which reminds me, Sophie, we'll be having a talk once we get home about what you said to the mayor today."

She had hoped that her parents would have forgotten the matter in light of the afternoon activities. "Have you seen Dusty?"

"He might be at the fair still." Her father removed his hat to scratch his forehead. "With that big basket of food he bid on, he probably doesn't want to get on a horse right away."

"He knows the way home," David chimed in. "I wonder if he ever misses being a cowboy, riding the range."

"Farming is real honest work, boy. Don't you doubt it."

Sophie's brother wisely kept quiet for the remainder of the trip. As the horses pulled the wagon up the winding path to the house, Sophie saw Dusty coming from the barn.

"I'll unhitch the wagon and take the horses for you, Mr. Charlton."

Her father eagerly handed him the reins and climbed to the ground. "Thank you, Dusty. It's been a long day."

She didn't want to go into that house just yet and have the promised discussion of her voting cause with her parents. "Daddy, can I look on Bess? I want to see how her hoof's healing from that infection she had last week." Sophie referred to her favorite mare.

Her mother arched a smoothly plucked eyebrow. "Do it quickly, and come right into the house. Your father and I will be waiting in the sitting room."

David whispered to her as he got out of the wagon. "You're not escaping this one."

Sophie waited for her family to go into the house. She observed Dusty as he unhitched the horses from the wagon. "How was your Hoppin' John?"

He removed the leads from the harness with quick efficiency. "Just fine. Miss Margaret's a good cook."

Sophie placed her hands behind her back. "You didn't seem all that hungry at the picnic table. I thought you may have lost your appetite."

"I got caught up in good conversation. Miss Margaret was nice company." He led the horses into the barn, where the setting sun provided a dim light of the interior.

Sophie walked up beside him. "You're fibbing, Dusty. I saw you looking at Chad and me while we had our picnic. You weren't thinking at all about Margaret."

"Is that so? You must not have been troubling yourself much about that banker boy if you had time to look my way." His mouth tilted up in humor.

She felt her skin tingle where blood rushed to her face. "Nonsense. Chad is very engaging."

"Could've fooled me." He folded his lean-muscled arms across his chest. "What made you stop paying attention to him, then?"

"You are mistaken."

"Am I?" He stepped toward her. She took one back.

"Yes. I'm simply not concerned about you."

"That would hurt if I believed a word of it." He reached out and snatched her in for a kiss.

Sophie had no time to react. The retort she was in the process of making died on her lips as he smothered them with his own. The stubble from his jaw scratched her chin. This was no sweet, innocent kiss from a boy, but a firm and certain one from a man. He continued to lay claim to her mouth until she yielded.

A fluttery feeling developed in her stomach, making her warm inside. Sophie's hands came in contact with hard muscle as she splayed her fingers against his shoulders.

Wait. Why was she letting him take control of her senses like this? She pushed against him until she was free, losing her bonnet in the process.

"Dusty Sterling, how dare you?" She seized the bonnet up from the barn floor and settled it back upon her head. The horses flicked their dark gazes to her.

He gave her a wink. "That was my congrats for winning the town belle contest."

"I should tell Daddy."

Dusty chuckled. "You won't do a thing. You enjoyed that as much as I did, else you wouldn't have kissed me back."

She put a hand to her lips. Despite the coarse way in which he kissed her, it hadn't been altogether objectionable. He would never hear her say so, of course.

Dusty regarded her with a bold confidence that set her on edge. "Now what were you sayin' 'bout you and Chad Hooper?"

She couldn't remember. The shock of his audacious move made her forget why she ventured into the barn in the first place. "Chad will call on me soon, and there's nothing you can do about it."

"We'll see."

"I'm done speaking to you." Sophie whirled on her heel to leave.

"Aren't you going to check on your horse's foot?"

"Not with you around." She kept walking toward the house, knowing that if she glanced behind all she'd see was a big wide grin.

She marched through the front door and ventured toward the stairs. Dusty's scent lingered on her nose, a combination of earth and leather. She willed herself to think of the expensive cologne Chad wore that day instead.

"Sophie." Her father called her from the sitting room.

She reversed direction and went to her parents. Her mother reclined on the ivory settee while her father stood by the mantel. The dormant fireplace at his feet was covered with an elaborate screen.

"Yes?" Sophie folded her hands in front of her and looked serene. Her mother's gaze shot straight to the top of her head.

"Why is your bonnet askew?"

Sophie fidgeted with it in the reflection of the glass cabinet beside the fireplace. "It fell in the hay." That was partially true at least. "What did you need to speak to me about?"

"You already know." Her father gestured for her to have a seat on the settee. "This cause you devoted yourself to for the town belle contest is inappropriate for a young lady of your standing. You'll need to inform the contest committee that you'll be changing it."

"But, Daddy, I can't. I stood onstage and told the town that I'd be involved with women's voting on school elections."

He gave a firm shake of his head. "No daughter of mine will be picketing in front of the mayor's office and pumping her fists in the air like a rabble-rouser. You were raised to be genteel."

"Your father is right," her mother added. "The cause should be one that reflects who you are. A lady."

"A lady that can't vote," Sophie muttered. Her parents heard.

"Where does this interest in voting come from all of a sudden?" Her father moved to sit in his favorite plush chair. "Did someone suggest it to you?"

"I thought of it when nothing else came to mind."

Sophie's mother clucked her tongue. "In that case, think of something else to do. Why not bake cookies for my ladies' tea social? Or you can donate your old dresses to the less affluent girls of the town."

"Mother, Mayor Hooper said to choose a worthy cause. Ladies would indeed like clothes and cookies, but that sounds...well, lighthearted." Sophie recalled Chad's response to her choice. "People expect me to do those things. This would come as a surprise."

Her mother crossed a leg. "Remember when we lived in a one-room house in Louisiana? Your father has worked hard so that this family could raise its social standing. Don't endanger that."

Sophie winced at the displeased expressions on her parents' faces. "I don't mean to sound ungrateful. Just permit me to keep the cause."

Her father sighed. "Why?"

"If I change my stance, people will think the task was too hard for me. I'll be laughed at." Sophie went to his chair. "Daddy, you even said so yourself last year that I could use more responsibility. Here's my chance."

"I said that when I scolded you for gossiping about the Reverend's wife. This matter is unrelated."

"But it is related."

"How?" Both parents asked in unison.

She thought fast. "I could show the town that I've improved. I can follow after you, Daddy, and have the Charlton name be associated with progress. You helped bring the railroad and businesses here. I can convince Assurance that the women's vote, too, is needed for advancement."

He had a gentle laugh. "You are a persuasive talker. When you put it that way, perhaps you could play a small role in the election."

Sophie was pleased by the turnabout.

"David, do you mean to tell me you are fine with the idea of our daughter being a *politician*?" Her mother's voice shrilled. Sophie quieted so her parents could debate amongst themselves.

"Of course not, Lucretia. She wouldn't be running for office. She'd be encouraging women to perform their civic duty and—how did you say it, Sophie?—advance our town. Apparently, she believes we're not forward-thinking enough."

Her mother touched the cameo brooch at her neck. "I don't like this notion."

"I'm not altogether fond of the idea either, but Sophie feels she can make a difference. If she agrees to undertake this cause *and* stay with it, she'll have my support."

"Thank you, Daddy." Sophie smiled at him.

He gave her a serious face in return, but the twinkle in his blue eyes told a different tale. "Your mother and I are entrusting you to conduct yourself properly. The minute you do otherwise, you won't be permitted to continue. Is that understood?"

"Yes, Daddy."

"Off to bed, then. I suspect you'll have your work cut out for you in the next few months."

"Thank you. I promise I won't disappoint." Sophie kissed her mother and father goodnight.

Sophie all but skipped into her room, washed, and changed into her nightgown. As she lay in bed, she thought of what her first course of action could be to get women the right to vote. Maybe she could visit Mayor Hooper at his office on Monday and ask. No, too soon. He needed to get over his mad spell. Once Chad returned from his trip, she'd ask him to help her get into his father's good graces again.

Sophie closed her eyes in the darkness and thought of Dusty. That kiss. Chad could never know about it. It was her fault for letting Dusty get too close. She resolved not to make the same mistake twice.

CHAPTER 5

HREE WEEKS WENT by with no visitors to the farm. Dusty knew Sophie was bluffing about Chad coming to call upon her. If the mayor's boy was intent on such a thing, he would have been out for a visit by now.

Confident in his deduction, Dusty loaded the last of the dirty straw into the wheelbarrow. The barn was finally swept clean, but work on a farm was never done. Tomorrow it would be time to plow the eastern field for the wheat crop to be planted. Wiping his face on his sleeve, he walked to the water pump and filled a bucket to wash up for supper. Mr. Charlton ran a tight ship, but at least he treated his workers with decency by letting them eat in the house.

Dusty anticipated sitting across from Sophie at the table. As the cool water ran down his face, he smiled, thinking about that kiss he gave her weeks before. Nearly three years he'd been waiting to plant a kiss on those pink lips. It was worth it. He hoped it wouldn't be another three years before he got a second chance.

"You. Worker."

Dusty raised his head and turned. Chad Hooper rode up to him on a gray gelding, stopping within five paces of the water pump. "I remember you from the festival. Basket bidding, wasn't it? I've seen you at the bank once or twice, too."

Dusty stared at him. He went to the bank at least once a month, and the mayor's son still didn't know who he was.

Chad pushed his brown curving-brimmed bowler at an angle atop his head. He was dressed in a matching three-piece suit with a burgundy diamond-patterned wide necktie. The man was fit for a Sunday. Too bad it was Tuesday afternoon.

"Can I help you?" Dusty rubbed his face dry with the edge of his shirt collar.

"Yes, I'm here to see Miss Charlton. Is she in?"

"The house, you mean? I reckon so." So much for Sophie's bluffing. There her gentleman caller was, looking down upon the world from his high horse.

"Would you mind taking my horse?" Chad dismounted and handed off the reins to Dusty. "Don't give him too much water. He's had plenty at the lake on the way here."

Chad walked with a purpose up to the house and knocked on the front door. Dusty had half a mind to tell him to tether his own horse when the door opened and Sophie breezed out. Her red and white pinstriped dress billowed in the wind, making him think of peppermints at a confectioner's store. Her curly blonde hair framed her face in a windswept halo.

"Chad, you're just in time for dinner."

"I hope you prepared something special for me."

Dusty raised an eyebrow. No one said anything about him coming over to break bread with the family. He observed as Sophie preened like a golden bird before her guest.

"I've prepared a four-course dinner with egg custard for dessert," she announced with pride.

"Then let's not waste time standing here while the food gets cold." Chad waved to get Dusty's attention. "Sterling? That's your name, isn't it?"

Dusty was surprised he knew. He nodded to Chad.

Sophie glanced at him with an indeterminable expression. He longed to know what she was thinking.

"On second thought, give my horse water. And some oats. I may be here for a few hours." Chad disappeared into the house behind Sophie without giving him another glance.

Dusty stood alone in front of the house. The handle of the water pump creaked behind him as the wind pushed at it. The gray gelding snorted and pawed the ground.

"Come on, then." He led the gelding into the barn and placed him in a stall beside Bess. He shut the door a little too forcefully, making both the mare and gelding turn their heads.

He returned to the water pump. David came out from the kitchen entrance of the house with a bowl in both hands covered with a checkered napkin. "Ma says to bring you this. We're having company over tonight."

Dusty intercepted the lukewarm bowl of beans and cornbread, leftovers from the midday meal. He imagined the fancier fare that Sophie would be serving her dinner guest. "Thanks. I guess I'll eat it outside the bunkhouse."

"Mind if I join you?" the sixteen-year-old asked, but was already following him across the field.

"Don't mind if your folks don't."

"Nah. Ma and Pa just want Sophie to impress Mr. Hooper. They don't care if I'm at the table or not. They don't notice me anyway."

"That can't be true."

"Sure it is. All Ma and the girls talk about is sewing dresses and going to tea parties. Pa only talks when the subject's on farming or business."

"I suspect that's 'cause he enjoys what he does." Dusty deposited himself on the stoop in front of the small bunkhouse. Sophie's brother sat on the step below him.

"Yeah, but not everybody wants to take after him, pulling

35

roots out the ground and breaking their backs to push a plow."

Dusty bit off a chunk of cornbread as he considered where the conversation was heading. "You don't wanna be like your pa?"

David looked down and twiddled his thumbs. "He works hard and all, but I guess I'm wanting to do something else."

"Like what?"

"I don't know. What made you become a cowboy?"

Dusty set the bowl of beans down. It had been a long time since anyone asked him about his way of life before he arrived at the Charltons. He didn't have an answer prepared. "I guess I never thought of being much else. My father was a rancher. Same as his father. Been around horses and cattle all my life."

The boy's eyes lit up. "I don't remember you saying your family owned a ranch. Guess I wasn't payin' attention. Where is it? Down in San Antonio?"

A wistful feeling settled over him and he wished he had something else to occupy his thoughts with. Thinking about Sophie wouldn't help. She was in that house cooking for someone else. "We had to sell it after the war. Didn't have the money to keep it running." Dusty studied the white clouds rolling across the sky above the wheat field.

"Where are your folks now?"

"Still in San Antonio. They live in a nice house in the city. My youngest sister's fixing to get married this summer."

"How come you didn't stay?"

How could he put it in words a sixteen-year-old would understand? "Ranching's in my family's blood, but I guess the Lord put a little bit more in mine than he did the rest of my folks. After we sold the ranch, I wanted to see if I could strike out on my own, so I took jobs as a hired hand on other folks' ranges."

"I bet you liked that."

He groaned inwardly as he considered the number of odd jobs he held in the past five years since he left home: ranch hand, wrangler, livery worker, farmhand. If his family's ranch hadn't gone under, he would have had his own ranch by now, or at least be in line to inherit one, but the closest he ever got to it was being trail boss for a man whose longhorns had to be turned away at the station for having Texas fever.

If he owned a ranch, it would be him in that house dining with Sophie, not outside playing stable boy to some silver spoon's horse.

He picked up the bowl of beans and forced a cold, mushy spoonful in his mouth. Thinking about the past and wondering about Sophie's dinner with Chad took away his appetite.

David picked up pebbles in front of the steps and threw them into the field. "Will you teach me how to tie a lasso sometime?"

"Maybe, if I can find a good enough rope around here."

"I'll look for some." David leaped up and disappeared into the barn.

Dusty dumped the remaining portion of beans into the hog trough and made for the direction of the house. He saw lights from two of the windows in the kitchen and a flurry of movement in front of the stove. The fact that Sophie was working hard to impress that spoiled banker made him clench his jaw. The evening wind gathered enough force to push at his back.

You shouldn't have let Chad talk to you like that. He's not your boss.

He agreed with the inaudible voice, though there was little he could do about it. As a hired hand on the farm, he

37

was expected to tend to his work and anyone on the property that needed assistance, whether they asked nicely or not.

Laughter carried from the dining room. He heard silverware clink against porcelain dishes as he stepped inside the kitchen. Sophie appeared in the doorway as he put the bowl in the copper sink. She rested her hands on her slender hips.

"What are you doing in here?"

Sophie didn't wait for an explanation from Dusty as he stood by the wash basin, dirty as a dung beetle. He seemed to prefer walking around in that fashion as of late. Likely it was to embarrass her in front of Chad. As her mother said, the condition of a woman's household is known by the appearance of the help. "You need to leave. Immediately."

"I was returning the dish your brother took outside for me."

Sophie looked over her shoulder at the dining room table. Chad carried on a discussion with her parents about the railroad while two of her siblings ate their meals in silence. No one heard Dusty come into the kitchen, thankfully. She ventured to the cabinet for an extra serving spoon, her original intent. "You know I don't want you embarrassing me while Chad is here."

Dusty still didn't move. He was quiet for a long moment. When she looked into his eyes, they were angry. She had never seen him like that before. He was always so unassuming and good-natured. In that moment she assumed Dusty could bite the head off a bear, fangs and all.

Without a word, he exited the kitchen, letting the door bang shut behind him. The sound reverberated through the cupboards and along the walls.

Sophie cringed as the dining room became quiet.

"Sophie, are you alright in there?" Her father was the first to speak. "Do you need help?"

"No, I'm coming." She took the serving spoon and returned to the dining table. All five faces expressed bewilderment.

"What was that I just heard?" asked her mother.

Sophie allowed Chad to seat her. "It was just Dusty returning a dish to the wash basin to be cleaned."

Chad scoffed as he sat down and pushed his chair closer to the table. "How rude of him. He knows you have company this evening."

Sophie didn't remark upon that being the very reason why he slammed the door. "You were saying, about your railroad capping investment."

"You mean capitalist. Yes, I think it is staging to become a very lucrative venture, especially within the next decade. You might be interested, Mr. Charlton. I could show you some figures I put together at the bank."

Sophie picked at her plate of veal and roast vegetables. Chad certainly had grown more business-minded over the past year. She let her mind wander from the conversation at the table to the one she had with Dusty before she'd gone and made him mad.

Maybe she had been a bit harsh. What harm was there in him returning a dirty dish to the basin? He appeared to have been minding his own business before she came into the kitchen. Dusty was many things, but he wasn't rude. He wouldn't have barged into the dining room on account of not being invited to the table.

She looked out the dining room window facing west. The setting sun cast a shadow over the pane preventing her from seeing where Dusty was in the field. She would go out and have a word with him after Chad left, provided he hadn't retired to the bunkhouse for the night.

Dinner ended at a quarter past eight. Sophie's father shook Chad's hand when he stood up to leave. "We really must have you over for supper again. I'll come to the bank this week to look at those investitures."

"Very good, Mr. Charlton. Enjoy the rest of your evening. The supper was very pleasant."

"I'll see you to the door." Sophie rose from her chair, feeling the lethargic effect of the heavy meal beginning to work its course.

She walked down the hall ahead of Chad. He reached for his coat and hat on the peg before going onto the front porch. "Where's Sterling? He should have my horse waiting for me."

Sophie scanned the area for Chad's gelding. "You did tell Dusty that you would be here for a while. I'll get your horse from the barn."

"You certainly will not." He stopped her with a touch on the arm. "You're a lady. You shouldn't have to go behind the workers to finish their tasks."

"Dusty must still be working. Otherwise he'd be here to assist you."

Chad shook his head. "You're too lenient with him, especially when your father's paying him good money to help keep the farm running."

His strong words cast away her drowsiness, as did the evening chill that crept through the thin sleeves of her dress. She rubbed her arms. "We all work on this farm. It's no trouble for me to get your horse." She went down the porch steps before he could protest further.

Dusty hadn't completely forgotten about Chad's horse; he left a lamp and a set of matches near the door. Sophie lit it before entering. The smell of freshly laid hay filled her nostrils as she located the gelding in the stall beside Bess. "Hello, Bess, my good girl."

The animal raised her chestnut mane and nickered. Sophie entered the mare's stall to inspect her hoof. The appendage was healing neatly between nail and skin. Dusty did a commendable job caring for her. Sophie reminded herself to thank him even as she wondered where he was. It wasn't like him to leave the premises when he knew he might be needed.

She left the barn with Chad's horse minutes later. He remained standing on the porch, arms crossed. "You should report this incident to your father."

"I will if it happens again." She knew it wouldn't. Dusty was fastidious with his work. Tonight had been the only slip. "Thank you for coming."

His countenance changed in the moonlight. Annoyance no longer showed on his face. "I thought more about your cause. I could ask my father about what you should do to get school elections on the ballot, and letting women vote in them."

Sophie experienced a warm glow of hope. "You mean, you're agreeing to get involved? I'd love to have someone who knows these things assist me, but I fear I made the mayor uncomfortable."

"Let me speak to my father over breakfast tomorrow. I'll let you know what he says."

"I'm most thankful."

He took the reins from her, letting his fingers linger momentarily over her hand. "May I call upon you again?"

"Yes, of course," she gushed, smiling up at his face. With the hat and expensive suit, he looked positively dapper. She rather liked being the object of his attention.

"Have a good evening, Sophie."

As he rode away from the farm, she took the lamp and went around the house. Crickets chirped in the grass and a hog grunted in the pen. The unplowed wheat field, gray and flat in the dark, stretched across the distance.

Dusty may have retired for the night. No light shone in the bunkhouse. She waited in case he came from the shed or chicken coop, so that she might be able to make her apology now instead of having to delay it until morning, but nothing stirred. As the hour grew late, the blackness of night threatened to swallow both her and the sliver of light in her hand. The wind began to howl, and she shivered.

When Dusty didn't show, Sophie went inside the house, strangely unsettled. The dinner had been a success, and she looked forward to seeing Chad again. So why did she find herself worrying about Dusty?

CHAPTER 6

THE WHEAT FIELD took three days to plow with a team of mules. Dusty saw no other people besides David and Mr. Charlton for the expanse of time. The three of them started work at sunrise. When they returned to the house at midday and suppertime, meals were already placed on a table outside the kitchen.

As Dusty hungrily tore into a chicken leg one afternoon, he spared a thought for Sophie. He hadn't seen her since that night Chad came over for dinner. He wondered if Sophie and Chad had seen each other since then.

Dusty couldn't remember the last time he had gotten so angry. He was glad it was in front of Sophie and not her father, else he could be in town looking for another job. The Charltons were kind enough to let him eat with them most of the time. It was their house after all, and he was the hired help as Sophie had so readily reminded him.

So why was it getting harder to accept his place?

"You're quiet today, Dusty." Mr. Charlton stirred butter into his mashed potatoes. "Anything wrong?"

He could never share his thoughts about Sophie to her father. "No, sir. Worn out from plowing, is all."

"We still got half a field left, so don't wear out just yet." The patriarch lifted his sunburned face into a smile. "You and David are doing good work. This time last year we weren't even a quarter of the way through."

"I wish we were done already," David grumbled over his plate of food.

"Patience, son. Hard work doesn't always yield quick payoffs." Mr. Charlton stood up to get more water from the pump.

"Ain't that the truth," David said when he was out of earshot. "Wish I could be practicing on that lasso." In their spare time, Dusty had shown him a few maneuvers.

Dusty chewed on a gristle. It may have been a bad idea to humor Sophie's brother. He should have carried on about how rewarding it was to plant seeds and wait for the harvest.

He just had to convince himself of it first.

Mr. Charlton returned with water to refill their canteens. "Dusty, I need you to make a run into town for me. We're short on seed. David and I can work on that last field until you get back."

"Yes, sir." Dusty was happy to be relieved of the back-breaking drudgery for a good portion of the afternoon.

"I'll get you some money. Don't take too long in town. These fields have to be finished tonight. We'll work through supper if we have to."

David grumbled. Dusty felt guilty for wanting to do the same.

Close to an hour later, Dusty purchased five bags of wheat seed from the general store in town. The clerk chatted with him as the purchase amount was totaled. "So Charlton's getting the fields ready, is he?"

"Yep, almost done. How's business?" Dusty handed him the money.

"Growing now that we have a rail station. I never sold so

many travel sundries before. Business would be even better if I could get those men over by the stove to actually buy something when they come in." The clerk gestured with his chin toward the back of the store.

Dusty swiveled to see a handful of older gents playing a game of chess atop a stack of crates. On a table nearby rested a coffee pot and tin mugs.

"Yes, sir," the clerk griped. "I thought to draw customers in by having a chess table and a pot of hot coffee on the boil. All I did was turn the store into a free social club. Those men do nothing but talk weather and keep track of those outlaws."

"Outlaws?"

"Sure. The Lubbett Brothers. They robbed two banks in Texas. Last I heard they went through a reservation in the Territory and made off with a couple hundred dollars and a musket from one of the chiefs. They're gonna have the marshals after 'em real soon."

"I used to travel through Indian Territory when I ran cattle up to Abilene." As Dusty talked, memories of his former life surfaced—days spent riding beneath the open skies with nothing but longhorns, a few wranglers, and a chuck wagon driver for company. It was hard work, with rough terrain, snakes, and cattle thieves, but each day brought something different. A challenge that refreshed the soul and gave purpose.

"You need help getting that seed onto the wagon?"

"I got it. Much obliged, though." Other customers had come in, and Dusty didn't want to keep the clerk from assisting them. He lifted two of the thirty-pound sacks and carried them out the store to the wagon.

Dusty went back inside and hefted the other three sacks. He tottered to the door, intending to kick it open. His foot met an opposing force. He heard someone grunt out a sound of surprise and pain.

"Careful there, stranger."

"Beg your pardon." Dusty peeked around the bags of wheat seed. He lost his grip on the top bag and sent it plopping to the floor. It burst open at the top and spilled golden kernels across the threshold and onto the sidewalk outside.

"It looks like you got your hands full." The man bent down and picked up the bag. It contained about half its original contents.

"Thanks." Dusty sighed. He had some sweeping up to do.

"Is that your wagon over there?"

"Yeah, just set it behind the bench." Dusty followed with the two intact bags. He glanced at the man's face as they loaded the cargo. He was deeply tanned, almost leathery, and dressed in layers of a brown jacket, gray striped shirt, kerchief, heavy canvas trousers, and boots. "I don't think I've seen you in town before. Name's Dusty Sterling."

"Eli Mabrey." The man shook his hand. "I moved here a week ago. I bought a ranch about five miles outside town. Well, it will be a ranch, soon as we get the property fenced in."

Dusty's curiosity piqued at the mention of a ranch close to town. "What are you raising?"

"Cattle. What else?" Lines formed in the man's face and around his eyes when he smiled.

"I thought you couldn't raise longhorns in Kansas 'cause of the law."

"You're from Texas, aren't you? God made more types of cattle than longhorns. I have Herefords at my ranch."

Dusty consulted his knowledge of the breed. "I knew a man who tried to keep them on his land in central Texas. They didn't do so well in the heat."

Eli agreed. "But this land here's good for them. Plenty of grass to graze on and more rainfall than in the south."

"Herefords can be a hardy breed, I guess, once the conditions are right. You're in a good place too, market wise. That

Katy rail here will let you ship them up north and back east when it's time to go to market."

"You sound like a man who knows his cattle."

"I've been around 'em long enough."

"Ever been on a drive?"

"I took the Chisholm, the Santa Fe, and the old Texas Road up here." Dusty was prepared to thank Eli and head back to the farm when the man said more.

"So what's a cattleman doing buying wheat seed?"

"I work for a farmer in town."

"Does he have a herd too?"

"Not unless you count the pigs and two milk cows."

Eli laughed. "If you don't mind my asking, do you like the work and pay he's giving you?"

Dusty didn't want to say anything negative about Mr. Charlton to a stranger. Farm work carried a different set of aches and pains than ranching, but it was still decent work. "I'd say it's been good for the past couple years."

Eli's eyes were keen enough to see right through him. "You don't sound convincing."

He touched the blistered sunburn on the back of his neck. His back hurt from bending over a plow. "We've been real busy this week. It should get better once the crop's sown."

Eli nodded as if he still didn't believe him. "I'm not a man out to take another's employee, but if you're interested in having a look at the ranch, it's down the road going to Claywalk. Ask for me and I'll be glad to give you a tour."

"Thanks, Mr. Mabrey."

Eli pushed one of the wheat bags into a position where it wouldn't fall over. "I won't take up the rest of your afternoon. Good day, Mr. Sterling."

After Dusty had swept up the spilled wheat, he set off for the farm, his mind fixed on the rancher's words. The prospect of working on a ranch again was tempting, but he couldn't

47

just up and leave the farm during the middle of sowing season. He berated himself for even letting the idea sink into his head. The Charltons needed him, and he couldn't think of abandoning his chances of courting Sophie someday. All the longhorns, shorthorns, and remaining bovine in the world wouldn't tear him away from that opportunity. Let her feign interest all she wanted to with that stuffed shirt Chad. One day she'd come to her senses. And he would be waiting.

You think she wants a man that works for her father? He heard a voice on the wind that zipped through the trees.

Dusty ignored it. Folks around these parts always said the devil was in the wind, taunting men and women alike with their worst fears. He supposed that was the locals' way of explaining why there were more twisters than soft breezes. Well, Texas had its share of strong winds and twisters too. It'd take more than puffs of air to make him change course.

And the devil had a challenge if he thought to make Dusty leave Sophie alone.

As he reached the farm and saw Sophie and her mother greeting ladies at the front door for their weekly tea social, his mood lightened considerably.

Sophie spotted Dusty driving the wagon to the back of the house. She had a mind to make her apology to him today, as soon as the weekly tea social came to a close.

The ladies gathered in the sitting room. Rosemarie squirmed next to Sophie on the settee. Sophie stilled the girl's restless hands while the guests, an assortment of her mother's friends from church and their sewing circle, talked.

"What beautiful draperies, Lucretia." Mrs. Gillings, the town physician's wife, admired the lacy white fabric hanging from the tall windows. "It makes your house look so airy."

"Thank you, Anne. I had them sent from a textile house in England. Clara helped me."

"You have excellent taste," Clara Rheins demurred.

Sophie watched her mother beam from the compliments. Her father worked hard to have their beautiful house built, and her mother spent large amounts of time seeing that it was properly furnished and decorated. Having multiple rooms alone was a vast improvement from their humble dwelling in the Louisiana bayou.

"Sophie, your mother tells us that young Mr. Hooper came over for dinner a short time ago," Linda's mother, Freda Walsh, commented with a telltale smile. The other ladies tittered. "Do tell us more."

Sophie helped herself to powdered sugar cookies being passed around on a silver tray. "We all enjoyed Chad's company. Mother helped me prepare the egg custard."

"We made a four-course meal that night." Her mother sipped tea from a dainty floral cup before setting it back on a gold-rimmed matching saucer. "I think we can expect Chad to call upon Sophie again soon."

"I should say," Mrs. Gillings conspired. "He did spend a pretty penny on your basket, didn't he, young lady?"

Sophie nodded. "Chad also said he would help me get school elections on the ballot so that we can vote."

The effervescent mood of the tea party changed. Her mother cleared her throat. A cup clinking against a saucer sounded like a crashing cymbal.

Mrs. Walsh spoke first. "Is that really what you prefer to do for your cause, my dear? If you want to do something more suited for feminine tastes, Linda and I could help you sew quilts for the sick and shut-in."

Sophie swallowed a cookie. "Thank you, but I've already started my course of action. I'll speak to the mayor shortly after Chad helps me get a meeting with him."

Mrs. Walsh made a face while she drank her tea, giving the impression that it was her drink that was offensive. "Forgive me, but I find the whole thing distasteful. What is there on the election ballot that concerns ladies, anyway?"

"I agree," said Mrs. Rheins. "I'd much rather my husband trouble himself with political matters. I have other things to concern myself with."

"I know Dorothea would enjoy being able to vote." Mrs. Gillings referenced her daughter.

A small silence fell. The women were uneasy with Dorothea too, a rather independent woman who had become a doctor like her father, but they daren't say so in front of Mrs. Gillings.

Mrs. Charlton finally said tactfully, "Not every lady feels as Dorothea does."

Sophie ate another cookie in silence.

"Oh, my dear." Mrs. Rheins noticed when she didn't speak. "We don't mean to be wet blankets. We'll stand by you if you want to get school elections on the ballot. We just won't picket or protest, but you have our support in every other way."

"Thank you." Sophie was uncertain as to what extent they would actually be involved, but she remained polite. She added another sugar cube to her tea before drinking. The awkwardness of the subject was still in the room.

Her mother switched the topic. "Sophie is expecting Chad to call upon her again this week."

"How wonderful." Mrs. Walsh's tone made it sound truly monumental. "Has he asked for permission to court your daughter, Lucretia?"

"Not yet, but it has only been a month since the Founders Day Festival."

"Not yet. I adore your optimism. Cheers." Mrs. Rheins lifted her teacup.

"Cheers." The women imitated her.

Sophie stole glances at the clock on the mantel in hopes that the awkward tea social would soon come to an end. At least talk of Chad brightened the mood of the occasion where politics made it uncomfortable. The ladies approved of her association with the mayor's son. That was something she could be happy about. She chose to focus on that victory and worry about the voting campaign later.

Chapter 7

No sooner had the ladies left than Sophie escaped through the kitchen door and crossed the yard to the wheat field to find Dusty. She took a big breath of fresh air to steady her nerves. It unsettled her that she was going out of her way to make amends with him. She'd never done so before, but after the dinner incident she felt compelled. What would Dusty make of her?

Her father and brother were preparing to store the plows in the shed. "You finished early," she observed.

Her father wiped his sweaty brow on his shirt sleeve. "We still have to finish planting the remaining wheat tomorrow. Is supper ready?"

"Almost. Do you want me to bring it out here?"

"No. David and I will clean up and eat inside."

"And Dusty?" She searched for him across the field but found only newly plowed rows for the wheat.

"Putting the mules in the barn. I told him to come in once he's finished."

"The sun burned him on the back of his neck," said David.

"I'll get some salve from the kitchen." Sophie went back inside and retrieved the jar and a cotton dish cloth. Her mother and Rosemarie were at the copper basin, washing the teacups and saucers. She slipped into the dining room and out the front door to head to the barn, pausing to wet the cloth at the water pump.

The mules rested in their stalls, eating from recently filled troughs. She heard Dusty moving around in the back. She passed the stalls and found him putting the mule harnesses and collars on the wall hooks.

He heard her approach and turned. "Sophie?"

She held up the jar of salve. "David said you got sunburned. I'll leave it with you."

She heard the amusement in his voice. "The burn's on the back of my neck. I can't see it. You mind telling me how bad it is?"

Sophie bit back a soft gasp. He had to be teasing her. But no—he met her appraisal with a patient, inconspicuous air. She feigned indifference and shrugged. "I suppose not."

His hazel eyes reminded her of a tabby cat's as they turned from brown to golden in the soft light. "Need me to sit down?"

He produced an empty bucket from one of the stalls and turned it on its head then plopped down in the middle of the barn, back facing the wall. Sophie skirted around him, a flicker of apprehension making her steps slow and stiff.

She studied the angry red skin that flamed the nape of his neck. She peeled back the collar of his shirt to see that the sunburn had spread across his shoulders. The action felt scandalous. She prayed her father wouldn't come charging through the barn door and hoped that her mother couldn't see them from the house. "It's blistered. How does it feel?"

He pulled away from her to remove his shirt. "It stings a little."

Sophie figured that was an understatement. She pressed the tip of her index finger against his skin, trying to ignore every other detail of his shirtless torso save for the sunburn. "What about that?"

"Yep."

She dabbed at his neck with the wet cloth, recalling why she ran out of the house to find him in the first place. "I'm sorry for what I said to you when Chad came over for supper."

"No, I shouldn't have gotten mad and let the door slam behind me."

She fanned his skin dry. "I suppose I could have told you in advance."

"I'm just the hired hand. You don't have to tell all your business to me."

Sophie paused. The admission was uncharacteristic of Dusty. "You sound pitiful. Are you sure the sun didn't give you a fever too?"

He twisted around and gave her a wink. "Would you nurse me back to health if it did?"

"Turn your head back to that barn door before I pinch the sunburn off of you." She threw the washcloth, splashing water droplets, while he chuckled. "You can't even accept an apology with dignity."

He rested his hands on his knees. "What do you want me to say? I was vexed when it happened days ago."

Was that his way of saying that she should have apologized sooner? An awkward embarrassment crept up in Sophie, almost as strong as her reaction toward seeing Dusty shirtless. Even now she couldn't help noticing how the subject of their conversation made him tense the muscles in his back. Very distracting. Was that how he was able to sit so tall in the saddle and walk so confidently?

Sophie shook her head, wishing the action really could force her thoughts to fall appropriately into place. She attempted to inject some humor into the situation to take her focus off both her clumsy apology and her admiration of his physique. "I hope I didn't offend you worse than Old

Ned. You held a grudge against him for over a month when he crushed your hat."

Dusty groaned. "That dumb mule should've been put out to pasture. You know how much I paid for that hat? It was my first Stetson, a Boss of the Plains the make was called."

Sophie held in her laughter and opened the jar of salve. It smelled of comfrey and a pungent ingredient that made up the base. She applied it to his sunburn, feeling the muscles along his back move beneath her fingers. Dusty wasn't a thick, brawny man, but he was lean and strong. "Am I hurting you?"

"A touch from you, and the pain goes away." He moved his head to give her a sly, sideways glance. Something in his eye hinted at more than teasing, as if he meant it. His gaze slid to her mouth. Her lips began to tremble under his scrutiny.

The barn grew very warm and stifling all of a sudden. Not quite as warm as his skin beneath her fingertips.

Sophie drew her hand away from him. "I see why you took to cattle and not Shakespeare." She hastened to screw the lid back on the jar. "I'll see you in the house for supper."

"When do you expect your gentleman caller to return?"

"I don't believe that's any concern of yours."

"Is he courting you?"

"He hasn't officially asked my father for permission, but he will." Sophie could look at Chad and tell there was interest. Her mother taught her that kindness or cunning could always be found in the glimmer of a man's eyes. She didn't know what to make of the look in Dusty's eyes at that moment. It wasn't cunning, but it certainly wasn't all sweet kindness, either. If she stood close enough, he'd probably try and kiss her again. She retreated several paces.

Dusty stood. "Supposin' I present a challenge to him."

She hid her smile. Dusty never was good at being subtle.

"How? I've told you for years that I don't want you courting me. You don't listen."

"You've been saying it, but that kiss told me a different story."

He had to bring it up again. Sophie folded her arms across her chest in a show of nonchalance. "You merely surprised me. I wasn't expecting you to seize upon me like a swamp alligator."

He formed a lazy smile at her comparison. "You didn't put up much of a fight."

She commanded her face to remain placid but it was difficult. "Nonsense. You imagine things if you think I enjoyed being hauled up like a sack of flour and slobbered upon."

"It was nothing like that and you know it."

She stiffened. "Put any notion of courting me out of your head, Dusty. Don't challenge Chad."

He put his hands on his hips. "Afraid he'll lose?"

"I don't want to see you humiliated." She walked out of the barn and left it at that before he could goad her further.

A week went by with no word or visit from Chad. Sophie put together reasons for what kept him away. She knew the bank drew in more customers since the town expanded, but it still closed its doors at five o'clock each weekday. Nothing stopped him from inquiring about her in the evening.

"It's a game he's playing." Linda offered her opinion as the two of them attended Sophie's trousseau one afternoon after Linda finished work at the seamstress shop. She folded an embroidered tablecloth and tucked it into the light oak hope chest. "He doesn't want to seem too eager."

"But he bid on my basket at the festival, and he promised to speak to his father for me concerning the women's voting cause." Sophie put in the matching linen napkins. "I already know he intends to call upon me again."

"Then why are you so worried?"

"I'm not worried. Just curious."

Linda held up a sheer, flowing white garment. "Oh, I adore this peignoir. Did my mother sew it for you?"

"No. My mother did." Sophie touched the beaded sleeve of the nightgown, intended for after her wedding. "It took her weeks to get the draping right."

"Silk is difficult to arrange. Have you ever wondered about what it would be like to live with your husband, Sophie? After the wedding?"

Sophie let the silk glide off her fingers. "I haven't thought about it much."

"But you have thought about it some."

"A little. Even though Mother says ladies aren't supposed to ponder such things until after they're married."

Linda appeared chagrined. "I guess so, but how can you not wonder?"

Sophie agreed. The peignoir was more ornate and delicate than any nightgown she had at her current disposal. It was meant to drape artfully over her form, to be looked at and admired. "I do wonder who I'll wear this for."

"Maybe you'll marry Chad."

"Linda!" She took the garment from her friend and set it atop the other items in the hope chest. "That's putting the cart well before the horse, wouldn't you say?"

Her friend shrugged. "Well, whomever you marry, you're still preparing for a life with him. Have you started thinking about your wedding dress?"

"No, but I found some glorious designs in *Godey's Lady's Book*. The magazines are downstairs in the sitting room. We can look at them while I brew us some tea."

They finished organizing the trousseau and filed down

the steps. A pleasant breeze came in through the open windows of the sitting room. The lace curtains swayed in a languorous dance. Sophie took a tea set from the glass cabinet and carried it into the kitchen to arrange. She put on the boil a pot of the new bergamot tea her mother had purchased. Soon the house smelled of bright citrus. Once the tea was steeped, she loaded it onto the tray along with slices of cinnamon bread left over from breakfast that morning.

Linda had half of a *Godey's Lady's Book* read by the time she carried the tray into the sitting room. "You should have a look at this wedding dress. I think it suits you."

She set the tray down on the side table next to the armchair and peered over Linda's shoulder at the page in the magazine. A drawing of a young woman stood out. The figure was adorned in a white wedding gown with a floral beaded bodice and ruffles along the neck and sleeves. The skirt had extra flounce, with the bustle padded in multiple layers of ruffles and tulle before graduating into a train that trailed several yards behind. "It's marvelous, but do you think I can wear so many layers of ruffles? I'm small."

"You can remove one layer at the hem and bustle. Maybe shorten the sleeves."

"Short sleeves on a wedding gown? I'd be a laughingstock."

"Not if they're three-quarters length. Wear lace gloves. I think it would look beautiful."

"You're the seamstress. I'll ask Mother if we can start fashioning a pattern. My own wedding dress. I can't wait to see how it turns out." She clasped her hands in glee.

Linda's eyes sparkled at that. "How exciting."

"What are you two ladies carrying on about?" Dusty stopped in the doorway. Sophie unfurled her hands and sobered. Linda closed the magazine and drank her tea. Why was Dusty always so nosy?

She hoped that by giving a little information to him, he

would be satisfied enough to leave. "Nothing you'd be interested in. Linda is helping me arrange my trousseau."

"Your what?" He frowned and entered the room.

"My trousseau. It's what a lady prepares in expectation of her wedding."

"Every well-brought-up lady," Linda supplied.

Dusty raked a hand through his sand-colored hair. Sophie never could tell whether it was dark blond or light brown. She started calling him Dusty after first seeing it. "I don't recall my sister ever putting together something like that. What goes in a too-so?"

"Trousseau," Sophie corrected. "All sorts of things to make a home. Linens, tablecloths, cooking utensils. Items for the bride as well, such as her dress and shoes." She intentionally left out a description of the peignoir. The thought of it made her bashful.

"You have your wedding dress already made?"

"Not yet, but it soon will be. Linda and I have thought of a pattern."

He made that low, slow whistle of disdain she had come to dislike. "I always thought women had to get proposed to before they went ahead and made wedding dresses. That's like putting the cookpot on the fire before you've caught the rabbit."

Sophie bristled at the condescending remark. "Some of us ladies choose to be diligent in our preparations."

"Dusty, why didn't your sister prepare a trousseau?" Linda asked.

He shrugged. "She was too busy helping run the ranch and break in horses. Besides, that sounds like it may have been too rich for our family's blood."

"Your sister worked on the ranch?" It was Sophie's turn to ask the questions. The thought of women running ranches and breaking in horses intrigued her. Although she liked tending to her horse Bess and had expressed interest in training others, her mother insisted she leave the task to the men.

Dusty nodded in answer to her question. "My whole family did. You seen Mr. Charlton about? I need him to inspect the new door I put on the chicken coop."

"He's in the dining room going over records." Sophie started to ask another question about his ranch when Dusty proceeded to leave.

"Bye, ladies. Sorry to disturb you." His footsteps resounded down the hall.

Linda huffed. "That was very rude of him barging in. He's supposed to be outside working, not sticking his nose into our conversation."

"You sound like Chad." Sophie told her how he reacted upon Dusty leaving his horse inside the barn. "He says I'm too lenient with Dusty."

"I agree with him, Sophie. You do let Dusty get away with saying all sorts of unseemly things to you."

Sophie felt cornered. "I put him in his place every time."

"Do you?" Her friend opened another issue of *Godey's Lady's Book* and flipped through the pages. "He's been giving you lip ever since your family hired him. I don't know too many farm workers who talk back to their boss's daughters the way he does you."

"It's nothing, Linda. He's not cruel with it."

"No, but he is awfully familiar. Why doesn't it bother you?" Linda took her eyes away from the magazine and tilted her head at Sophie. A sage expression came over her face as she raised an eyebrow. "I think you like the way he talks to you."

Sophie drew in her stomach as though she were being corseted. "I like no such thing."

"Then why do you allow it to continue? Maybe that's

why Chad hasn't called on you since last week. He probably thinks you're too free around Dusty."

"Surely not." Sophie weighed Linda's words. Was that why she hadn't seen Chad, because he was displeased with the way she interacted with Dusty? Her breath wedged in her throat as she recalled that night after the festival when he kissed her.

Dusty crossed the line. Very much so, but he couldn't take all the blame. Sophie knew he wouldn't be so bold if she didn't talk back to him or play coquette all the time. Was Linda right? Did she secretly like the way he talked to her? Kissed her, even?

Sophie resolved never to tell a soul of what transpired that evening. It would cost Dusty his job and her reputation. "What should I do to make Chad think differently?"

Linda rose from the armchair. "Treat Dusty like the hired hand that he is. Don't speak to him anymore."

"He eats at our table most nights. I can't refuse to acknowledge him."

"Then find some way to make him realize his place. If you don't, your chances of Chad courting you are slim to none."

Sophie's discomfort grew at the thought of turning strict.

"Do it," Linda insisted, "or those linens we folded in your trousseau will never see the light of day."

CHAPTER 8

*D*USTY LAUGHED TO himself when he thought of Sophie and Linda poring over those dog-eared copies of that ladies' fashion magazine. Sophie wasn't even engaged and was already talking about patterning a wedding dress. Imagine that.

It never failed to amaze him how the well-to-do folk carried on. His sister was to be married later this year, and as far as he knew, she was going to wear their mother's hand-me-down wedding dress. He should write to her and ask if she had a trousseau. Either she'd ask him what it was or giggle that he thought she possessed one.

Dusty pictured Sophie in a gown of white. She was already a pretty little thing, with gold hair and eyes blue as his mother's china tea set. No doubt she'd take everyone's breath away when her wedding day came.

He wanted to be there to see it, and not in the church pews with the guests. He wanted to be standing to the right, in front of the preacher, waiting for her to come down the aisle to be at his side.

Lofty dreams for a farmhand. The breeze trickled in through the entrance of the chicken coop.

Dusty awaited Mr. Charlton to give his opinion on the new door he installed. His boss tested the hinges, nodding his approval when they moved without squeaking. "It appears sturdy. It should hold tight against wind and rain this summer. Good work."

Dusty normally felt pride in a job well done, but today he was just eager to get the workday over with. The chicken coop was hot inside, and he needed to go into town to address a matter with the bank. "I finished mucking the horse stalls. Anything else you need me to do?"

"No, that's it. I'll let you end the day a couple hours early. Take your wages and buy a steak at McIntyre's." He reached into his pocket and withdrew twenty-five dollars from his billfold.

"Thank you, Mr. Charlton." Dusty accepted his monthly pay and went to the bunkhouse to get cleaned up. He washed and changed into more respectable clothing: a white shirt, necktie, gray waistcoat and trousers, and his black Sunday boots. He checked to make sure the shoes were free of scuffs on his way out the door.

"Ready to head into town, Gabe?" he asked his horse once he had the animal saddled and out the barn. The stallion tossed his dark mane and swished his tail at flies.

Dusty tucked his wages into the inside pocket of his waistcoat, grateful that he didn't have to wait until Monday afternoon to deposit the money in the bank. If his book-keeping was accurate, he should have almost a thousand in his account, counting the payment he saved from his previous jobs. Cattle driving didn't pay much, but he made the most of what he received. One day he was going to purchase property. Perhaps he could start investing to help his savings grow.

The town square in Assurance was busy. Inside the bank, he waited in line behind eight customers. Only one teller was on duty. The poor man looked like he had seen enough moneybags and account books to last him till next

Christmas. Dusty scanned the area of small offices adjacent to the bank counter. The three doors were closed.

"Can I help you, sir?" His turn finally came. The teller pushed spectacles higher upon the bridge of his aquiline nose.

Dusty put his wages upon the counter along with a deposit slip. "I need to deposit this into my account. Also, I wanted to look into investing."

The teller jabbed a thumb at the office doors. "One of the bankers went home early today. If you can wait about ten minutes, I'll see who else is on duty to advise you. Have a seat on that bench over yonder."

Dusty did as he was told and waited for the teller to finish attending to customers. Ten minutes turned into twenty, and a half hour passed before the teller was able to come from behind the counter and knock on one of the office doors. Dusty twiddled his thumbs as he waited. The bench was hard beneath him, and the summer wool of his trousers itched. Would that dress clothes were made of breathable fabric like his work shirts.

The teller came to him. "Mr. Sterling, you're in luck. Mr. Hooper is available to advise you."

He didn't rise from the bench. "Did you say Chad Hooper?"

"Yes. Mr. Hooper is the chief advisor here when it comes to investitures in local business and industry. He has clients from other county seats as well."

"Uh huh." Dusty's attention waned as the teller continued to sing Chad's praises. The last person he wanted knowing his business was the mayor's boy.

"Were you looking to finance in a different market? A stock exchange, perhaps?"

"No. Is Hooper the only person I can speak with?"

The teller nodded. "Today, yes. Our other advisors deal with property and loans, and they won't return to the bank until Monday. What business did you say you wanted to invest in?"

"I didn't. I needed to know the best way to increase my savings."

"Then Mr. Hooper would be the best man to assist you. Come with me."

Dusty crossed the floor of the bank and waited behind the teller to be announced. He considered doing his banking at one of the offices in the next town. But when would he have the time?

Chad waved him into the expensive but tastefully furnished office. "Mr. Sterling, have a seat."

Dusty crossed the point of no return. His boots sank into the plush rug on the floor. Without looking at the other offices, he knew that Chad had the best one. The banker sat at his heavy mahogany desk, polished to a gleaming black perfection, surrounded by tidy stacks of brown envelopes and correspondence written on fine quality stationery. Two inkwells rested at the desk's right corner, along with an assortment of fountain pens and decorative quills. Chad sat in a dark brown leather chair, studded with shining brass medallions along the front and down the arms.

Dusty slid into a smaller version in front of the desk.

"What can I do for you today, Mr. Sterling?" Chad asked with professional politeness, closing a portfolio he was working on. His hair had the same sheen as his desk. Dusty wondered if it was indeed furniture polish he used to get the effect.

"I want to start investing some of my savings into a business."

Chad raised his eyebrows ever so slightly. "Did you have an idea of what type of business you wanted to put your money in?"

"I figured the railroad would be a good choice. I hear the Katy's doing real good in this area."

"The Missouri-Kansas-Texas Railroad is expanding, but so is their stock price, I'm afraid. Given your occupation, I'm not certain of your ability to contribute on that level. Let's have a look at your bank records and see what we can do."

Dusty gnashed his teeth together while Chad thumbed through his account information and deposit slips. He hated being talked down to, especially when Chad flat-out assumed that he couldn't afford to put stock in the railroad. For all that man knew, he could have accounts in other places.

And my horse has wings. He chastised himself and attempted to give Chad the benefit of the doubt. Hooper was doing his job this afternoon, not playing gentleman caller to Sophie. Dusty wanted to let that very concerning matter rest for the moment, but it refused to go away. Something about Chad stank of smug.

"You have just over twelve hundred in the bank, Mr. Sterling. We require you put at least five hundred in railroad stock if you choose to invest collectively with our clients."

"Why so high?"

"It helps absorb any losses to the stock price if the railroad loses money in a given year. Also, our clients chose that number to invest with."

Dusty figured that the clients were Assurance's wealthier residents, who could afford to part with five hundred dollars. That was almost half his entire savings. If he lost the investment, he'd have to start from scratch. "Can't I invest on my own?"

"You could choose to invest individually, but your stock price will be higher. Seven hundred, in fact."

"I can't do that."

Chad's gaze flicked over to the bookcase along the wall. "I could show you more affordable stocks. It may help to start investing in those and work your way up to one of the rail-road companies. Would you be interested?"

Dusty shrugged. "I came here to invest in something."

"Excellent." Chad went over to the bookcase and with-drew a green ledger. "The textile industry has been doing well for the past several years."

"I know Sophie would be amused to hear I was buying stock in clothing."

Chad raised his nose from the ledger book. "Do you always refer to Miss Charlton by her first name?"

Dusty straightened his back against the cushioned chair. "I've worked for her father for three years. She and I have become acquainted in that time."

"Have you?" The mayor's son stood over him. The suit made Chad resemble a big black crow, and his eyes glittered just as attentively as one. "And does she address you as Mr. Sterling?"

"Only when she's teasing. Usually she calls me Dusty, the nickname she gave me on account of my hair color. But when she's mad, I get addressed by my full name." Dusty stopped talking when he saw Chad glaring daggers at him. "You wanted to know, didn't you?"

"Don't you think it inappropriate for a man of your sta-tion to talk so to your employer's daughter?"

"Man of my station? Wait now." He heard his own Texas drawl deepening, and knew it was a sign that he needed to get a hold of his temper. "I may not be highfalutin, but I'm not common, either. I've always been courteous to Sophie."

Chad closed the ledger book, holding his place with an index finger. "See that you're very careful with what you say to her then, Mr. Sterling. You don't want to jeopardize your work position with the Charltons."

Dusty got to his feet. "Is that some kind of threat?"

"Of course not." Chad walked behind his desk with an air

of calm. "Merely a friendly warning." His smile was just as artificially perfected as his hair. "Did you still want to decide on investments?"

"I think I'll mull it over for a while. Thank you for the advice all the same." Dusty left the office without shaking Chad's hand. Outside, customers watched him with detached interest as they waited in line for the teller. He marched out of the bank and into the town square.

So much for trying to increase his wages outside of earning them the old-fashioned way. All he got for his trouble was a confrontation. Chad Hooper really procured himself a pack of nerves since he spent time away at college. He must have thought his fancy education and money made him a man to contend with.

Dusty slapped his hat on his head. He may have come from more humble means, but at least his folks taught him to respect others, no matter their station in life. What did Sophie see in Chad to make her want him to keep coming around?

"He can provide for her," he said aloud, paying no mind to the people that gave him puzzled looks as he walked by.

The reason was not a completely shallow one on Sophie's part, Dusty reasoned. She was accustomed to the best clothes and the finest food. He wanted to be in a position to give her those things, but twelve hundred dollars in the bank wouldn't be nearly enough to support a woman of her caliber. It wasn't enough even for a bare-bones cowboy to settle down with.

A train whistle pierced the air. He wished he had gotten in on the railroad stock before it grew to the size of Texas. He'd be sitting on the front porch of his own ranch house now, telling *his* hired workers what to do. And maybe, just maybe, Sophie would stop to look his way once or twice.

Dusty saw his reflection in the windows of McIntyre's

Restaurant as he approached. He couldn't give up on his ambition that easily. He had to better himself, not just for Sophie, but for his own peace of mind. Buying stock wasn't the only way to do it.

He recalled Eli Mabrey and the invitation to come to his ranch for a tour. Mr. Mabrey seemed friendly enough. He probably wouldn't mind being asked questions about how to get a ranch started.

Dusty worked out the details in his head. He wouldn't have to work next Saturday, as Mr. Charlton was planning on making a day trip to Claywalk with his family. That was the best time to head for the Zephyr Ranch.

He changed his mind about going into the restaurant. The steak could wait. His money had to be saved for worthier investments.

CHAPTER 9

$\mathcal{S}$OPHIE NOTICED A change in one of Dusty's habits. Usually, he treated himself to a steak at McIntyre's when he got paid each month. This time, he ate supper with her family.

She sat across from him at the table, wanting to ask how his afternoon in town went, but she refrained on account of Linda's advice not to become overly familiar with the hired help. It didn't feel right not to acknowledge a grown man at the table. However, Dusty was too absorbed in downing his chicken and gravy to be engaged in any form of discussion.

She gave scant attention to her mother and father as they talked about next week's trip into Claywalk. Her thoughts came back to Dusty and that remark he made about growing up on a ranch. He obviously enjoyed being around horses and had mentioned his love of roping and riding. Why did he leave that type of work to farm instead?

Perhaps her father knew. He would never hire a worker without inquiring about previous employments. She had to figure out a way to ask without appearing conspicuous.

Sophie peered through her water glass at Dusty while taking a sip. The easiest way to find out about his past was to simply ask him, but then she'd be harvesting more familiarity.

"What are your plans for tomorrow after you do your chores around the house, Sophie?" her mother asked.

"I'll head to the general store in town to see if they have new copies of *Harper's Bazaar.*"

"Rosemarie and I will work on our samplers. And boys? What will you do?"

Sophie's brothers David and Bernard looked up from their plates. Bernard had gravy smeared across his chin. "Dusty's gonna finish teaching me how to lasso, and then I'm going to show Bernard," David answered.

A look passed on their father's face. "You'll take your sister to town first."

Sophie recognized when he was displeased. David had better be careful. Dusty, too, since he was the one doing the instructing.

Supper ended, Dusty went to the bunkhouse, and Sophie passed the evening by reading a novel. The next afternoon after the chores were finished, she rode with David to the general store. The clerk was reading a newspaper behind the counter when they came in. Her brother scooted off to find rope for another lasso.

"Do you have the newest edition of *Harper's?*" She caught part of the headline on the front page before the clerk set the paper on the counter. Something about Lubbett Brothers. A new rail company, in all likelihood. They changed names every day.

"There should be some on the stand beside the stationery." The clerk pointed her in the right direction.

Sophie wandered past the chess players by the stove. The area smelled of stale coffee. She perused the stand until she found what she was looking for. Illustrations of well-dressed fashionable ladies smiled up at her from the brand-new copies. She had to crouch to get them from the lower shelf.

"How did I know you'd be here today?"

She raised her head to find Chad standing by a rack of periodicals. He was dressed in a suit as though he had momentarily left the bank. A bundle of eastern newspapers was tucked under one arm.

"Chad, how good to see you." She rose, careful not to trip over her hem. It would be awful to fall in front of him. He was neat from head to polished toe. Not a hair out of place. She drew her hands in closer to her body, not wanting him to see how dry they were from wringing out laundry that morning. She should have worn gloves.

He put a newspaper back on the rack and came her way. "I feel the need to apologize for not calling upon you earlier in the week. We've had an increase of clients at the bank."

"You didn't take my advice about not letting work make you a stranger." She kept her tone light. "That's alright, though. I've been quite busy myself."

Her added touch of intrigue produced the desired effect of making him curious. "What has kept you occupied?"

"Linda and I have been working on a particular task. I can't tell you what it is."

He played along. "Would it be related to women's voting?"

"Not exactly, although I have given much thought to that cause too."

"As have I." Chad moved aside so that a customer could squeeze past the two of them. "I spoke to my father. He said that he would be able to meet with you Monday morning at nine o'clock to discuss your objectives. I know it leaves you with less than two days to prepare, but no doubt you have a list of things to discuss."

Sophie thought to bring her little sister's outdated primer as proof that school elections were needed to improve the town. "I'll be ready on Monday. Thank you so much for doing this."

"It's nothing. Would you like to go to the lake with me today? We could walk the new promenade."

"That sounds delightful." Sophie remembered not to make

her smile too broad. A lady must never appear too eager to have company with a gentleman. "I'll tell my brother where I'm going." She caught sight of David walking around the back corner of the store. She gave her brother a brief description of where she would be for the rest of the afternoon.

"Bye." David never looked up from the four types of rope he was debating on purchasing.

Sophie paid for her magazine before meeting Chad at the door. "My brother can amuse himself here in town until we get back."

"No need. David," he called. "I will take your sister back to the farm before supper."

David nodded, and Chad offered her his arm. She accepted and allowed him to lead her from the store and into the small black buggy outside.

Excitement curled in Sophie's stomach at the idea of going on a promenade with the mayor's son. Thank goodness Linda had been wrong about Chad's reasons for not coming to call on her. It was all a simple matter of him being busy with his work. Her friendship with Dusty had nothing to do with it.

She reclined upon the cushioned bench as Chad drove the buggy beneath the shade trees toward the lake. Sparrows chirped in the branches above. Sunlight filtered through the pale green leaves that fluttered softly, still days from reaching their full bloom.

The lake area was populated with three wagons and picnickers taking up choice spots along the shore. A fishing boat glided out toward the center of the water where it was quiet, its two passengers getting ready to cast their lines. Chad offered Sophie his arm again as he walked her to the newly cleared promenade that circled around the water before returning to the main path. Residents of the town waved as they passed by.

Sophie made small talk. "I heard that the promenade might be getting paved soon. Wouldn't that be nice, having a brick walkway around the lake?"

"If it can fit within the town budget this fall, you could be walking on it next summer."

"I want to thank you again for offering to take me back to the farm. You've made David happy by giving him more time to practice his lasso."

"Lasso? I thought your family did mostly crop harvesting."

"We do, but Dusty's teaching him how to rope. Why, I don't know. We don't have any herds."

Chad's brows drew downward. Sophie grasped her mistake at mentioning Dusty's name, but it was too late. She bit her lip and attempted to regain control.

"The two of them are always sharing work on the farm. David doesn't have a brother close to his age to talk to. I guess that's why he's always trailing after our farmhand."

"And your father doesn't mind?"

Sophie saw the image of her father at the supper table the night before, wearing a frown. "He knows the workers he hires can be trusted." She maintained a light grip on Chad's arm as they approached the first bend in the walkway.

"Dusty was at the bank yesterday."

"He usually goes once a month when he makes his wages." Sophie grimaced at her runaway mouth. Why was it so hard to stop voicing all her knowledge of Dusty's routine?

"You seem most familiar with his habits."

She wished she could retract her words. "It's just an observation. He's worked with us for a long time."

"He might be in the process of making a change."

"I beg your pardon?"

Chad paused for another couple to walk by. "I'm not permitted to say in detail, but his business at the bank yesterday afternoon wasn't entirely related to his work on your family's farm. I'd say he's considering other ventures."

Sophie was too struck by the news to keep walking. "Other ventures? You mean, new employment?"

Her promenade companion lowered his eyes. "I could be wrong, but I thought you should know."

"But he's been working on our farm since he came to Assurance. Surely he's not considering other prospects."

Chad squeezed her hand. "I didn't intend to upset you. As I said, I could be mistaken."

The sounds of people talking and children splashing their feet in the lake became muted in Sophie's ears as she absorbed what Chad told her. No wonder Dusty was acting a bit strange. He hadn't gone quiet because she hurt his feelings. He was making plans to leave the farm. That also explained why he ate with her family last night instead of having steak at McIntyre's. He was saving his money in the event that he would be without a job while searching for new employment.

Sophie couldn't help feeling betrayed. Why was Dusty being deceitful? "That's unlike Dusty to not say anything. My father will have to keep an eye on him then." She planned on doing the same when she got home.

"It's the best thing to do until you know more, but that's hardly a thing to discuss on a day like today. Shall we keep walking?"

Sophie resumed her promenade with Chad while her mind traversed back to the farm. Dusty told her very little about his previous jobs, but she just couldn't see him not working with her family. Passing by him every day on the farm as she went about her chores had become second nature.

She and Chad had the lake circled within the hour. The excursion, though pleasant, left her a little overheated from the sun. She welcomed the shade of the buggy as she settled back in for the journey up the road home.

"It's going to be a hot summer," Chad remarked. "I can tell already, but I'm sure you're used to this weather from living in the bayou."

"I do believe New Orleans had a cypress tree or two more to lessen the sun's sting. I thought this prairie land was a desert when I first arrived here, all scrubbed bare of tall foliage and hung out to dry."

Her observation brought a flash of humor to Chad's face. "You always did have a colorful way of seeing things. You're not like other girls here in Assurance."

"I hope you don't mean I'm worse off."

"No, livelier, and perhaps more outspoken."

Sophie looked to her lap and played with the folds of her bustle front. "I like to talk. How else do you get to know someone? My mother tells me that a lady should observe more than she should speak, but I don't see why she can't do both. The Lord gave women voices as He did men."

"To nurture and soothe."

"To cajole and put things to right too, if need be."

Chad made a sound of disapproval, but she was fairly sure that it was all in jest. "My father will have himself a challenge with you on Monday."

"Not at all. I'm quite knowledgeable of how to conduct myself before a public official. I'm aghast that you'd think otherwise."

He raised one hand in mock surrender. "I think nothing but the highest thoughts of you."

"Please do good to continue." She smiled, beginning to think that Chad could be a potentially enjoyable person to banter with. Not as quick as Dusty, but decent enough. But why was she comparing the two men? Chad was her gentleman caller, and soon to become her beau if she kept his interest. Not Dusty.

Chad slowed the buggy the closer they got to the farm. "Last summer you were a frequent guest at socials. I thought you'd be married by the time I finished college."

So did her parents. Sophie remembered her father presenting her with the hope chest for her trousseau. "Why? You were only gone for eight months."

He shrugged a shoulder. "So many men had an eye for you. I'm surprised you accepted my invitation to the Claywalk festival and not someone else's."

She shifted her position on the bench. The subject of the Claywalk festival last summer was not one of her favorites. "You give yourself very little credit, Chad. I enjoyed your company."

"Well, you did make it clear at the time that you preferred Reverend Winford to be your escort instead of me."

Sophie cleared her throat. Not a fond memory at all. The festival ended in humiliation when the Reverend declared to her that he had eyes only for another. "I've gotten past that. I hope you can too."

The barest trace of a dark emotion crossed Chad's face, making his countenance dim. Then, as a gloomy cloud would part for the sun to shine through, he returned to his normal state. "Forget what I said. This is a new day."

"Yes, it is." Sophie fought off the chill that abruptly settled at the base of her spine and snaked upward.

They arrived at her house. The door was left open and rugs and upholstery coverings were hanging from the rails of the porch. "My mother's cleaning. I should assist. Will I see you in church tomorrow?"

Chad nodded. "It may just be my father and I. My mother's been down with a headache since this morning."

"Please tell her I hope she feels better. Thank you for

taking me on the promenade." The buggy was low enough for her to step down on her own. Chad held her hand as she did so, and continued even though her feet touched ground.

"Stop me if I'm being too forward, but would it be alright if I asked your father's permission to court you?"

A tight knot formed in Sophie's chest, and she didn't know whether it came from happy anticipation or anxiety. Her palms grew moist. She hoped Chad couldn't tell. "Y-you want to court me?"

"If you think it's too soon—"

"No. I don't. I think it grand that you want to do so." Her words came out hollow, like another woman was uttering them. She didn't understand why her body became so tense. This was supposed to be good news.

"I'll speak to your father tomorrow after service."

She managed a bobbing motion with her head. "See you tomorrow."

"Sophie, you forgot your magazine." Chad handed it to her.

As she started to go into the house, a tall and lanky figure moved near the barn. She knew it was Dusty. As much as she wanted to go over and talk with him, it had to wait until Chad went down the road.

But by the time he was out of sight, Dusty had disappeared as well.

CHAPTER 10

$\mathcal{D}$USTY KNEW WHERE Sophie had been the moment that costly black carriage with the cushioned bench came up to the house. David told him that she decided to go walking by the lake with Chad. He wished he could read her mind, because the way she stood before Chad at that buggy was pitiful. Chin hanging down, shoulders drawn in to make her look more fragile than a newborn filly. If Hooper said or did anything to hurt her, the man was going to answer for it.

Dusty didn't get his chance to inquire of her Saturday. Sophie stayed around her family all evening. He wondered if he was imagining things, or if she was speaking less and less to him. When he offered his opinion on a new field plow that Mr. Charlton brought up in discussion, Sophie just peered at him with those blue eyes he enjoyed staring into. Only this time, they were as clear and cold as the lake in winter.

Early Sunday, he readied himself for church and left the bunkhouse to saddle his horse. Sophie was by the barn waiting for him in the cool of the morning. None of the other Charltons were yet outside the house. A peach shawl draped her delicate shoulders. Dew dampened the tops of her two-tone shoes as she stood in the grass.

"Mornin'," he greeted. "A bit strange seeing you out here so early on a Sunday."

"I have a bone to pick with you," she replied, her airy, genteel voice calm and even, belying her words.

"Is that so? You didn't seem too eager to say much to me yesterday at the supper table. Figured I had gone and done something to get you riled."

Long eyelashes swept down and up. "You would tell me—my family, rather—if you were on the verge of a change, wouldn't you?"

Either his mind was still asleep or Sophie had learned to speak Greek overnight. She wasn't making sense.

She pulled the shawl closer about her. "It's come to my attention that you may be leaving the farm."

"That's news to me. Who said anything about me leaving?"

"It's just something I heard, is all."

"From who?"

When she didn't answer, Dusty tallied through a very short list of people who could have given her that wrong information. "Chad Hooper made up that lie, didn't he?"

She lifted her eyes. They were not as frigid as they were yesterday. "You're not looking for a different farm to work on?"

"No, but Chad ought to look for a job that doesn't require him to keep his mouth shut. He's in the wrong line of work." Dusty bristled at his own lack of good sense for agreeing to have Chad as an advisor. He should have followed his first mind and waited to see a different banker, even take time to make the trip to Claywalk. "I was at the bank to ask about investing in the railroad. That's it. I guess I don't make enough money to afford discretion."

Sophie looked appropriately shamefaced. "He thought to warn me in case you did look for other work."

"Trying to make me look dishonest is more like it. You know I wouldn't do that to Mr. Charlton. I've always given advance notice to my employers *if* I was going to leave, but I'm not going anywhere."

She sighed. "That's good to hear because you're a hard worker. My father would hate to lose you."

"Would you?" he dared to ask.

Two splotches of apricot appeared on her cheeks to match her shawl. Was she being bashful at having been asked a bold question, or was that an unspoken admittance of the truth?

"Why else do you think I'd come out here to catch you before you left for church?"

That didn't quite give him the answer he was looking for.

"I don't know. Maybe to brag about how Chad took you out on the promenade yesterday."

Her eyes rounded. "How did you know that?"

"Just something I heard, is all." Despite being angry over Chad's blabber-mouthing, he took a moment to savor the look on Sophie's face as he teased her. If she could only see the cute wrinkle in her nose when she scrunched her features together.

"Just for that, I'm going back into the house. But you should know that Chad intends to ask Daddy's permission to court me."

Dusty's moment of hilarity deflated. "Sophie, don't you think that's unwise? He's a liar and a manipulator. Look what he tried to do to get me in trouble with your family. You sure you want to be courted by someone like that?"

His strong words made her clamp her jaw tight. "You don't need to resort to name-calling. I know you two are not fond of each other, but I don't believe that Chad is malicious."

"He sure seems to believe in cutting down his fellow man just fine. You'd think he was worried about me being competition."

"I've assured him that there is no other suitor."

Sophie's words stung but he couldn't let it show. After all, he never ventured to court her properly. Perhaps it was time to stop acting the part of a schoolboy and make his intentions known. "Where I come from, a man that constantly needs to be assured and coddled has the maturity of a child."

"And where do you come from, Dusty? You hardly ever talk about your family. How can you expect to court me if you don't tell me the truth about yourself?"

The side door of the house pushed open and Sophie's father strode out to get the wagon ready. Their talk was going to have to cease.

"It was hard on my family to lose that ranch. That's why I don't talk about it much."

Sophie saw her father, too, and hurried to say her final words. "You should have. It would have made a difference."

"Why? Would you have let me court you knowing I wasn't always a hired hand?"

Sophie moved her lips as though she were about to speak, but as her father approached she retreated to the house.

"Why are you out here so early?" Mr. Charlton asked his daughter. "Your mother's looking for you to help set Rosemarie's hair."

"I was just having a word with Dusty."

Dusty suffered the brunt of Mr. Charlton's probing stare. Sophie's father didn't earn his success by being a fool. He knew something was stirring in the pot. "Well, get back in the house. We don't want to be late for service."

Sophie trotted away. Mr. Charlton swept a keen eye over Dusty and the barn behind him. "What's going on? Why does my daughter need to have a word with you before breakfast?"

Dusty remained still under his employer's scrutiny, not wanting any shifting movements to give the wrong impression that he was hiding something. "Sophie was wondering about my days of ranching. She thought I wanted to go back to doing that, but I told her I planned to keep working on the farm."

It wasn't a very tidy explanation. Mr. Charlton shook his head. "What gave her cause to think you wouldn't?"

"I went to the bank to invest my earnings. Rumors started that I was doing that for reasons other than to save money." Dusty disliked having to tell all his business, but in this instance, it was necessary.

His boss *tsk-tsked*. "Rumors. You'd think folks in this town would have learned by now to worry about the dirt littering their own front porch. Is Sophie gossiping again? I disciplined her for that before."

"No, sir. She was only concerned about your farm."

Mr. Charlton stepped inside the barn to get the horses for the wagon. He led a mare outside with a rope bridle. "I know about that new ranch opening outside town, Dusty. Would this business have anything to do with it?"

Of course he would find out about the Zephyr Ranch. Sophie's father was a prominent citizen and made it a point to keep himself up to date on Assurance's progress. Dusty rubbed the sunburn on his neck that had begun to itch. "No, sir. I never set foot on that place."

"You said you were at the bank to invest. Do you need more pay?"

"I do well with what I earn, but if you feel like I deserve it, I won't turn it down."

He chuckled. "Don't ever be too modest when someone offers to give you money. I make it a habit to treat my workers fairly, especially the hard-working ones. You let me know if there's anything you need. Understand?"

"Yes, Mr. Charlton." Dusty took hold of the mare's bridle while Sophie's father went to get a second horse.

"And if my daughter comes pestering you with questions

again, send her to me. She knows I don't stand for that conduct."

Sophie could never be a pest to him. He would regret it if he caused her to get in trouble. "Don't scold her on my account. She said nothing uncivil."

Mr. Charlton gave him the reins of the second horse while he began fastening the harnesses. "Help me with this, and then go have some breakfast. Lucretia's making eggs this morning. After that, we'll see you in church."

They would be seeing Chad Hooper, too. Dusty wished he could intervene to stop that man from asking to court Sophie. If only he had the money, the right standing to approach her father and get permission to court her first. He would have been able to do it once, when his family owned six hundred head of longhorns and a ranch spanning almost three thousand acres. Why did God allow them to lose all they worked so hard for?

As the sun rose higher in the sky, the last of the morning chill carried on the wind. *God's got you in a low place now. Might as well sit in it.*

Dusty attempted to shrug off the bothersome faint voice. It wouldn't do to go to church thinking ill thoughts about the Lord and bemoaning his station. Still, it was getting harder to ignore the fact that he was stuck in a rut.

After hitching the horses, he straightened his shoulders before meeting the Charltons for breakfast. No matter what, he had to make Sophie see that he was just as worthy to pursue her as any politician's son.

Sophie twisted in the pew at church to see where Chad was seated. Due to the town's growth over the year, the sanctuary filled up every Sunday with new faces. She had to search the crowded rows. The mayor and his family usually sat near the front. They were going to be late today. The service was to start in a few minutes.

Her father said nothing on the way to church about her talking to Dusty. She was relieved, as she knew her behavior could be regarded as unseemly if Dusty wasn't known for his truthful nature.

She swiveled in her seat again, this time to look for Dusty. He sat toward the middle pews. He normally sat close to her family. It had to be because of what they talked about that morning. His words still rang clear in her head. *Would you have let me court you knowing I wasn't always a hired hand?*

She grappled with her reaction. Dusty was different from the type of man she had been groomed to favor. A man like Chad came from good stock, was wealthy, educated, and schooled in the proper customs. Dusty was rough-hewn like the rope he used for a lasso, and his ways were as homespun as a colorblock quilt. No amount of money and upward station could change that about him and, oddly enough, she liked that.

"What has gotten into you, Sophie?" Her mother laid a hand on her arm. "You're as jumpy as your little sister, and she's more composed than you today."

Sophie regarded Rosemarie, who was quite calm, seated beside their mother wearing a new dress of floral calico. Her sister gave her a superior smile.

"Tell me what you're anxious about," her mother pressed. "Is it about Chad?"

She nodded, glad for the distraction. "I think he's going to ask Daddy for permission to court me."

The news pleased her mother. "Wonderful. I understand now why you can't sit still, but do try."

Sophie faced the front of the church. As the organist played, she heard footsteps and a rustle of fabric brushed her arm.

"May I sit here?" Marissa Pierce—Mrs. Marissa *Winford*, Sophie had to remind herself—stood in the aisle, waiting for her answer. As uncomfortable as the situation was to sit beside a reformed saloon girl, she couldn't deny the Reverend's wife a seat close to the altar. She moved over and signaled for her mother and Rosemarie to do the same.

"Thank you." Marissa offered her a quiet smile and settled into the pew. She faced forward to watch the choir as they began to sing a welcome hymn. The congregation rose to its feet.

Sophie felt like a stump when she stood next to Marissa. Undoubtedly other members of the congregation knew about their past strife and were commenting on the sight of them standing beside each other. The newly married and the still unspoken for. She tried concentrating on singing the hymn, but maintaining pitch was never her strong suit. She mouthed the words instead while she searched the sea of faces in the sanctuary. Was Chad going to be present or not?

CHAPTER 11

To Sophie's relief, Chad and his father came striding down the left aisle during the second verse of the hymn. Immediately, two rows of people shifted to make room for them. They moved into the third pew from the front. Chad found her gaze and acknowledged her with a nod. Her mood lifted. He dressed as he always did in his tailored suits. The mark of a gentleman. Every day was his Sunday best.

The choir led the church through two more songs before the congregation returned to their seats. Reverend Winford came up to the altar to deliver the sermon. Sophie picked up her Bible and turned to the corresponding book and chapter. For the next half hour she put aside the distractions of Chad and Dusty.

When service ended she got a tap on her shoulder. She craned her neck to look into Marissa's face.

"Sophie, we haven't spoken for a while. How have you been?"

Awkwardness settled upon her person. She hadn't said anything to Marissa since she attended the woman's wedding last autumn, and then it had been mandatory to at least congratulate her and Reverend Winford on their nuptials. She always found a way to avoid Marissa since. It wasn't going to be easy to escape a brief conversation with her today.

"I've been well. How about yourself?" With Chad waiting outside to speak with her father, Sophie wasn't in the mood for social niceties, least of all with someone she considered a former rival.

"Very good. It's been a happy season for Rowe and me. We've been married for over half a year now."

Sophie knew that she spoke without an ounce of spite or ill will that Marissa was simply blissful in her marriage, but it still made her uncomfortable. Must she be reminded of her past follies? She mustered up her decorum. "Yes, you have. If you'll excuse me, I'm going to stand at the door."

Marissa raised her hand in greeting to Sophie's family before parting ways to go stand beside her husband and shake hands with the congregation as they left the church.

"Your time will come too, my dear," Sophie's mother spoke low. "And perhaps in the near future, if what you say about Chad is true."

Sophie filed out of the pew along with her family. Margaret and Linda chatted together, waving when she walked by. They followed her out of the church. Once Sophie's mother found herself in conversation with Mrs. Euell, Sophie fell in step with her friends.

"We heard that Chad took you on the promenade yesterday. How was the walk?" Linda asked.

Margaret also expressed interest. "Did he hold your hand?"

Sophie felt better instantly. "He offered me his arm. It took almost an hour to walk around the lake. Afterward, he drove me home in his new buggy. Well, I should say it looked new."

Linda clasped her hands together in excitement. "He sounds like the hero in *The Adventures of Lady Whitecastle*."

Margaret rolled her eyes. "You and your dime novels.

I should think you had better things to do than read that drivel."

"It's not drivel," Linda defended. "Those stories are very engaging. Sophie reads them."

Margaret turned to her. "That isn't true, is it?"

Sophie chuckled. "They are entertaining, Margaret. You really should try reading one. I have several stories that you may borrow."

"No thank you."

"Sophie, your father is talking to Chad." Linda indicated to the two men standing near the tethering post.

Sophie's pulse increased as she witnessed Chad make true on his word. "Chad's asking my father for permission to court me."

"I knew he would. He's quite smitten with you," Margaret said. "I could tell at the Founders Day Festival."

Sophie studied her friend. "But how could you know, Margaret? You were sharing a picnic with Dusty."

"I could hardly eat a thing, I was so insulted. That Texan didn't like my Hoppin' John."

It was hard to suppress a giggle, but Sophie succeeded. "Never you mind Dusty. He didn't mean anything by it."

Linda agreed. "You can try a different recipe next year."

Margaret shook her shiny dark curls. "I don't intend on being unspoken for next year. I will have a suitor, I assure you."

"As will I." Sophie saw her father and Chad shake hands before departing from the other. "I'm twenty-one years old, after all. And eligible."

Upon saying good-bye to her friends, she traversed the steps leading from church to return to her family's wagon. Dusty was at the tethering post, talking to that tanner Wes Browman. They smiled and laughed. She liked when Dusty smiled. Grinned, was a better word. Her father told her that life wasn't easy for some people living on the plains, and more than a few men barely managed a smirk, but that never stopped Dusty from being good-humored and genuine.

Except when you make him mad, a little voice inside her head reminded. *You've been doing that frequently in recent days, haven't you?*

She turned her back on Dusty and Wes as the wagon drove off. No use in harping over old events. If Dusty was going to get upset because Chad was courting her, there was nothing to do about it. He was her father's employee. How did he expect to call on her if he was out working in the fields from sunup to sundown every day?

She banished the thought from her mind. To entertain the idea of him as a beau was laughable, at least her mother would say so. Ladies did not accept the attentions of those beneath their station. Social rules were meant to be adhered to.

"Sophie, I spoke with Chad concerning you." Her father brought up the subject of the day as they drove from town. "I think you already know what he asked. I gave him my permission to court you so long as his intentions are honorable."

"And, of course, we can expect nothing but propriety from the young man," her mother added.

Sophie's three siblings crowded the wagon with her. "So you're gonna marry the mayor's son?" Bernard asked. David yawned and Rosemarie folded her Sunday school lesson into the back pages of her Bible.

"That's moving rather fast, Bernard. Your sister and Mr. Hooper will have to go on an acceptable number of outings first to make their courtship known." Her mother recited the well-known practice. "Perhaps by the end of summer you may ask that question again." She patted Sophie's hand. "I'm so proud of you."

Sophie didn't feel like she accomplished anything. Chad was the one that did the asking. Still, praise didn't come lightly from her mother so she would take what was given. "Thank you, Mother."

Dusty didn't want to spend money at McIntyre's, but after church he found himself being dragged along by Wes, Taylor, and Matt Briggs from the livery stable. They sat him down at a table and thrust a plate of roast beef and a mug of sarsaparilla before him.

"Eat," Wes Browman commanded. "I hate seein' a man pine after a woman."

Taylor Hastings snickered and mimicked a lady's high-pitched voice. "Even a woman like Sophie Charlton?"

"Especially Miss Charlton." Wes swigged his drink and set it back down on the table with a thud. He let out a belch. "I saw Sterling make eyes at her all during church. Sorriest sight I ever did see."

"Come on," said Dusty. "I wasn't looking at her all the time."

"No, only when the congregation wasn't reading from the Bible. We had one verse to read today. One."

Dusty let the men rib him while he tasted the sarsaparilla. He wasn't going to share with them his courting troubles, or lack thereof. He just wished he hadn't been so obvious about it in public.

Wes stuffed a chunk of steak in his mouth and chewed loudly. "I'll tell you what you need to do." He talked with his mouth full, letting pieces of meat fly on the table. "You need to get off that farm. Three years is too long to stay in one place, especially if you don't plan on making it a trade."

"Get off the farm, you forget about her," Matt supplied.

Dusty sidestepped the reference to Sophie. "I get good pay. Why would I wanna go and do that?"

Wes wiped his mouth on a napkin, leaving a greasy

imprint. "We're not talking money. We're talking about you chasing after Goldilocks. How long you been trying to get her to pay you some mind?"

"Too long." Taylor took the words out of Dusty's mouth. "I don't think he's looked at another girl since he came to town."

"Not good. That Sophie's nothing but trouble. She snubbed five men last spring alone. That's before the Reverend came. Then she threw herself on him, but he wasn't about to stand for any of that."

Dusty put his fork down. "Mind yourself, Wes. You can say all you want about me, even get a good laugh or two out of it. But don't talk about Sophie in that manner. I mean it. That goes for all of you."

The table fell silent as he stared the men down. Wes recovered and drank the rest of his sarsaparilla. "I won't mention her name again, but you need a change. You're a rancher, a cattle driver. I know you don't plan on working on that farm for the rest of your life."

"No. I plan on having my own ranch someday."

Matt flagged down the waiter for more food. "You won't get any closer to making that happen by raking up pig slop. You hear about the Zephyr Ranch outside town?"

Dusty began to wonder if Eli Mabrey hadn't hired people to go around and remind him of that place. "I met the owner at the general store last week. He said I could go there and have myself a tour of the ranch."

"So why don't you? Sounds like he's fixing to offer you a job."

Wes had his food gobbled down. "You know why he hasn't been there to visit." A warning look from Dusty and he changed his course.

"As a matter of fact, I thought about going there to have a look-see." Dusty defended himself.

"When are you goin'?" Matt held up his glass for the waiter to refill. "I might come with you. I could use some extra pay."

Dusty hesitated to tell them. He didn't want the whole town following him out to Zephyr Ranch next Saturday. "I'll let you know when I decide."

He heard Taylor snicker in his glass. "You're not going, are you?"

"We'll see."

"You mean we'll see you at that farm for the next ten years."

Dusty took out money from his billfold and put it on the table next to his half-eaten plate. He pushed his chair back and stood. "Thanks for the company. Be seein' you."

He passed the waiter on the way out. The man gave him a perplexed glance before seeing to the other diners. Wes followed him outside.

"Hey, Sterling, we didn't mean to make you all thorns and horns. The boys and me think you're a good enough fellow. You should go where your work's appreciated." He clapped Dusty on the shoulder. "Besides, what's gonna happen when Miss Charlton does get herself married? You'll be there to watch the wedding, and she won't care."

The tanner had a point. Dusty couldn't fault him for his observations on the stagnant work on a farm, but he didn't want to believe what was said about Sophie. "You don't know her like I do, Wes. She's not an uncaring woman."

"But it don't look like she sees you the way you see her. I could be wrong, but women like her aren't wanting hard-working men. They marry gents who are already made."

Men like Chad Hooper. Dusty fathomed that man could sit at home all day if he wanted to and never go to his job at the bank. His wages were long since deposited by some wealthy ancestor. Was that the reason why Sophie preferred to be courted by him? The only reason?

A bitter tang of jealousy formed in his mouth. It didn't seem right how some men accumulated all and did little to earn it while others had to scrape and claw in the dirt to barely get by. The loss of the ranch in San Antonio cost his family their savings and their assets. Apparently he was still paying for an event beyond his control.

A gust of wind stirred up dirt to the sidewalk. *Sophie is shallow. Let her be.*

No. Sophie may like her pretty clothes and her daddy may have spoiled her for a time, but in this last year, she'd shown she could work hard. And she had a good heart. She used to bring him soup in the winter when he came down with a cold.

Any lady of the manor would make sure her help was healthy enough to keep working.

And that time the plow was broken, she sat and kept him company while he repaired it. She didn't have to, but she did. Way down there on the inside, Sophie wasn't a fair-weather person. Dusty believed that with his entire mind. "I've got to get back to the farm, Wes. Nothing to do in town anyway 'cept spend money in the restaurant."

Wes didn't bother to hide his opinion. "You're hopeless, Sterling."

CHAPTER 12

ONDAY MORNING, SOPHIE chose her clothing carefully for the meeting with Mayor Hooper. She had to look respectful and capable. That meant no excess of ruffles or light-colored garments.

Perusing her wardrobe, she withdrew a dark blue gown that was en vogue three seasons ago, but still fashionable enough to be seen in town. She chose one of her best corsets to wear underneath, a whalebone apparatus that reduced her waist to little more than a wisp. Rosemarie or her mother would have to help her get it on.

She chose to enlist her little sister. She needed to borrow Rosemarie's school primer anyway to show the mayor the sorry state of the school supplies. "Rosemarie, are you awake?"

Across the bedroom, her sister rolled over with a sleepy yawn. Part of her hair had come out of its braid where she slept on it. "What is it, Sophie?"

"I need two things from you. One, your school primer, so I can show it to Mayor Hooper. The second, your help in lacing me into my corset."

"Where's Mother?"

"Downstairs cooking, I'd imagine. Please, I only need you for a few minutes, and then you can go back to sleep."

"It's already almost time to get up."

"Then this should not be too much of a bother to you."

Groaning, Rosemarie complied. They tackled the corset first.

Sophie felt Rosemarie tugging on the laces. She looked over her shoulder. "What's taking so long?"

"I can't get it to lace. You've gotten bigger."

"Nonsense. You're just not strong enough. Try pulling harder." Sophie grabbed the bedpost again while her sister made a second attempt.

"No good, Sophie. You've gained weight."

"I have not. I wore this corset only two months ago to Linda's birthday party. If it fit then I know it fits now."

"Are you holding your stomach in?"

"Of course I am." Sophie held her breath and imagined flattening her belly button to her spine for good measure. Rosemarie pulled the stays again. Any more and Sophie knew she wouldn't be able to breathe. "That's good. Tie them." She held her breath again until the laces were securely fastened. On the exhale, her ribs stopped short of expanding against the iron-tight boning of the corset.

She stepped into her dress and let Rosemarie button it for her in the back. The youngest member of the Charlton family was only eight, and yet she was shooting up as high as a cornstalk. Sophie had no desire to anticipate how tall her little sister would be by the end of summer. Already the girl's nose was on the same level as hers.

"Daddy says that I'm going to be taller than Mother when I finish growing," Rosemarie chattered as her small fingers buttoned up Sophie's dress in rapid succession. "How come you're so short?"

"I am not short. I am what the French call petite." Sophie held her head high as she gazed at her reflection in the mirror atop the dressing table. If she wore her hair in a high bun, then the illusion of height could be achieved. When Rosemarie finished getting her into the dress, she combed her hair back and swept it atop her crown. "Hand me pins as I go, Rosemarie."

Her sister dutifully stood by with hairpins in hand while Sophie sat at the dressing table, arranging curls. "Why do you need my primer? You already finished schooling."

"I told you, the primer is outdated. Your school needs new ones. I have to show it to the mayor so that he will put it on the ballot this year."

"Why can't the school just buy primers from the general store, or have them shipped on the train?"

Sophie took a hairpin from her. "It's more complicated than that. The town has to vote on new primers, but we don't have school elections in Assurance yet. Other towns in Kansas do, and the women can cast ballots. If I can make the mayor see how important this is for the town's progress, then we will have school elections and ladies can vote like men do."

She had said a mouthful. Over Rosemarie's head, from the quizzical frown her little sister gave. "Why do you have to do that just to get new primers? Can't you ask people to give money to buy them?"

"You're not understanding me. Or maybe I'm not articulating very well." Sophie opened a pin with her teeth. She had better get her words in order before she set foot inside the mayor's house, else he'd see things the way Rosemarie did.

But Chad might be there to help her. The thought gave her a measure of calm. Then again, it was her cause. She needed to see it through on her own, even if her new beau helped open the door to Mayor Hooper's office.

Sophie used a total of twenty pins to get her hair to stay in place. She topped her coiffure with a small hat and pinned it at her crown, giving the hat a jaunty tilt. Very Parisian. "Do I look presentable?"

Rosemarie ignored the question. "If I give you my primer, I want one of your books."

"I don't have any primers. The ones I used to read were passed down to you and Bernard."

"No. One of those books." Her sister pointed to a small stack of dime novels on Sophie's bedside table. "I want to read *The Adventures of Lady Whitecastle*."

"Those novels are too old for you. I have a volume of fairy tales you can read instead."

Rosemarie shook her head back and forth in apt protest. "I want to read *Lady Whitecastle*. My teacher says that my marks in reading and grammar are high. The words won't be too hard for me at all."

Sophie curled her stocking-clad toes in frustration. Her sister was making her late with pointless arguing. "It's not the words. It's the subject of the books. I'm afraid they're a little too advanced for a girl your age."

"I already know what's in those books. Sarah from Sunday school told me they have pirates in them, and knights and gunfighters who rescue the princess from the dragon. Those pirates kiss the princesses, too, but I'm old enough to know that."

"Pirates don't kiss princesses, and gunfighters don't slay dragons." Sophie caught herself. Why in the world was she schooling her sister on the plot devices of dime novels? "Fine. Choose any novel over there that you want, but leave the one that I'm still reading. Don't let Mother catch you with it, either. You know she'd rather you practice your French over the summer."

A triumphant Rosemarie skipped over to the bedside table to choose her reward. "The primer's on my bookshelf next to *Little Women*."

Sophie let her amuse herself while she retrieved the primer. The cover of the thin book was falling apart at the seams, the yellowing pages held by unraveling thread. The crumbling sight of it surely would help her case for getting school elections on the ballot.

She took the primer downstairs, where her mother was setting breakfast on the table. The smell of fresh-baked biscuits and warm honey made her stomach rumble. The whalebone corset pressed against her belly in reminder to abstain. "I'm off to meet with Mayor Hooper. I should be home before noon."

Her mother nodded stiffly, evidence that she still was uncomfortable with her decision to pursue the cause. "Don't stay in town too long. We have shirts to mend today. David and your father are already out milking the cow and gathering the eggs."

Sophie's tense nerves stretched taut with more anxiety. "Did they forget? Who's going to ride with me into town?"

"Dusty will. He's waiting outside for you."

Her nerves snapped. On no account whatsoever did she want Dusty taking her into town. What if Chad saw them? Or worse, what if Dusty said something that would embarrass her? The whole thing spelled disaster. "Can't Daddy take me?"

"No, Sophie. Your father has work to do that cannot be interrupted by this pursuit of yours. I'd rather Dusty go along with you than your brother, as you and David tend to dawdle."

In the sitting room the mantel clock struck half past seven. If she waited any longer to leave the house she was going to arrive late. Sophie committed the image of the buttery, golden biscuits to memory before meeting Dusty in front of the house.

He was already waiting with his horse and her mare Bess, both animals saddled and ready to go. If she had known she was going to sit on a horse, she would have donned her riding habit. Sophie cast a doubtful eye upon Bess's sidesaddle. She was hoping to take the wagon. Riding in the elements was going to do her hair something awful.

Dusty tipped his Stetson to her. Beneath the brim, she saw his eyes take in her blue ensemble. "You look right pretty today."

She murmured her thanks, feeling warm under his smile. "Why aren't we taking the wagon into Assurance?"

"It's faster on horseback. Mr. Charlton told me you needed to see the mayor by nine. We'd better get a move on, or these horses are gonna have to gallop all the way."

"Not with me dressed like this, they won't." Sophie handed her sister's primer to him to place in his horse's saddlebag. She reinforced her hat pin before approaching the mare. The left stirrup rested three feet off the ground. She didn't see how she was going to get her foot in there without baring a leg or doing a most unladylike hop. "Would you mind looking the other way for a moment, Dusty?"

"How about I help you, instead?" He came around to her side, knelt, and cupped his hands. "Ready when you are."

Where was that mounting block? Sophie scoured the yard for it, but the little wooden structure was nowhere to be seen. Dusty must have hidden it on purpose.

She put one foot in Dusty's hands and stepped off the ground. He boosted her up to the saddle, where she made haste to position herself and get her skirt properly tucked into place to keep it from blowing about. He put her foot in the stirrup, his touch gentle and steady at once.

Her heart stirred within her chest as he tended to her comfort and safety, making sure that she was in no danger of falling from the horse. A rugged confidence graced his movements as he inspected the saddle straps and made sure Bess's bridle was set in place. He moved to Sophie's right, brushing against her hand. His canvas shirt had been washed enough times where she could feel the heat of his skin through the soft fabric. He was close enough for her to reach down and touch his face.

Why was she thinking of touching his face? Sophie kept a tight grip upon the reins and forced herself to pay attention to the sun rising above the wheat fields in the distance. Dusty finally climbed into the saddle of his horse and led the way down the road.

As the path widened for them to ride alongside each other, Sophie matched her horse's stride to his. Dusty stared at the road ahead, one hand holding the reins, the other resting on the saddle's pommel. He wore a reflective countenance. "Guess Chad's asked for permission to court you now, hasn't he?"

"Yes." Admitting it brought a sense of discomfort to her, when yesterday she had been eager to share the news with Linda and Margaret. "You didn't have to escort me into town if you didn't want to."

"Mr. Charlton told me to."

"He doesn't know that you and Chad don't see eye-to-eye." Sophie pushed a long branch from a tree out of her way as Bess walked beneath it. Morning mist rose off the lake as they passed by. The peace of the forested area, enlivened with the occasional birdsong, made her imagine she and Dusty were the only two people in the world.

"It's not about me and Chad agreeing with each other. I don't think he should be your beau."

Sophie wanted to ask why, even though she knew the answer. "That's not your decision."

"Maybe not, but I'm entitled to an opinion, at least. You could do better."

"Oh, I can, can I? And who could possibly be a more eligible bachelor than Chad Hooper? I see no other man in this

103

town who's a banker, a representative for the Katy rail, and whose father is mayor."

That old twinkle returned to Dusty's eyes as he took his gaze off the road. "All that doesn't mean a horseshoe in a bucket of hog slop. What do high and fancy titles have to do with him courting you?"

"Plenty."

Dusty persuaded her to elaborate by raising his eyebrow.

"For starters, it shows that he's a diligent worker."

"Or that the position was handed to him."

"No, Chad rightfully earned his place. He studied to be a banker."

"That still doesn't show how he's suited to court you."

Sophie threw one hand in the air. "I knew you'd show out. Please don't talk like that in front of the mayor."

"Don't you mean his boy?"

"Chad too. And he's not a boy. He's twenty-four, about the same age as you."

"Why, Miss Sophie, I'm surprised you know that much about me." He pushed his hat down to avoid the sun's glare as they rode in its direction but his mischievous smile was plain to see.

"Only about as much as you'd care to tell." She sat stiff as a board in the saddle, thinking of what to quip next. Bess made a misstep as her hoof connected with a wagon wheel rut in the road. Sophie slipped, grabbing the horse's mane and the lower pommel over her left leg to keep from falling.

A strong hand grabbed her arm and held her in place. "You got your balance?"

Sophie repositioned herself and hooked her right leg more securely over the top pommel. "I wasn't expecting Bess to falter like that."

"Her hoof may still be bothering her. I'll have a look at it again while you're talking with the mayor." Dusty released her arm but the warmth remained where he made contact. A look passed between them. At that moment their prior quibbling, albeit all in good fun, was pushed aside. He may joke and flirt with her like a schoolboy but he was a man. One that didn't hesitate to protect her when necessary.

They rode the rest of the way to town in silence.

Assurance was alive with shopkeepers opening stores for the day and travelers leaving the hotel to take a stagecoach to the station. Sophie and Dusty cut through the square and rode to the residential areas. The further they ventured away from the square the bigger the houses became, until they reached the largest one, a two-story structure complete with eight windows that faced the front alone. A white picket fence lined the house's perimeter and shielded a budding flower garden from being trampled.

"Mayor's house seems to get bigger each election." Dusty took his stallion to the tethering post by the fence. "I'm expecting a butler to open the door."

"Hush. They might hear you. Help me down, please."

"Not if you tell me to hush, I won't." He pretended to take his time to get to her. "You'll just be late for your meeting."

Sophie wasn't worried. "If you insist." She unhooked her foot from the stirrup and slid out of the saddle. Four feet was a longer descent than she expected. Her skirt fanned out and smacked the ground, stirring up a ring of dust.

"Sophie, you could've hurt yourself." He scolded her while rushing to her aid. "Don't do that again."

She straightened and brushed herself off. The force of her previous impact drove the corset into her ribs, where the boning of the garment dug and rubbed against her flesh. She longed to take a deep breath to regain herself, but was allowed no more than a few shallow, useless gulps. "I am not so helpless as to let you win at this game."

"What game? You knew I was teasing, and that I was

coming to help you down." He took her shoulders in a possessive gesture. "What if you had landed the wrong way and broken your ankle? Mr. Charlton would have my head on a stick."

She shot a glance at the door of the mayor's house, hoping no one could see them. She wanted to know what Dusty's true motivations were before she went inside. "Is it the pursuit of my affection or my father's wrath that spurs you?"

He dropped his hands from her. "Why do you do keep testing me to see how much it takes before I get angry? Stop rubbing your courtship with Chad in my face." He backed away and took Bess to be tied to the post.

Shocked, Sophie was motionless as he left her to tend to the horses. She expected him to toss a barb back, not get offended and stalk off. Once again she discovered that she did not have anything clever to say. "You brought up the whole thing on the way here about Chad courting me."

His back was toward her as he lifted Bess's hoof to inspect it. "No, that was you. I'm just doing my job by seeing you into town."

"If you don't like how I tease, then why don't you ever say anything ahead of time before you go and get mad?"

Dusty removed Rosemarie's primer from his horse's saddlebag and gave it to her. He took too long in answering the question. When he did, she wished she never asked. "You're a lovely lady, but sometimes, Sophie, what you say just isn't cute."

CHAPTER 13

$\mathcal{S}$OMEONE THAT APPEARED to be a butler opened the door when Sophie knocked. The white-haired man greeted her in a respectable suit of summer wool and polished brown shoes. He wasn't there the last time her family had visited. "Can I help you, ma'am?"

She was unsure whether to think of him as a butler. Such help was nearly unheard of in Kansas. "I'm Sophie Charlton, here to see Mayor Hooper. I was scheduled to meet him at nine."

"Yes, he told me to expect you. I'm Jarvis Shaw, his new assistant. Come in."

Sophie stepped through the open doorway, leaving her disagreement with Dusty and his horrible opinion of her outside with the horses. *Sometimes what you say just isn't cute.* His words were a song that played over in her head, stinging repeatedly like a wasp. Time enough to think about him after the meeting when they had to ride all the way back home together. She'd make sure it was done in silence too.

"Wait here." Mr. Shaw left her standing in the hallway while he entered Mayor Hooper's office. Sophie busied herself by studying the portraits hanging from the walls. A family portrait took up the center. Chad was a baby in his mother's arms, all pink and swaddled in a long infant's gown.

A cap of snowy white sat on his bald head in imitation of a miniature bonnet. He appeared fussy.

Mr. Shaw reappeared in the hall. "Mayor Hooper says you can come in."

Sophie patted her hair into place before entering the office. The mayor was at his desk, surrounded by plaques that decorated the walls. The Hoopers were Yankees, having accumulated modest wealth in Philadelphia before heading to Kansas to invest it in railroading. Their journey to good fortune was illustrated in the tintypes that also gave the office its décor.

As Sophie took in the empty settee and chair, she realized that Chad was not present. Perhaps he was coming, on his way from a different part of the large house.

The mayor greeted her. "Good morning, Miss Charlton. I'm glad you were able to make it to town. Please sit down. Would you like some coffee while you're here?"

"No, thank you." It was always odd to hear him call her Miss Charlton, when in years prior to her coming of age, he and Mrs. Hooper called her Sophie. Primer in hand, she reclined on the settee, at least five steps away from the mayor's desk. Why would he have guests seated so far from him? "Will Chad be attending the meeting as well?"

"No, Chad left for the bank about an hour ago."

"Oh." She had hoped he would be there to help her convince the mayor to put the school elections on the ballot. He knew it was important. Did he think that merely arranging her meeting with his father would be enough?

She couldn't afford to let her temper smolder in the company of Chad's father. Sophie convinced herself to see reason. Perhaps Chad thought she was well able to seek the mayor's aid without his help. Hadn't she told him that she was capable? It was time to illustrate that fact to Mayor Hooper.

She squared her shoulders and raised her chin. "Sir, I

know you're well aware of why I'm here. I mean to stand by the promise I made at the town belle contest by working to get women in Assurance the right to vote on school issues. As I recall, both schoolhouses are in need of instructors and administrators. Surely the names of those people can be put on ballots this year." She ended her speech slightly winded. Rosemarie laced her stays tighter than she realized.

Mayor Hooper listened with a patient yet undecipherable expression on his face. He folded his hands atop the desk. "I understand that you want to give ladies the right to vote in our town, Miss Charlton, but it's not that simple. You can't just put together a school election. Our children's facilities aren't large enough where they require someone to run a campaign to be voted as administrator."

Sophie ran her fingers over the fraying spine of Rosemarie's primer. "What about a vote for new school supplies instead? This is my little sister's reading primer. Look at the state of it, outdated and falling apart. Can't we do something?"

Mayor Hooper accepted the primer from her when she stood and walked five paces to hand it to him. He flipped open the faded cover with his index finger and flicked through the worn pages. "I don't see anything wrong with this book, Miss Charlton. It's aged, but the words and illustrations are still highly legible."

"Mayor, that primer dates before the start of the War Between the States. If the teacher were not present, boys and girls wouldn't know if the North or South had won."

"But there is an instructor to guide the children."

Sophie was taken aback by his glib remark. "Surely you don't think that's acceptable?"

Mayor Hooper closed the primer. "Young lady, when I was a boy in school, we didn't have primers. I learned to read with whatever literature my mother had in our house, which wasn't much. When I went to the schoolroom, I practiced my letters and grammar on a slate. In my humble opinion, what the students have now is a vast improvement."

"I'm not speaking ill of your schooling, Mayor, but Assurance can afford to purchase new supplies for the children. The railroad brings new resources to our town nearly every day."

"Are you taking a stance for the schoolchildren, or for the potential women voters that you hope will participate on account of these elections?"

Sophie fell silent as she scrambled for the right words. "Well...both."

Mayor Hooper shook his head, his smile fatherly and a bit condescending all at once. "Now you realize how politics are played. In order for you to get what you want, you have to use other means, even other people, to get it."

Sophie stiffened in vehement protest. "I would never use innocent children as a means to further my agenda. We have a terrible misunderstanding if you think that's what I'm doing."

He kept his outward composure leveled. "How will you convince the citizens of that? If there was another way to allow women to vote in this town, would you have still touched upon school elections?"

"I don't think that's a question for me to answer. The state constitution made it so that women can only vote in school elections. A better question is why Assurance leaves the election off the ballot." Awareness dawned on her, and made her cross. "I should think men want to keep women away from the polls."

"I assure you, Miss Charlton, that it's not deliberate. Assurance is still growing." The mayor's tone grew terse. Sophie was pleased that her argument was getting through to him. She only wished she had taken more time to educate herself in the way of legislation and current events.

"The town is still growing, but not progressing in its view

of citizens being equal. We don't want to be the laughing-stock of Kansas." The more she defended her stance the more intriguing the subject became. Why shouldn't a woman's vote count?

"I'll tell you what. If you can show me that people in town share your sentiment, I will find a way to put school elections on the ballot this year. Bring me a petition with as many names as you can find."

Sophie became heartened by his willingness to reex-amine the town's election policies. Or perchance he was doing it simply because he wanted her father to vote him in for another term. No matter. As he implied, more than one end could be accomplished in politics.

"Thank you, sir. I will get started immediately."

He chuckled and returned to being the patriarch of the house as opposed to the mayor of Assurance. "Not too imme-diate. My wife learned that you were coming and wanted to spend a few moments with you. She's in the sitting room, waiting with tea and scones."

Sophie refused the offer of coffee earlier, but after such an adversarial debate she welcomed a respite. She had argued like a man before the mayor. Her mother would be most dis-pleased if she were to find out.

Mayor Hooper led Sophie into the sitting room, greeted his wife, and left the two of them to return to his office. Sophie returned Mrs. Hooper's polite salutation. "How do you do, Mrs. Hooper?"

"I hope you didn't give my poor husband too much trouble with the election ballots." The mayor's wife patted the chair next to her for Sophie to be seated. She poured two cups of tea.

"No, ma'am. Mayor Hooper was willing to listen."

"You have my son Chad to thank for that. You take sugar, don't you?"

"Yes, two lumps."

"He's very fond of you."

Sophie accepted the cup from her. "As I him."

"Oh, I'm certain, as you had shown by attending the festival at Claywalk with him last year."

Sophie stopped in mid-sip, raising her eyes over the teacup. Had Chad spoken to his mother of the fiasco, when he caught her voicing aloud at the festival her preference to be escorted by another man instead?

Mrs. Hooper did not give an outward indication that she knew anything to be remiss. "I wished at the time that something could have come of your association, but Chad left for his studies in the fall. Better late than never, I should say."

Sophie nodded and let her talk.

"His time away at college has made him more reflective, but you must not be alarmed. He always was a quiet, serious boy."

"My mother says those are very good qualities in a man. It makes him more apt to listen to a lady."

"Lucretia is wise." Mrs. Hooper stirred honey into her cup. "But I think you will make a fine match for Chad. Your conversation and effervescent spirit are sure to please."

Too bad Dusty didn't find her conversation pleasing. She remembered him as she looked to the window. Her view of the tethering post was blocked by a hedge in the garden.

Mrs. Hooper clinked her spoon against the teacup. "But Chad is stationed at the bank here in town, so you will not have to worry about him leaving again."

"No, I would not." Sophie ate a scone. Dusty was going to have to get used to Chad being a fixture in her life, plain and simple.

She sat with Chad's mother until the tea was finished. After Mr. Shaw showed her the door, she walked with apprehension back to the tethering post. Dusty leaned against the frame of the picket fence, waiting.

"How'd your meetin' go?"

"What I had to say was well-received." She searched for traces of previous anger in him, but Dusty had returned to his normal nature, carrying himself in an unhurried, relaxed stance. "Dusty, about what I said to you before I went inside the house—"

"Let it be. I forgot about it."

Sophie wasn't sure he did, but did not press the matter. She was learning that even Dusty was not immune to constant jibes, particularly where it involved her choice of beaus. Better to tease him on gentler subjects, or not at all, for the time being.

This time she waited dutifully for him to help her back upon the horse. "I need to make a purchase of stationery at the general store before we return home. Mayor Hooper wants me to get a petition started."

"For what?"

"For women to vote in school elections, of course. You think women should be able to vote on the state of our schools, don't you?"

He climbed astride his own horse and set the pace for them. "Never thought about it much, to be honest."

"Why not? You don't seem the kind of man to want to keep women from the polls."

"No, I never said that. I just always had other things to do, like helping my family or working. Most of the time, I didn't get out to the polls myself."

"You mean while you had your ranch?"

"Not my ranch. My parents'."

Was he finally willing to talk about his past? Sophie deliberated whether to encroach upon the subject as they rode the horses back to town square. "You can tell me about your ranch and family if you want to."

He sat astride the stallion as if he were bored, looking out at the people walking in the streets. He rested a hand at his hip. In that moment he appeared out of place among the shops and busy chatter, better suited for riding the open range. "Not much to tell. My family owned a ranch. Now we don't. They still live in Texas. I'm up here."

He didn't say that he lived in Kansas. How odd, that after being here for three years, he still didn't consider it home. "Maybe your family can start over. That's what my father and mother did." What was Dusty staring at, that he refused to let his eyes meet hers?

"Cattle costs more at the start than purchasing seed to plant. Anyway, you'd better get what you need at the store so you can make it back home before noon. I'll be out here, waiting."

Sophie gave up for the moment. He couldn't be pressed no matter how gentle her persuasions. Maybe he thought she was incapable of understanding, but as the oldest, she had known hard times. Her parents too. The Charltons just made sure to not let anyone else know.

"Sophie."

She turned to view Dusty's half-smile. "I'd like to be the first to sign that petition. After you, of course."

CHAPTER 14

W AS HE A fool to be so nice? Dusty wondered after signing Sophie's petition.

He was doing her another favor, right after taking her to town to see the mayor and waiting outside the house like a loyal hound dog. Sure, part of his job entailed looking after members of the Charlton family if need be, but that didn't make it any easier to accept that the girl he was sweet on accepted the courtship of someone else.

He was glad he didn't run into Chad while waiting for Sophie's meeting to end at Mayor Hooper's house. Things would have been said that shouldn't and he'd find himself in trouble with somebody, be it the mayor, Chad, or Mr. Charlton.

"I can't keep doing this," Dusty said to his stallion as he groomed the horse in the barn stall later that week. "I wasn't raised to keep my head down and be wary of folks talking about me, trying to threaten my work."

Gabe agreed, or seemed to, by shaking his black mane. Dusty fed him a handful of oats before brushing the horse's back.

"I'll go to that ranch on Saturday," he promised for the fifth time in four days. Saying it aloud made him feel better about his choice.

What harm was there in touring the ranch? He might

learn something and put it to good use on his own ranch someday. It was just the thing to liven his spirits. "Never hurts to store things away for the future."

Gabe smacked loudly on the oats.

"You'll be glad to see herds again too, won't you, boy?"

Inside, he felt like a liar. It was going to take more than seeing cattle to make him happy. The discontent started small, and moved to settle on his insides.

"Do you always talk to that horse?" Sophie appeared in the open doorway, leading Bess.

Dusty smirked. She never missed an opportunity to berate him for talking to Gabe whenever she caught him doing so. "Not always, but he was my only company on the trails."

"I don't believe that. You couldn't have driven cattle north all by yourself."

"Those other cowhands weren't as sociable as Gabe." He put aside his humor and considered the potential conse- quences of the situation. "What did you hear me say?"

She shrugged and walked Bess to her stall. "Nothing important, since you're talking to an animal. Just that he or you would be happy seeing herds again."

Good. She didn't hear the part about him going to the ranch. "Do you want me to groom Bess for you?"

"I can do it." Sophie wore her work calico, a simple brown dress that had seen better days. Bess clopped behind her as she went to get a brush from the tack wall.

Dusty waited for her to make another remark, to jest about his equine companion or rib him on being a silly cowboy. When no quip came, he was let down. So this was to be the extent of his interactions with Sophie while Chad was courting her. All primness and no sass. Not much of it, anyway.

"Will you help me make rounds on Saturday to get my petition signed?"

He paused at the question. She waited with a pleasant, unassuming smile. "I had something else to do that day."

Her smile faded into a nod of resignation. "I suppose I did ask at a moment's notice. You sure have become busy in the past few weeks."

He hoped to deflect her curiosity before she asked where he was going on Saturday. "Naturally. Can't expect me to sit around by my lonesome while you have all the fun, now can I?"

She marched back to him with brush in hand. Her mare gazed after her in possible bewilderment before entering the last stall to find hay to eat. "Are you calling upon a lady in town, Dusty?"

"A gentleman never tells his business."

Sophie made that puckered face where it looked like she swallowed a mouthful of mustard greens and vinegar. "You are seeing someone, aren't you? Who is she?" She followed him from the barn, waving the brush. "Is it Margaret?"

"You'd best go back and close that stall door on Bess. You don't want her wanderin' the fields at night." He increased the speed of his stride. Behind him, her footsteps quickened into a light run.

"Answer me. Are you seeing Margaret Rheins?"

"You're asking me more than I need to tell you." He walked faster to the bunkhouse. The soles of Sophie's boots slapped the dry ground twice for every one of his steps.

"It is her, isn't it?"

"I didn't say that."

She sprinted in front of him. Out of breath, she stopped and bent over, resting her hands on her knees. "Don't try to fool me...I talked to Margaret at church Sunday... She said she didn't plan on entering the town belle contest again next year."

"And?"

"And...that must mean that she has a gentleman caller now. One who is very, very promising." She peered at him through the heavy gold fringe of her lashes.

Was that supposed to intimidate him? Dusty had seen scarier looks on cornered rabbits, and those downy little creatures could growl if the need arose. "Just never you mind about Miss Margaret. You have your own beau."

That gave her pause. Her pink lips trembled. He wanted to kiss them again. "If you are courting Margaret, I will find out. I'll know something tomorrow when I go to her house with that petition."

"Do what you think you need to. I'm going to clean up for supper." He veered around her and climbed the two steps to the bunkhouse, leaving her in the field still holding the grooming brush. "Let me know how that petition signing goes."

Dusty saddled Sophie's horse for her before he left for town on Saturday morning. She and David came out of the house after breakfast. Sophie moved with a nervous energy, clasping her petition and pencil case, while her brother trudged along beside her, yawning and doing his best to appear bored and bothered.

"I don't care whether women can vote. How come I have to go with you?" he asked with petulance not yet outgrown.

Sophie wore her gray riding habit today and had pinned her hair back in a severe bun underneath what was fashioned to look like a gentleman's top hat. Her gloves were black to match her shoes. In Dusty's opinion she made herself look too solemn, but he guessed that was the whole point.

If Sophie wanted to be taken seriously, dressing in her usual colorful frilliness wasn't a smart way of going about it.

"I cannot go to town unescorted, that's why. It's unseemly. Dusty would go, but he has other things to tend to today." She shot him a crushing look. Dusty tipped his own hat to acknowledge her greeting.

David lost interest in sparring with his sister. "Where are you going, Dusty?"

"He won't tell you. He won't tell anyone. Dusty's become a man of secrets." Sophie's skirt swished as she walked up to him. Dusty presented her mounting block so she could climb in the sidesaddle. He offered to assist. She held onto him for half a moment, her dainty fingers resting on his hand just long enough for her to get on the horse. She pushed her own foot through the stirrup.

"You look pretty today, as always."

She adjusted her skirt before peering down her pert nose at him. "Flattery will get you nowhere."

"All the same, though." He knew she was burning up inside, wanting to know his plans for the day, hating that he kept mum. He patted the horse's flank. "I'd better get goin', too. Wouldn't want to miss my engagement." Dusty held back a chuckle as Sophie bit down on her lips to hide a nervous tic.

"I'll see you in town."

"Maybe. Have a good day, Miss Sophie. You too, David." He felt Sophie's eyes on him as he turned to the barn to saddle up Gabe. He'd give Sophie and her brother a head start before leaving. They should be onto the first house by the time he rode through and out of town.

He considered simply bypassing Assurance and following the Katy tracks, but that was out of the way. Zephyr Ranch was close to the main road, if he remembered Eli correctly.

He had dressed in a different style that day, and was surprised Sophie hadn't said anything. He wore a blue and white striped chambray shirt with a thin necktie, black pants, and boots with his best spurs. The rowels flashed silver in the sunlight. The shanks were engraved with a calligraphic S for Sterling.

An heirloom passed down from his father, the spurs jingled softly as he walked. Perhaps he could put them to good use again soon and do his family name proud.

After thirty minutes he rode into Assurance. Knowing Sophie, she probably started her petition in the more affluent section of town near the mayor's house and close to the square. He maneuvered his horse through the square as quickly as he could, not stopping to greet anyone.

Outside of Assurance the main road was a narrow dirt path, just wide enough for a schooner to push through. Maybe next year it would be expanded for more travelers, but Dusty doubted it. With the new train station in town there wasn't much need for wagon travel.

Tall green grass waved him onward as dandelions drifted in the air. He broke his stallion into a trot, and then a full-on gallop. Dusty held on to his hat as the horse ran into the wind. It felt good to race across the plains, away from the ever-increasing number of shops being built and people coming into town. Assurance was getting more cramped by the day, and he felt trapped.

He wondered why he didn't feel that way when he lived in San Antonio, a city ten times the size of Assurance. His family had miles of land to roam on outside the city. He enjoyed going into town in those days, when he had money to spend and cattle to bring to market. Now his ventures into town consisted of playing errand boy and chaperone.

To a girl who knows you exist, but doesn't care. The wind

whipped through his shirt and threatened to take the hat off his head. Dusty pressed the top of his Stetson down further.

He wouldn't go so far as to say Sophie didn't care. She did express curiosity as to his whereabouts today. She played right into his teasing by assuming that he was out courting another girl, and she wasn't pleased about it.

It doesn't mean anything. Sophie will still keep Chad as her beau whether you court a girl or continue to chase after her.

Dusty let go of a sigh. The Zephyr Ranch showed up ahead on the left, the first of several fenced-in areas. He pulled on the reins to slow his horse down and led him off the road.

A sign hung from a newly built gate. Letters spelling out Zephyr Ranch in iron-wrought curlicues resided next to a figure of a wild mustang standing on its hind legs, mane and tail carved to appear as though they were blowing in the breeze. Dusty couldn't help but grin. Mr. Mabrey wasted no time in making sure his ranch had flair.

Dusty scanned through the front fence and saw men riding out among the cattle in the fields. The reddish-brown Herefords lumbered out of the way when a cowhand rode his horse by.

Should he just mosey on in or tether Gabe to the fence? Dusty tried to get the cowhands' attention by waving. When that didn't work, he cupped his hands over his mouth. "Hey, there."

One of the men raised his head, saw him, and steered his horse in the direction of the front gate. "Howdy," he called back.

Dusty waited for him to reach the gate. The man got off his horse and strode up to him. "What can I do for you?"

Dusty was momentarily struck by the cowhand's appearance. He was a big man, easily over six feet tall with a wide, muscled neck and shoulders that stretched his gingham shirt. More striking than his build was his skin color. The man swiped a large hand across his black face to wick away the sweat.

"My name is Dusty Sterling. I'm here for a tour of the ranch. Mr. Mabrey said to ask for him when I got here."

"The boss headed to town for more supplies. You lookin' to get hired?" The man rumbled in a deep voice, although his tone was friendly.

"We'll see. I'll look around before I make a decision. I'm working for someone else right now."

"Who?"

Dusty didn't want to give away the name. "A farmer back in town." He jabbed his thumb in the direction of Assurance.

The man nodded. "Don't mind me for askin'. We get folks coming this way to be nosy. Last week we caught a dairy farmer from Claywalk sending one of his workers out to see whether we were in competition."

"That's not why I'm here."

"You said your name was Dusty Sterling? I'm Joe Emmers."

"Pleased to meet you, Mr. Emmers." Dusty stuck out his hand.

Joe gave a surprised pause, but then smiled and shook his hand in a strong grip. "Not often that a white man greets me respectful like that. Call me Joe. The only person 'round here that gets a 'Mister' in front of his name is the owner."

"What work do you do on the ranch, Joe? I saw you with the Herefords a minute ago."

"I do the husbandry work. Might say I'm a cattle doctor." He laughed. "I inspect the herd for diseases, hoof rot, insects, and the like."

"I do a little of that with the horses on my employer's farm."

"This weather's been bad on the animals' feet, hasn't it? I've seen more hoof rot on the horses than I care to count."

Dusty thought of Sophie's horse. "I had to keep several bottles of vinegar on hand to treat one of the mares. Linseed oil too."

"Yeah, easier to put the ointments on than it is to keep their hoofs wrapped and dry. Our horses chew through the wrappings."

"Put some hot pepper sauce on it. My boss's family is from Louisiana, and his daughter makes this spicy red sauce that goes in rice dishes. I guarantee that horse won't chew through the wrapping again."

"Hot pepper sauce? You don't say. Come on. I'll show you around."

Dusty liked Joe. He felt like he met a kindred spirit, one who enjoyed being around animals as much as he did. It was good to talk to someone who shared similar interests.

He rode his horse into the ranch and listened to Joe explain the workings of the property. Though new in town, it seemed to have everything that a proper ranch should. The property, previously an old farm, consisted of wide pastures and a healthy herd. The new bunkhouses were much bigger than what he currently resided in. But he wasn't interested in the bunkhouses.

He gazed in admiration at the ranch house in the middle of it all, fenced in proudly with a water well. The front of the one-floor structure alone boasted large windows, through which he could see hand-tooled leather furniture and gleaming wooden floors. "Mr. Mabrey's family sure must live well," Dusty remarked.

"Mr. Mabrey doesn't have any wife and children," Joe answered. "Says he'll worry about that when he gets the ranch up and runnin' more. That's wise, I suspect."

"Yeah." Dusty looked to the house again. Five rooms from what he could see, and built to take on additional levels, if the owner should choose. It would take him years to make enough money to build a house like that. What woman would wait that long? Not Sophie.

There he went again, letting his mind take off in the wrong direction. Sophie was a farmer's daughter, and a pampered one at that. She was no rancher's girl. That life required everyone to work, and not just simple chores, either. She might have shown her ability to lend a hand around the farm but a ranch would be another story.

"You married, Dusty?"

"Nope."

"Got your eye on a gal?"

"Yeah, but she doesn't seem to have her eye on me. At least not all the time."

Joe chuckled. "A charmer, is she?"

"Indeed she is, but I'm not sure how she'd fare on a ranch." Sophie enjoyed riding and taking care of her horse, but would she understand his attraction for the open range and big herds of cattle? Dusty fidgeted in the saddle, uncomfortable at revealing details of his life to his new acquaintance so soon. He flipped the table. "Do you have a family?"

Joe nodded. "A wife and a daughter. Another child on the way soon."

"That's something to be right happy about."

"I think it'll be a boy this time. I thank the Lord every day that I got taken on to work here. I don't know how I'd provide for my family any other way."

Dusty's ears perked at the information. "I take it Mr. Mabrey pays well?"

"You can start out makin' thirty-two dollars a month if you know your way around a cattle brander and a lasso. More if you prove you can work hard."

That was significantly more than he was making. With those wages, he'd be able to build his savings by Christmas, and have some left over to invest. The railroad stocks wouldn't be too far out of reach. Temptation whispered in his ear to apply for the job. "How do you get hired?"

"Talk to the boss. I thought you said you already did that."

Dusty cleared his throat. "I didn't agree to anything last time we spoke."

"Don't wait too long. Mr. Mabrey's lookin' to hire three more hands before the end of next month. Won't need any more once midsummer's passed."

Dusty nodded. He had to give a definitive answer soon before Joe and Eli Mabrey both thought him unstable. "Thanks for the tour, Joe. I suppose I'll be 'round this way again soon."

"Good meetin' you. I think you and the other workers would get along." Joe turned his horse and showed Dusty back toward the ranch entrance.

On the return trip to Assurance, Dusty fought the guilt that settled over him. He hadn't accepted any offers to work at the Zephyr Ranch. Why did he feel like he was betraying the Charltons? He didn't believe Sophie's father really expected to keep him as a farmhand forever. A man had to make a living. Might as well be doing what he was meant to, if it was possible.

The trail was changing direction. A new destination. He felt it in his blood, even if it did leave a distressing sensation in his stomach.

CHAPTER 15

"I DON'T KNOW ABOUT this petition, Sophie." Linda cast a doubtful eye on the second page of the document where a white space awaited her signature. She rolled the pencil across the counter of the seamstress shop. "Are you sure I won't get into trouble for doing this?"

Sophie stifled her annoyance at her friend's hesitation. Linda wasn't the first woman in town to consider the consequence of upholding the voting cause, and she would not be the last. All morning Sophie dealt with upstanding ladies turning her down as soon as she uttered the reason for her visit upon their doorsteps. The simple fact that Linda was her closest friend and therefore, supposed to be her staunchest supporter was what upset her patience. "Mayor Hooper wants women to sign the petition in order to see how many of us wish to vote."

Linda read the names on the list. "I just don't know. My mother wouldn't like it."

Sophie knew Mrs. Walsh and the other ladies who attended her mother's tea socials said they would back her efforts, so long as they didn't have to get directly involved. Little help silent support made. "You're my closest friend, Linda. If you don't sign this petition, what will it look like to everybody?"

"That I'm choosing to follow my mother's lead."

Sophie approached the subject another way. "You'll inherit this seamstress shop someday. As a future property owner, shouldn't you also be able to cast your vote? Don't you think your name should carry weight in our town?"

Linda's stiff posture began to bend. "I guess so, when you put it like that. But I'm not married yet. What if my future husband disapproves of women voting and he finds out that I signed this petition?"

"You didn't say you had prospects."

A soft blush crept onto Linda's apple cheeks. "I don't, really, but Wes Browman sat next to me in church Sunday. He was very polite."

Sophie couldn't imagine how that tanner, with his coarse speech and manners, could show a modicum of civility. "Is he calling upon you?"

Her friend found a length of measuring tape to play with. She unfurled it instead of meeting Sophie's eye. "Oh, no, but I thought.... He was just kind to me, and maybe, one day, I'll have a real gentleman caller too. It doesn't have to be him, of course."

"You fancy Wes Browman, don't you?"

The blush darkened to a crimson hue. "I didn't say that."

"You don't have to. You're as red as a beet and your hands are jumpier than a cricket being chased by a cat. Why didn't you tell me?"

"It's nothing. I told you, I don't fancy Wes Browman."

Sophie rose on the balls of her feet and propped her elbows on the counter. "It isn't good to lie."

"What about you and Dusty, then?"

A rock landed in her stomach. She sank back to the floor. "What about me and Dusty?"

Linda rolled the measuring tape. "Isn't he escorting you around town while you get your petition signed?"

"No, my brother is. Dusty had other things to do today.

He wouldn't tell me where he was going, either. He's so infuriating." She caught her friend's small smile. "What?"

"You don't sound very pleased that he has other plans."

"Only because Dusty is more accommodating when asked to help. David is always fussy when he has to travel with me into town."

"Or maybe you fancy Dusty more than you care to let on."

"Hush. How can you say that, knowing I have a beau already?" Sophie whirled around to see if anyone had entered the shop and overheard. "You know with absolute and indefatigable certainty that I do not, nor have I ever, fancied Dusty Sterling."

"I don't know anything, except that you can't seem to stop talking to him, even after he mocked you for wanting to fashion a wedding dress before you were engaged. And look." Linda flipped the petition back to the first page. "He was the very first person you asked to sign."

Sophie's tongue stuck to the roof of her mouth as she studied the neatly scribed letters of Dusty's full name. "He wanted to. Why would I tell him he couldn't?"

"Sometimes I think I hear more about Dusty on any given day than I do about Chad."

She reeled from her friend's teasing accusation. "When did you get so bold? My guess is since you've been entertaining the company of a certain tanner."

Linda deflected. "Prove I'm wrong, and that you and Mr. Hooper truly fancy each other."

Preposterous. How in the world could she show that without engaging in a public display of affection with Chad? Sophie returned to the petition on the counter. "Just sign this."

"Prove I'm wrong, and I might sign my name."

"Never mind, then. I'll go across the way and see if there are any ladies at the hotel interested in the petition."

She heard Linda mutter behind her. "I knew it."

"Fine, Linda. I'll go to the bank right this minute and speak to Chad. I'll ask *him* to sign the petition. Then you won't have any reason to think I only wanted Dusty to sign it. What do you say to that?"

"Wait until my mother comes back from the post office. I'll go with you."

The move was daring, asking Chad to sign. He said he wanted nothing overt to do with her cause, but Sophie refused to allow Linda to think she went out of her way to get Dusty to support her efforts. Once Chad saw how many names she collected, he might be persuaded to change his mind about getting more involved. Hadn't she done enough since the Founders Day Festival to prove she could devote herself to something that wasn't frivolous?

Sophie stayed in the shop until Mrs. Walsh arrived ten minutes later. Linda told her mother that she needed a few minutes to go outside and took her leave with Sophie. They walked to the bank.

David caught up with them. "Are you done with your petition signing yet?" He matched steps with his sister. "The livery's gonna charge us for the whole day if we don't get the horses out in the next hour."

"Go get them. I'll be ready to leave as soon as I go to the bank."

"No woman works there."

"No, but Chad does, and his signature might be the most important one I get." Sophie raised the hem of her riding habit and took longer strides to the bank. Linda increased her pace as well.

The harsh light of day receded as they pulled open the bank door and entered the dark recesses of the building. Furniture polish and the stale smell of old paper reached Sophie's nostrils.

"May I help you?" A teller from behind the caged counter lifted his eyes from papers in front of him.

"Is Mr. Hooper available?" She clasped the petition to her chest.

"He may still be in his office. He works only a half day on Saturday." The teller unlocked the door to the counter and came out to stand in the small lobby. "Of what purpose is your visit today, Miss Charlton?"

"I need a document signed."

"Mr. Hooper doesn't do notaries."

"I don't need a notary. This is something else. Miss Walsh and I can see ourselves in, if you don't mind."

The teller gave a long speculative stare at the two women before shrugging. "It is the close of business. Go ahead. His office is to your left."

Sophie found that the door wasn't completely closed. Chad's head was down as he rifled through one of his desk drawers. He looked up at the sound of her knocking. "Sophie, I was about to leave. What brings you by?"

Linda followed her into the office. Sophie turned the petition in her hands. "I've been getting people to sign my petition today. I wanted to know if you would care to put your name on the list." She slid it across the desk.

A muscle in his jaw ticked. He didn't as much as glance at the list before him. Instead he raised his dark eyes and peered at her from beneath his black brows. "I expressly told you that I wasn't going to get involved like this."

Sophie balked at the hard edge underlying the low, even tone in his voice. "I thought that since you helped me get this started you might want to see it through to completion."

"Will you excuse us for a moment, please, Miss Walsh?" Chad waited for Linda to depart and went to close the door behind her. Sophie sensed the tension emanating from him, hard to be contained within the four walls.

"While I do enjoy seeing you, Sophie, I'm not overly fond of surprise visits, especially when they involve you asking me to do something that I refused earlier."

The office became too cramped. She searched in vain for a window. "I hoped you would change your mind once you saw how many signatures I've collected. Don't you think women should have a vote about school issues in our town?"

Creases formed along the shoulders of Chad's coat when he crossed his arms and studied her. "This is my father's campaign, now that you've given him a way of influencing more voters. Newcomers to Assurance complain that our laws are backwards. Allowing women to vote in the next election will put him on par with the rest of the state's leaders."

Sophie noticed that he never answered her question. "I don't understand how that can be a problem."

"As a banker, I need to be neutral. It's hard to do when my father is the mayor."

"I don't think you could ever avoid being associated with him."

"I did avoid the reelection campaign until you brought that list of names in my office."

Pain stabbed Sophie's chest. "Why didn't you say that before you helped me? A man shouldn't court a woman if he finds it too demanding to be honest with her."

As you were honest by telling him that you and Dusty shared a kiss? The revolting little voice whispered in her ear. She stared at Chad's shoes in momentary shame.

"A woman as lovely as you should never hang her head. I'll sign your petition if it will make you feel better."

Sophie's head shot up. She didn't intend for Chad to think that was why she stared downward, but his name on the paper would certainly bring her good cheer. "Thank you. I won't involve you in this cause any further."

"Will you seal that promise with a kiss?" His eyes hooded

as he gazed at her with the assurance of a man used to achieving his goals.

Sophie expected her heart to respond positively at the prospect of being kissed for the first time by her beau. She experienced a peculiar emptiness where excitement and giddiness should have taken over. "After you sign your name."

"Always the coquette, aren't you?" He lifted the petition from the desk and flipped it over to the first page. His mild expression turned cold. "Why is Sterling at the top of this list?"

Sophie tugged at her high-necked collar. "He wanted to show his support of women voting on school elections."

"I didn't take an unschooled cowboy for a forward thinker."

She bristled at the remark, even though it was not intended for her. "One doesn't need a formal education to be progressive."

"From my experience, it helps."

Sophie fanned her face. "I'll have you know, Mr. Hooper, that my father did not attend your college, but he has single-handedly managed to bring the railroad to Assurance and make what was once a tent city into a town on the state map. Will you dispute that?"

"I meant no disrespect to your father. We all are grateful for Mr. Charlton's efforts in growing our town. I only meant it in reference to Sterling. He doesn't sound like a man to be a suffragist."

"Don't let the drawl fool you. Dusty Sterling is many things, but he is not ignorant."

"You never cease in telling me all the things that Mr. Sterling is to you." Jealousy settled across Chad's face. "I don't like how you always see fit to defend him."

Sophie had dug herself into a hole that was getting to be too deep to claw her way out of. "I don't like defending myself, much less Mr. Sterling. I agreed to let you and only you court me."

Chad opened his mouth to reply, but clamped down at the last moment. He turned the petition to the second page and reached for his fountain pen, jabbing the instrument into the ink well on the desk. He wrote his name with large flourishes, taking up three inches of blank space where four more names could easily have fit.

"There is my fulfillment of our bargain. It's your turn."

His attempt at being flirtatious sounded like a demand to her ears. He motioned with one finger for her to come to him. Was he not going to get up from that chair?

He remained seated as she stood over him. Conquest shone in his eyes as he allowed the barest of smiles to reach his lips. Sophie waited for him to take her hand, gather her near, or do whatever it was that gentlemen were supposed to do before embracing ladies. He never moved.

This was to be her first kiss with Chad, he reclining and making her do all the work? Indignation flared in Sophie's chest. Even when Dusty stole that kiss, he had the decency to spring for her. Granted, it was unwelcome at the time, but at least he put forth the effort. That was more than she could say for a man wagging his finger at her as though she were a small child learning to toddle across the floor of the nursery.

She bent over and planted a quick kiss on his cheek. His skin was smooth and cool. Strange images of cold, day-old catfish came to her mind.

Chad had his eyes closed. He popped one open. "That's all?"

"Until you rid yourself of doubt and start courting me properly, Mr. Hooper, I'm afraid that will be the extent of my affections. Good day to you, sir."

He stood up so fast she thought he would send the chair sprawling. "What about my signature on the petition?"

Without hesitation, she picked it up on her way out. "Never you worry. It's big enough for all to see." She closed the door behind her.

Chapter 16

I can't believe you did that, Sophie," Linda exclaimed as they left the bank. Sophie told her everything that took place in Chad's office. "He may not want to court you anymore after you refused to give him a proper kiss."

"I wouldn't say that." She handed the petition to Linda so she could see Chad's grandiose signature looming on the second page. "Both of them have signed it now. I did what I could to lay his fears to rest about Dusty. Your belief too, I hope."

Linda's face told that her beliefs were still alive and thriving. She walked with Sophie across the street where David had the horses ready.

"I know that look. What is it you want to say, Linda?"

"Petition signed or not, it still doesn't prove you don't fancy Dusty, or at least put up with him more than you should. I've watched the two of you go back and forth for years."

"It hasn't been that long."

"It is a long time, considering his type of work. Most farmhands leave after a season or two."

"Daddy pays him well." Sophie supplied the most logical reason available. "Are you going to sign the petition or not?"

Linda sighed and took the pencil she offered. "If my mother gets angry about this, I'll tell her you forced me."

"Before or after you tell her about Wes Browman?" Satisfied that she made Linda blush at the mention of her admirer's name, Sophie took the signed petition and tucked it safely in her mare's saddlebag.

David walked up to her with the horses after Linda returned to the seamstress shop. "Are you done yet?"

"For the time being. I should venture to the train station. Many of the signatures on here are from ladies new in town."

Her brother helped her onto her horse. "I'm not sitting at that depot all day."

"You will if Daddy says you have to come with me."

David mounted his own horse. "I'm almost seventeen. Both of you won't be able to boss me about for much longer." He rode ahead of her. "When I reach majority, I just might pursue a different calling."

Sophie made sure he could see her wrinkle her nose in distaste. "There's not much around here for amateur lassoists."

"I'm fixin' to be a cowhand, mind you. And just so you know, there is work to be found 'round these parts. While you were gabbing to Linda, I overheard some men talking about a new ranch outside town. The Zephyr Ranch, it's called. The owner's hiring."

Another sinking feeling came on. If David heard about a new ranch, then Dusty must also have knowledge of it. She gave Bess's reins a tug to make the horse turn left. "How long has the ranch been there?"

"I don't know. A few weeks. It's where farmer Crenshaw's old place used to be. They already put in a fence and started fixing up the main house, from what I'm told."

Sophie wanted to ask who had been hired, but remembered her father's warning about gossip. Ever since he severely admonished her last year for speaking about Marissa's saloon-girl past, she thought twice about returning down that old, worn road. "You'd still have to wait until you're older to work on a ranch. Daddy would never approve."

"I don't plan on telling him until I turn eighteen."

"We can all see how ill-contented you are. It's only a matter of time before he has a word with you." She hoped her father wouldn't blame it on Dusty, but there was no one else but him on the farm to inspire her younger brother to pursue a different calling.

What if Dusty felt the same way as David, but didn't let on? He never did say where he was going that morning. He was dressed like he was going to meet somebody important.

Sophie sped her horse into a canter, eager to get home and catch Dusty. It wasn't gossiping if she came straightforwardly and asked him if he paid a visit to the Zephyr Ranch. He couldn't lie to her. She had every nuance of his face memorized, from the cleft in his chin to the crinkles of his eyes when he smiled. She'd know if he wasn't telling the truth.

The ride back into Assurance was less disagreeable now that Dusty knew there were cowhands just down the road that he could swap stories with. No longer the only cowboy in town, he was thankful that his remaining in Kansas had not been a mistake. As to the matter of continuing to work on the Charlton farm and see Sophie's sweet face every day, he groaned at the restlessness nagging from within.

Their games of dally and tease were drawing to a close. Sophie wanted to get herself hitched to a wealthy man, not flirt with fellows that thought her pretty, but couldn't afford to put her up in the splendor she was used to. Too bad the things he knew how to do didn't pay much.

He hated the feelings that betrayed him. God designed

man to work, and to take pleasure in it. Whatever his hands found to do, be it to work a lasso or push a plow, he needed to do it for the Lord's glory. Dusty was able to abide by that before. Why not today?

One of the liverymen acknowledged him as he passed by. Folks in town would call him ungrateful if they knew the workings of his mind. At least he was making steady pay, had a good roof over his head, and had a place to lay his head at night, they'd say. Plenty of other folks didn't have those things. Count the blessings.

He always did. Dusty knew he was better off than he was before he rode into town with just his horse, some savings, and a spare change of clothes. The problem was in finding something more permanent. No man could be a roaming cowboy forever. Either he found himself a ranch to work on or he needed to take up another trade. Unlike his industrious father, who was a gun shop owner before he became a rancher, Dusty had no plans to take up residence in town and work in a store.

"Mr. Sterling."

Dusty moved his head left and right to see who called his name. When he looked past the head of his horse, he found Chad Hooper standing in the middle of the street. "Yeah?"

"A word with you." Sophie's beau appeared not to notice the dirt sticking to his shiny shoes and pressed suit.

"'Fraid you caught me on my way to someplace, Hooper." Dusty didn't bother to come up with specifics. The mayor's son might find a way to twist that around, too.

"It won't take long." Chad walked to a shaded spot on the corner of the road, under the storefront sign of what would soon be a hardware shop.

Dusty dismounted and led Gabe off the road. He kept the stallion's reins in hand instead of tying them to a nearby post. "Speak your mind." Air his conscience, was what Dusty really wanted Chad to do, but the banker didn't divulge.

"I spoke to Miss Charlton this afternoon. I noticed you were the first to sign her petition. How surprising to learn you were in favor of women's suffrage."

"I guess it would surprise you, seeing as how that information isn't written on any of my bank records."

One of Chad's nostrils twitched. "Actually, I meant given your past experiences driving herds up through cattle country. It isn't a cause that most men in your position would devote themselves to."

"Times are changin'. A man in my position learns to accept that and find his place in the midst of it."

"So you do understand where your place is, Mr. Sterling?"

Dusty thought of words he used to employ before he gave up swearing. This was an opportune time to reinstate them, but he didn't want to revive an old habit on account of a minor temptation. "I'm still listening for the point to this discussion."

A bead of sweat formed on Chad's temple and ran down behind his ear. Or was it hair lacquer? Dusty couldn't tell. "If you haven't heard, I'm courting Miss Charlton. I asked permission from her father to do so and was granted it. That means that she is not accepting of your attempts to woo her by showing an interest in her causes."

"You got all that from me signing a petition?" Dusty kept a straight face as both of Chad's nostril's flared. No wonder he didn't follow in his father's footsteps and run for office. When he got mad, there was no hiding the thoughts that expressed themselves on his face.

"She talks about you. I know you pursue her."

Dusty gloried in the small victory that he stayed on Sophie's mind, even while she was in the presence of her beau. Did she think about him as often as he did her? If so, he wasn't out of the running yet.

"To what extent have you tried to be amorous with Miss Charlton?" Chad displayed a knack for questioning. If his clients left him, he could always trade his bank license for that of an attorney.

Dusty recalled that evening of the Founders Day Festival, when he swooped Sophie up for a kiss. He could still feel her long lashes fan against his cheeks, her soft lips beneath his. Maybe he shouldn't have caught her off guard, but it was well before Chad Hooper made his intentions known. "I've done nothing since she told me that you were courting her."

None of his answers satisfied Sophie's beau. Chad's voice became strident. "What did you do before?"

People in the streets turned. Chad cleared his throat and waited for them to keep on their way. "Sterling, you are to leave Miss Charlton alone. Do you comprehend?"

Dusty wanted nothing more than to curl his fist and send the mayor's boy splattering off his high perch. The sheriff's office was just down the street though. He had better things to do than spend a couple hours in a cramped, dirty cell with the town's portly law official as his only company. "It must be the country boy in me, but I don't seem to follow these fancy rules of courtship. Down in Texas, a lady ain't spoken for until she has a ring on the fourth finger of her left hand. Why don't we let Sophie decide which man she wants?"

Chad spat out a harsh laugh. "Do you call yourself a rival for her affections?"

"I don't have to call myself anything. You're the one with all the fancy titles and accolades surrounding his name. We'll see if they mean something to Sophie." Dusty vaulted back in the horse's saddle.

As he rode from the town square, he knew the secret was out. He had practically declared himself a valid contender for Sophie's hand. Anyone that overheard him and Chad talking would get the word out to the rest of the town by nightfall. Airing that bit of business wasn't going to help his chances with Sophie. In fact, he may have shortened his stay at the farm. Still, an exuberance washed over him that was as fresh and exhilarating as any splash in the lake.

He smiled at the path leading home to Sophie. "May the best man win."

Sophie saw Dusty riding his stallion up to the house, wearing that grin like a harebrained fool. Did he pay a courting visit to Margaret as she originally assumed? He wasn't so happy that morning when he left.

"Miss Sophie." He tipped his hat in playful formality and kept right on for the barn. She considered leaving the laundry in the basket beneath the clothesline and going after him. That's what he wanted her to do. No, she'd stay right there and finish gathering the dry clothes before joining her family in the house to prepare supper.

He returned several minutes later, a jaunty stride in his step. "Did you get all the signatures you wanted today?"

She pressed her hands against the wrinkles in the home-spun floral calico she changed into to complete the last chores before Sunday. "Two pages' worth." A page and a half, not counting Chad's signature, but she wouldn't quibble over small details. "How was your day?" She fished for a way to get the subject of the Zephyr Ranch into the conversation.

"Oh, just fine. Ran into a friend of yours while I was in town."

She glanced toward the house to make sure the front door was closed and that no one could hear. She scraped her nails along the outside of a clothespin. "Dare I ask which friend?"

He sat on the grass near the basket. "Take a guess if you're brave enough."

"Margaret Rheins."

"How did I know you were going to say that?" He produced another grin. She was beginning to think him the inspiration for the Cheshire Cat in that illustrated book of Rosemarie's.

"If not Margaret, then who?"

"I'll give you a hint. He's always dressed for a funeral."

Chad's dark-suited image came immediately to the forefront of her mind. "Shame on you, Dusty. That wasn't very nice."

He snatched a blade of grass and chewed on it. "But you know who I'm talking about now."

"I won't dignify that comment with an answer." Sophie pulled a tablecloth off the line.

"Don't worry. I didn't show out, as you like to say. He came up to me and asked what I called myself."

"What?"

"He wasn't satisfied that I simply went by Dusty Sterling. He called me a cowboy, and I don't much mind that one bit."

"Quit teasing and get to the point. I don't like when you try to make me antsy."

The blade of grass hovered at the corner of his mouth. "He wanted to know if I was your courter or your wooer or his rival. I think that about sums it up."

Sophie let the last tablecloth fan in the breeze. Talk of the new ranch was going to have to wait. This meeting between Dusty and her beau took precedence. Scandal would break if Dusty led Chad to believe that he was also pursuing her. "What in the world did you say to him?"

"I told him to let you decide which man you wanted."

"You allowed Chad to think that you were also courting me? Why can't you leave well enough alone?"

"I didn't say anything." He got up from the grass, innocent and unassuming as a man with laughter in his eyes could look.

"That is strictly the point. Your refusal to dispute Chad's claim led him to believe you were sweet on me."

"I am sweet on you." He admitted words honest and plain as the buttons on his shirt. "And I'm waiting for you to proclaim you're sweet on me."

If he weren't such an uncomplicated man his statement would have sounded arrogant. Sophie went for the last tablecloth in order to have something to occupy her hands, an excuse to turn away from his earnest face as he stood much too close for her liking. Why didn't she have enough will to tell him to leave, that she didn't want him coming around anymore? She'd stay on one side of the farm, he on the other, and they'd only meet when her family invited him inside the house for supper. A very simple arrangement. "You may find the wait quite tedious."

"It's been three years since I first made your acquaintance. Most folk would say I'm a patient man."

Three years. It didn't seem like that much time had passed. Sophie remembered how slow and plodding the days were before he arrived on the farm seeking work. Having a tall, good-looking stranger walking about the property provided a pleasant distraction from household chores and helping to care for younger siblings. Best of all, he didn't stay a stranger but daily engaged her in conversation and bantering. She couldn't give her true feelings away, though. "Most people would say you're fooling yourself. How long do you think I'll be living under my family's roof, sparring words with you?"

The boyish gleam in Dusty's eyes became flat and dull. Marble-faced, he watched clouds float over the house. Sophie regretted the reaction she caused in him. She intended to disparage his advances, not to sound cruel. "I mean to say that I won't be an unmarried woman forever. Since I'm being courted, people are telling me that I shouldn't speak so common to other men. It's not proper."

"People, or one man in particular?"

Sophie didn't want to reveal that her friend Linda also agreed with Chad, that she should leave Dusty alone. If they knew the extent to which she flirted... "It doesn't matter who said it. You need to let Chad know that you are not contending for me."

"I never could lie very well. Hard to keep from smiling."

Sophie lifted the clothesbasket and held it in front of her like an awkward shield. "You can't court me. My father wouldn't grant you permission if you asked, and that's the only way to do it if you want to be proper." Her mouth betrayed her, stringing words together that sounded like she was merely warning him of the challenges he'd face instead of flat-out refusing his courtship.

Dusty conceded to her argument. "He might change his mind if he sees how well I'd treat you."

"He wouldn't. Besides, I'd refuse." She'd be expected to, for other reasons that she chose not to say out of fear of further damaging his pride. Dusty knew enough about the rigors of courtship and her family's expectations of gentlemen callers. Men were to show that they could provide for a future wife, to give her a life that was at or above what she was accustomed to. Her mother and father would never approve of her being courted by a cowboy, especially not one who worked for them, whose monthly wages were spelled out in their record book.

But was that being hypocritical, given their lean years in New Orleans? Sophie struggled to determine the answer. "I have to take this basket inside." She hoisted it higher and carried it up the steps. A movement occurred behind the drapes of one of the windows overlooking the front porch. Was David trying to eavesdrop? Rosemarie, maybe? Sophie balanced the basket on one knee and turned the doorknob.

The door opened without her pushing it. Her mother aimed down at her with stern eyes, hands placed beneath both sides of her tightly corseted waist. "You and I will speak in the kitchen this instant."

CHAPTER 17

*T*HE BASKET MAY as well have been weighed down with lead. Sophie's strength waned under the strict and uncompromising gaze of her mother. What did she see from that window? What did she hear?

"Set that basket down. Rosemarie will tend to it while we talk."

Meekly, Sophie did as she was told and trailed behind her mother. The kitchen was immersed in smells of roasted garlic and lamb, but her appetite retreated.

"What were you and Dusty talking about outside?"

Her mother's tone indicated that she already had an answer to the question and was only giving her a chance to reveal the truth. Still, Sophie wasn't sure how much her mother had actually heard. "Dusty was telling me about a friend he met in town."

"The two of you spent an awfully long time talking about this friend. Is the lady or gentleman a mutual acquaintance?"

"You might say that."

Her mother pulled out a chair from the kitchen table and indicated for Sophie to do the same. "Evasiveness is not a becoming trait for a lady. Tell me what was spoken or you will dine alone in your room."

Eating supper by herself didn't sound like a terrible punishment in light of revealing aspects of her discussion with

Dusty. Sophie met her mother's awaiting stare. She wasn't getting out of confession. "We talked about Chad."

Her mother's firm composure gave way. Never an encouraging sign. "Why would you talk to Dusty about a man who's courting you?"

Sophie shook her head.

"Or to anyone outside of your family or female confidants?"

"I don't have a good answer, Mother."

"No, I don't believe so. Your actions prove very discouraging." She launched into a lecture. "You know what I've said about being careful in how you speak to men. One misinterpretation of your words, one slip in the way you carry yourself, and your reputation is gone. Do you want that?"

Sophie shook her head again. It failed to stop her mother from proceeding as though she did damage her standing.

"Assurance is growing, but we still live in a small town. There's no returning after a fall from grace."

"Dusty wouldn't spread rumors about me."

"Someone need only see the two of you in deep conversation to draw vicious conclusions. Cowboys are notorious for sweet-talking impressionable young ladies."

In addition to Chad thinking her frivolous, her own mother presumed that she didn't have enough sense in her head to prevent being easily influenced. It hurt Sophie to see that two important people in her life had such perceptions of her. "There's no reason for you to change your opinion of Dusty. You and Daddy allowed him to ride into town with me when I went to Mayor Hooper's house, and other times since he's worked for us."

Her mother paused in silent agreement. "Dusty has proven trustworthy in the past, but that was before you had a real suitor like Chad."

"How does Chad being my suitor make Dusty suddenly dishonorable?"

"Don't be brazen with me, young lady. Shall I bring your father in here to speak with you?"

Sophie gave up trying to talk to her mother when she believed she was justified in her reasoning. "No. I'm sorry."

The apology calmed her mother down. "What I witnessed outside the house today between you and Dusty was too intimate. How long have you been confiding in him like this?"

Sophie traced her fingers along the grooves of the table where many a kitchen knife slipped and made its mark. "I wasn't confiding. Just talking."

"Call it what you will. You both looked to be on too dear of terms."

"He's friendly, Mother, and means no devious will."

"Your beau won't think that. Chad will consider his friendliness to mean more than you care to defend against. I will not have Mayor Hooper's son thinking my daughter common." Sophie's mother rose in one fluid motion, head held high and imperious.

Sophie sat in her shadow. What did she intend to do?

"From now on, Dusty will no longer break bread at our table. He will take his meals outside or in the bunkhouse. Your brothers will bring him his food."

Sophie flinched at the harsh sentence. Her breathing sped to match her erratic heartbeat. "Please don't punish Dusty when he did nothing wrong. I promise not to say more to him than is required."

Not one hair of her mother's tightly-coiled bun moved out of place as she shook her head. "There's no other choice. I've already sent your father out to talk to Dusty."

What would Daddy say to him? Sophie groaned.

"Don't make that guttural noise. You are not a sow."

How could her mother say that, when she felt lower than swine? Dusty did nothing to harm her, and yet he was to

151

be punished on her account, a potential prelude for worse things to come. Her father had the power to send him off the farm and withhold his pay. She had to do something to keep that from happening. "I'll take all of my meals upstairs when Dusty eats at the table."

"Don't be ridiculous. You are part of this family. It's a privilege that we even provide Dusty room and board. I know people that subtract that from their workers' wages."

Sophie stared at her mother in disbelief. She would never have said a thing like that when they lived in Louisiana, where Daddy worked as a hired hand himself. "But you and Daddy always tell us to have regard for men of different trades."

"This isn't about regard. This is about retaining your propriety. Now wash your hands and help me set the table." Her mother ended the conversation by going to stand by the sink.

Sophie went to her task and gathered the plates from the cupboard, minus one.

Dusty didn't notice Mrs. Charlton peeking out the front window until Sophie went to go inside the house. He hoped they didn't talk loud enough for her to hear, else he'd be in a heap of trouble for admitting his feelings for her daughter. What he needed to do was ask Mr. Charlton for permission to court Sophie, but how could he do that if permission had already been given to Chad?

He strode to the bunkhouse to wash his face and hands before supper. Like it or not, it was coming time to leave the farm. He needed to show himself sufficient to win Sophie's hand by increasing his earnings and making a home of his own. Those things couldn't be done while he was still in her father's employ.

Before there were no suitable prospects of employment.

Now he had one. If he kept sitting on the fence, his opportunities were going to pass by.

Dusty shut the door to the bunkhouse. To his surprise, Mr. Charlton was standing in front of the steps, waiting for him. He knew where Sophie got her ability to creep up on people.

"How're you doing today, Dusty?"

"Fine, sir." What an odd question to ask so late in the day when Mr. Charlton had the opportunity to greet him with it earlier. "Did you need to speak to me about something?"

"As a matter of fact, I do. It's about my daughter."

Dusty's hand remained on the door. What did she tell her father? "Is Miss Sophie alright?"

"She will be. Her mother and I thought it best to make some changes in the way things are going around here. Before I proceed, I want you to understand that no one is accusing you of reckless conduct."

Dusty wished he would make his point. What was it with the people of Assurance taking so long to state important matters? He hated being as fretful as the Christmas turkey on December twenty-fourth. "Okay."

Mr. Charlton didn't look mad, but he wasn't all smiles, either. "Sophie is being courted by a young man that her mother and I highly approve of. It's come to our attention that she isn't being... *mindful* of the importance of that association. If I'm correct, she's confiding in you about it."

Now he looked mad. Dusty didn't like the blue frost in the man's eyes. If not reckless conduct, what was Mr. Charlton accusing him of? "I know Chad Hooper's courting your daughter, sir."

"She admitted speaking to you about it this afternoon while she gathered the laundry. That's the truth, isn't it?"

"Yes." Dusty wondered if this was what men felt like when they went to stand before a judge. Accused and presumed guilty. "But she didn't say a word that would lower anyone's estimation of her."

"I still can't let my daughter carry on to anyone she chooses. I can see how she's gotten used to your presence over the years, but she needs to understand that you're not a relative that she can speak freely to. Until she learns to control her tongue, I'm going to have to keep her separated from you."

The blue frost left Dusty cold to the marrow of his bones. "What does that mean?"

"She won't talk to you unsupervised. I'll be watching her as she does her chores. And—I don't like this, but I feel it necessary—you won't be sharing any meals with the family. You'll eat in the bunkhouse or with the boys and me when we break from work."

Dusty had no entitlement to feel insulted but it came on anyway. Before this evening, the Charltons trusted him enough to let him eat at their supper table, and now he was being ordered to take his meals elsewhere as though he posed a threat. Did Sophie get angry enough to tell her father that she didn't want him around her anymore? It didn't sound like what she would do. "It's your household, Mr. Charlton. I'll do as you say, but I never meant any disrespect toward your daughter."

Mr. Charlton held up his hand. "At this time, Dusty, it's not about what you meant. It's about Sophie learning where her place is."

Far away from him, that's what her father should come out and say. Dusty took pains not to let his anger show. Sophie's parents were teaching her another lesson in decorum, and he was the one they picked to do the illustrating. He understood the need of a family to protect one of their own, but Mr. and Mrs. Charlton weren't shielding Sophie. They were shielding her reputation, her standing with Chad and the rest of the higher-ups in town.

They made their point clear. No Charlton woman was going to sully herself by talking to someone beneath the station they deemed fit for her to abide in. The truth he had been ignoring for the longest time came to stare him in the face.

"I'm glad you understand, Dusty. I'll send David out with your supper."

As Mr. Charlton disappeared into the house, Dusty realized that he had, in fact, received an answer as to when to leave the farm.

The Lord worked in mysterious ways, indeed.

Dusty ate his supper on the porch of the bunkhouse before he went inside. Banned from the Charlton home, where marbles and jack straws were played after the evening meal, he had nothing to do but tidy up his living space. He went one further and rearranged the bed and small table. Then he cleaned his revolver and Winchester rifle, two firearms that hadn't been put to any practical use since he came to Kansas. Might be a purpose for them on the Zephyr Ranch, if Mabrey decided to hire him. Dusty made plans to ask about it in church tomorrow if he ran into the foreman.

On Sunday morning he went to church by himself after getting the wagon ready for the Charltons. What was the sense in staring forlornly at the back of a wagon while everybody inside pretended he wasn't there, anyway? He tried to shake off his grumbling spirit that persisted as he saddled his horse.

The road to church was quiet without the chatter of Sophie and her siblings filling the air. A gentle wind drifted through the trees and moved the grass near the lakeshore, where the mud colored the shallow water. Despite the stillness of the woods, Dusty felt that a hundred pairs of eyes were watching him.

They treat you like a lowdown dog. The voice moved through the trees as he rode past. *Why are you still there?*

It followed him through the thicket of low brush. *You should've left a long time ago.*

And wound through a small clearing. *Don't you have any self-respect?*

He heard Wes Browman's words next. *That Sophie's nothing but trouble.*

Dusty resisted the lure of believing what Wes said at McIntyre's Restaurant last Sunday. It wasn't Sophie's fault that he had been ordered to keep his distance. If he hadn't talked to her while she was folding laundry, the two of them wouldn't be under her father's scrutiny.

You never want to blame her for anything, do you?

The church yard was bare when he arrived. Even the Sunday school teacher, Miss Kinsey, had yet to appear, judging from the lock on the door. He said hello to Reverend Winford and his wife as they came walking up the path. Their cabin wasn't too far away from the church.

"Good morning, Dusty. You're early," Rowe stated. "Where are the Charltons?"

"Still at the house." Dusty let his horse walk to an appetizing patch of grass flourishing under the shade of a tree.

"That's strange," said Marissa. "You usually come with them."

Of course they knew his habits. He should have stayed by the lake until a decent time had passed before traveling to church. "I thought I'd leave a little early today."

They frowned at the vagueness of his explanation. He considered changing the subject by asking how they enjoyed being newly married, but it was evident on their happy faces.

The Reverend held his wife's hand as they walked up to the doors.

"You can come sit in the sanctuary if you want," he offered. "You don't have to stand outside all morning."

"I'll be alright."

"Suit yourself." The door closed behind the Reverend and Marissa.

Dusty busied himself by reading a few passages in Genesis from last week's study of the Bible. Reverend Winford would conclude the sermon today on how Joseph was thrown into prison on the false accusation of seducing Potiphar's wife. He couldn't help but compare it to his own unfortunate predicament. He wasn't going to jail, and he didn't seduce Sophie, but it seemed like he was being penalized for a crime he didn't commit. At least Joseph could say he never fancied Potiphar's wife. For Dusty, being separated from Sophie was turning out to be a definite punishment.

Chapter 18

OLKS STARTED COMING from the direction of town. While waiting for church service to start, they stood near the fence, talking about subjects Dusty had little knowledge of. A snippet about a railroad acquisitions merger, details on another robbery in a town along the Kansas border. Dusty kept to himself and proceeded to finish the Bible chapters.

A half hour later, the Charltons arrived, driving their wagon close to the fence, so that the women of the family wouldn't get their pastel dresses soiled from walking in the road. Mr. Charlton got down from the fancy carriage to assist his wife first. Mrs. Charlton was dressed to the nines in her rosy gown, lace trimming every corner, with gloves and parasol to match. Dusty hid a smile at the overly corresponding ensemble.

The Charlton matriarch established a similar trait in her daughters. Little Rosemarie followed clumsily after her mother in a child's version of the same frilly dress, still unaccustomed to wearing long hems. Sophie then emerged from the carriage, and Dusty was glad a fence was there to keep him from stumbling backward.

She was radiant in a peach confection that flattered her coloring. Although not as showy as her mother, she drew glances from the male onlookers. Dimples appeared in her cheeks as she teased her youngest brother Bernard for trying to tip his hat to a female classmate. She then took Rose-marie's hand to keep the girl from tripping on the hem of her dress.

David jumped down from the wagon and landed on both feet. Spotting Dusty, he called out a loud hello. Dusty nodded once to the boy.

Hearing her brother shout, Sophie turned. Her eyes found Dusty. He was caught staring back like a sheep, and felt the same way. Was it proper to wave or better to pretend to stare at the steeple on the roof? With Mr. Charlton still in the wagon and having full view of the two of them, Dusty chose the latter. Out of focus, he was still able to see how she lingered in place, visibly uncertain of what to say or do. Her little sister made the decision for her, and tugged her arm to go into the church.

"Why are you standin' by the fence, Sterling?" Wes Browman marched up to him, raising an eyebrow at the open Bible in Dusty's hands. "Reverend Winford preachin' outside today?"

Dusty had no heart to laugh at his friend's lackluster humor. "Just refreshing my memory."

"Where's Goldilocks and her family?"

"Inside the church. Stop calling her that."

"No need to be jealous. I'm not studyin' her. Got my eye on sweet little Linda Walsh." The tanner smiled.

"The seamstress?"

"Who else in town goes by the same name? Yes, the seamstress. I sat next to her in church last Sunday, in case you didn't know."

"Can't say I pay much attention to where you sit, Wes."

His friend snickered. "No, you were probably staring at the back of Sophie's head, hoping that she'd turn around and look at you if you kept at it long enough. How's work on the farm going?"

"It's going." Like he soon planned to be.

Wes signaled to the road with a movement of his chin. "Here comes the high-falutin' Hoopers now."

Dusty saw the mayor and his wife ride up in the black buggy that Chad used to take Sophie on an outing. No sign of their son. Thinking about the man made him angry all over again.

Wes kept talking, oblivious to the change in Dusty. "That buggy must have been shipped on a train from back east. No one drives a contraption like that around here."

"You sound worse than a gossipy, snaggletooth old hag."

"Yeah? You're quick to scold like one. I know you, Sterling. You're thinkin' the same thing I am."

Worse, he was ashamed to admit it to himself. The out-of-place city buggy stood a better chance of withstanding his judgment. "Every thought doesn't need to be voiced."

"When I want a Sunday school lesson, I'll go see Miss Kinsey."

"Better not. Miss Walsh may get envious."

"I'm gonna look for her inside." Wes trampled off with his objective energizing his steps.

Dusty filed in with the other congregants and took a seat on a pew near the back. As the sanctuary filled, he searched the rows for Eli Mabrey. If the man was in church, he'd try to catch him after the service to have a word. He didn't foresee himself getting out to the Zephyr Ranch at any time during the week.

"Dusty?"

He looked up to see Joe Emmers. The man had his family with him. His wife stood behind him, the loose folds of her dress hinting at the swell of her pregnant abdomen. His daughter wore a simple cotton dress and stood taller than her mother. She looked to be about seventeen or eighteen. Dusty held out his hand to Joe. "How do you do this morning?"

This time, Joe didn't hesitate to shake hands, but warmly accepted the greeting. "I decided I'd take the family to church with me. Do you mind if we sit next to you, seein' as how you're a friendly face?"

"Don't mind at all." Dusty moved down in the pew so they could sit. He ignored the glances tossed his way by several people. He'd come to terms with the fact that Assurance was no San Antonio, where cultures largely mingled on a daily basis. At least Reverend Winford, his wife and some of the churchgoers were welcoming to visitors, regardless of skin color. Other folks would follow in time, Dusty guessed.

Joe introduced his family. "This is my wife, Helen, and my daughter, Violet."

Dusty greeted the women as they took their seats. "Is this your first trip into town?"

Violet leaned forward to see over her father's shoulder. "Papa took me to the general store last week to buy a new saddlebag. I help him train the cutting horses on our land." Her voice rose, hinting at a feistiness of spirit that Dusty often saw displayed in settlers.

Helen shook her head good-naturedly as she looked upon her daughter with pride. "She'll give me a head full of gray hairs soon."

Joe patted his daughter on the knee. "This girl will be runnin' her own ranch someday. Just wait."

The organist struck a chord for the latecomers to hurry and find a seat. Dusty stretched his neck to see if more people were coming through the doors. "Is Mr. Mabrey here?"

Joe shook his head and lowered his voice as the music quieted the chatter in the sanctuary. "He took the train to

Abilene to see about purchasing a new bull for breeding. You decided that you want to work at the ranch?"

Dusty ran his thumb along the leather spine of his Bible. "I'll talk more after service."

The Reverend proceeded to lead the congregation in a worship hymn. Joe's singing voice matched that of his speech, his deep timbre easily distinguishable from the people around them. Dusty muttered along to the song, grateful to have someone to drown him out. He never was much of a singer.

He glanced at Sophie down in one of the front rows and knew she was doing the same. Was their inability to carry the tune the only thing they had in common?

Mayor Hooper and his wife were situated in their usual pew closest to the pulpit. He wondered how long it would be before the mayor's son decided to make more public showings of his courtship of Sophie, similar to the way Wes showed his interest in Linda Walsh.

The more Dusty ruminated over Chad's status as Sophie's beau, the more he found it difficult to concentrate on the church service. Thinking about how Mr. Charlton told him in no uncertain terms to stay away from his daughter made it worse. Perhaps he should have stayed in the bunkhouse or headed into the next town to distract himself. No one would blame him, but he couldn't let his anger at the circumstances keep him from going to church and giving his time and offering to God.

He paid attention to the sermon and kept his focus by jotting notes inside one of the blank pages in the back of his Bible. As soon as church service ended, however, the negative thoughts resurfaced. Images of his former life came to mind, when he finished his days at the ranch in San Antonio or completed a cattle drive on the Chisholm Trail. No shortage of money to throw away at the time. If only he saved then instead of squandered. Things would be different today.

He waited outside for Joe while the man and his family greeted the Reverend. Joe emerged from the church shortly.

"You were sayin' about the ranch?"

Dusty walked with him. "I thought it over some. I'm looking to get hired as soon as it can be arranged."

Joe didn't ask what made him change his mind. "Mabrey should be at the ranch again toward the end of this week. Come by midday when we break for a meal."

His work at the Charlton farm rarely allowed him an afternoon reprieve. Sophie's father would raise his eyebrows at Dusty for asking to wander off at noon without a good excuse. "What about evening time?"

"That too, if you catch him before supper. I said midday because the foreman would want to see how well you can rope a calf or steer the herd. You got a cutting horse?"

"Gabe over there's had his share of that. He'll remember what to do once I get him 'round those Herefords."

"Come by when you can, then. I'll tell Mr. Mabrey to be expecting you." Joe reached his wagon, extending a hand to his wife to help her up. Violet climbed in after her.

Dusty spared a glance at the Charltons as they prepared for the drive back to their home. "If it's all the same with you, Joe, I'd like to keep this between us. I haven't said anything to my boss yet. I'm waiting to see if I get the job before I give him notice."

"Understandable." Joe got onto the driver's bench and drove his family away.

Dusty untied his horse from the post and prepared to ride back to the farm. Nothing else to do but wait for the end of the week to come. He looked over his shoulder and saw Sophie glance his way before her friends Linda and Margaret said something to make her turn around.

Sophie managed to catch a glance at Dusty when she was outside before and after service. She had even been tempted to sneak a wave at him, had he not been busy conversing with some of the new settlers. No doubt he was livid at her, thinking she had told on him to her family.

For the next three days her mother found more chores for her to do. On the chance that she had a moment to peek out the window, she'd find Dusty planting the summer hay in one of the fields or cleaning the hog pen.

At night, her family gathered around the supper table without him. His absence was a glaring certainty, so much that on the second night, his chair was removed.

"Where's Dusty, Daddy?" Bernard asked between a mouthful of peas.

Sophie's father cleared his throat. "He has more work to do outside, son. He takes his meals out there now."

"Doesn't he like us anymore?" Rosemarie chimed.

"Of course he does. Now, who wants a slice of pie?" Sophie had never seen her father hasten so fast into the kitchen. How long could he and her mother keep this up? Even her younger siblings knew something wasn't right.

On the third night Sophie witnessed her mother putting food leftover from the day before on a plate and ordering Bernard to carry it out to the bunkhouse. The scene made her think of that night Chad came over for supper. Grimacing, she visualized herself and her family carrying scraps of food outside to throw to a dog. All of them were guilty of treating Dusty appallingly.

Wednesday afternoon, a knock sounded on the door. "Answer that while I'm ironing, please," Sophie's mother said.

Sophie left the stifling hot kitchen and crossed over the hallway to the front of the house. The door jammed in the frame because of the sticky moisture in the air. When she finally tugged hard enough to get it open she discovered Dusty on the porch. Her stomach constricted at being in close proximity to him again and anxiety at being discovered by her mother. "Why did you knock?"

She felt foolish as soon as the question passed her lips. Of course she knew why he did it. He wasn't welcome to come and go through the house like before.

"Figured I need to." Dusty was gracious enough to say nothing beyond that. Sophie still could sink beneath the floorboards to the house's foundation. "This came for you."

She accepted a slender, wooden keepsake box from him. A simple notecard was attached to the ribbon, with her name written on the front. "Who brought it by?"

Dusty put his hands in the pockets of his suspendered work pants. "A teller from the bank. Said it was from Chad." He left the place where he was standing.

"Wait, Dusty." Clutching the box, Sophie let the hot wind from the plains blow tumbleweed and prairie sage into the house.

"Is that door open?" her mother called from inside.

Sophie talked fast before she had a chance of being discovered. "I hate what's happening. I only told them that we talked about Chad, but not the other things…you being a contender or a rival. They don't know that."

Her mother called louder. "Sophie!"

Dusty's face was stoic. "You'd best get back in the house. I don't want you in trouble because of me." He carried his back straight as he returned to the fields.

Raw disappointment lurched in her chest. He still protected her when her words did nothing to change the circumstances. She considered her attempt at explanation and apology to be a cheap consolation for her parents' decision to demote him.

Sophie closed the door on the tumbleweed and carried the box into the kitchen. "Chad had a present delivered to me."

Her mother set the iron upright to keep it from burning a hole in Rosemarie's dress she was pressing. Her eyes lit up as though she were the recipient. "It's always an encouraging sign when a gentleman bestows a gift upon a lady. Quick. Open it."

Sophie untied the ribbon and lifted the box lid. A single purple flower rested on the red velvet lining, along with a necklace. The same flower bud, crafted in gold, dangled from the chain. She lifted it for her mother to see.

"How pretty. Did he leave a note?"

Sophie withdrew the card stock stationery that had been tucked under the flower. She read the three lines written beneath her name. "I regret that my time at the bank has kept me away from you once again. Please accept these gifts as small tokens of my affection. Also, I would be pleased if you and your family would join me for supper tomorrow evening at six o'clock."

"A chance to wear your dinner dress." Her mother smiled approvingly. "Is it going to be held at a restaurant or his residence?"

Sophie read further down, but the note ended with Chad's large signature. "No address is given, so I assume it will be at the mayor's house."

"Chad invited all of us. That means that his parents will be present as well. Now we really do have to finish the ironing today. Go upstairs and bring me the dress and your Sunday petticoats. They must be taken out and starched."

Sophie laid the box and notecard on the table and set out on her new task. Chad offered a second apology for being occupied at the bank. On Saturday he told her that he didn't appreciate her surprise visit. Perhaps that was the real reason for the gift, to smooth things over. Or he had taken to heart her accusation that he wasn't courting her as a man should.

Whatever the cause, her family and Chad's parents were going to be present at their next meeting. They must never find out how she set him straight about his insecurity and jealousy of Dusty. If her mother and father had any more indications that she was on such familiar terms to the hired worker, defending Dusty to the man courting her, even, they would terminate his employment immediately. Sophie didn't know what to do if she cost Dusty his livelihood.

In her bedroom, she gathered the petticoats and her burgundy and navy plaid dinner dress with draped sleeves. A breeze from the open window made the curtains flutter their embroidered roses at her. She answered their beckoning to look down at the land below where Dusty worked tirelessly in the field, unaware that she continued to watch and yearn to speak to him as before.

CHAPTER 19

TWENTY-FIVE GOING ON sixty. That's how Dusty felt on Thursday after all the hay was planted and the hogs grunted at his feet while he scraped mud and filth from their trough. He thought about picking up some of that pain tonic being sold at the general store the next time he visited town. It started to look like a worthy investment.

The pain wasn't merely in his back, legs, and arms. Each time he caught a glimpse of Sophie from afar, knowing that he better not say anything to her when her father was around, was enough to make him feel like he had been thrown off a horse. Presenting her with Chad's gift after the bank teller left it with him was akin to being kicked by one.

Dusty finished scraping the dried mud off his boots when Mr. Charlton came from putting tools in the barn. "You can have the rest of the afternoon to yourself, after you harness the wagon. The family and I were invited to share supper with the mayor."

So that's what was in that gift box that reminded Dusty of a miniature pine coffin. "Have a good evening, sir."

"You as well." His boss cut a path to the house. Minutes later, the Charlton boys David and Bernard followed suit, exiting the chicken coop after emptying the nesting box.

Dusty raised his head to view the position of the sun. A little past three in the afternoon. If he hitched the wagon and got himself a quick scrub, he'd be able to make it to the Zephyr Ranch and back before dark.

Pushing aside the knowledge that his aching back would hurt more if he were asked to demonstrate his prowess as a cowhand, he put one tired foot in front of the other to reach the barn.

A half hour later he was on his way. The dry heat of afternoon had let off by early evening, but sweat still ran down the back of his neck. The nerves he was experiencing had more to do with his reaction to the weather than he cared to admit. Everything counted on his making a good impression at the ranch. If Mr. Mabrey didn't think he had what it took to keep the place running, he was going to have to settle on another job outside his training or keep ducking his head at the farm.

The sign above the ranch gate swung on its hinges as he approached. He prayed he was still making the right decision.

Sophie held still for her mother to finish arranging the folds of her dress over the bustle. Her appearance must be more than presentable. She stood in front of the floor-length dressing mirror in her parents' bedroom and admired how the lace collar of the gown drew attention to her face. The necklace Chad gave her glowed softly in the light.

"Sophie, I'm concerned about the fit of this dress. Turn around."

She faced her mother's critical stare. Her mother stood back and appraised her from head to toe, eyes resting longer on the middle. "You've put on weight."

Sophie shuddered with humiliation. Her pleasure at being able to finally have an occasion to wear the dinner dress deflated. "I don't think I have."

"I can see it. Look at yourself in the mirror from the side.

Do you see how the fabric puckers just beneath the bodice?" Her mother ran her hand along the seams. "I would say your measurements have increased by at least an inch."

Sophie noticed the expanse upon giving intense focus to that area of her body. It confounded her as to how the bit of excess crept up on her unawares. She wore corsets every time she went into town and was not idle when she was at home.

"That isn't the only place where you've gained. With that high collar you're wearing, I can see your cheeks have filled too."

Sophie touched her face. Her fingers made indents into her flesh as if it were a pillow. "Oh, no."

"It isn't terrible. Wear some of your hair loose in tendrils about your face, and don't pinch your cheeks to make them blush. But this weight about the waist, I don't think it can be hidden."

Her mother's tone gave her a sense of defeat. After being caught talking freely to Dusty last week, here she was letting her mother down again by failing to keep a dainty figure. "The dark colors of the dress disguise it."

"Perhaps, but you can't wear dark colors every day. Eventually someone will notice your peculiar dressing habits."

Outside the bedroom walls, Sophie heard her brothers tear down the stairs. It was almost time to leave for the dinner party. Knowing that her girth had increased took the pleasure out of anticipating the menu.

"You need to practice self-control in more areas than one." Her mother gave the final verdict.

Sophie faced the mirror again so her mother could finish arranging the dress. This time, she looked at the gilt frame of the mirror instead of her reflection.

Within the hour, Sophie and her family arrived at the Hooper residence. No other wagon or horse was stationed outside the fence. They would be dining alone with the Hoopers after all.

Chad was at the door to greet them. "I'm glad you could make it. My mother's prepared a five-course meal. Come in." He reserved a lingering look for Sophie. A measure of approval shone on his face when he saw that she was wearing the necklace.

"Thank you for the invitation," she responded.

"My pleasure. This way."

Following behind Chad and her parents, she stepped into the affluent interior of the house. Lights from the kerosene lanterns cast a warm glow upon the walls and the plush upholstery as they passed by the sitting room. In the dining room, the long table was set formally with a lace tablecloth and an assortment of fine-bone china. Linen napkins with an embroidered letter H rested near silverware that cast bright spots of light upon the fleur-de-lis wallpaper.

Chad pulled out a chair for Sophie before taking his seat across from her. She paid attention to the height of the table and how it covered almost half of her torso. No one would take notice of her waistline tonight.

Her mother and father sat on her left, Rosemarie to her right. Mayor Hooper sat at the head of the table, while his wife's seat was adjacent to his. Sophie's brothers sat beside Chad.

"I've prepared glazed vegetables with honey, one of my specialties when we lived in Philadelphia." Mrs. Hooper lifted the covers of the serving platters as she described each course. "Oyster stuffing, with the oysters brought in from St. Louis on the train today. Potato soup, stuffed peppers, braised venison, and breaded ham. The rolls are a secret family recipe. Dessert will be a surprise."

"It looks like you've outdone yourself," Lucretia complimented.

"Shall we say grace?" Mayor Hooper led them in prayer before the food was passed around the table, platter by heavy platter.

Sophie put a roll on her plate and helped herself to a good portion of the glazed vegetables that smelled at once both sweet and savory. The oyster stuffing had a golden crust that called her name. She speared a chunk of the braised venison. Rosemarie passed the tray of breaded ham her way. Sophie went to take a slice of the meat when a subtle but unmistakable glance of caution from her mother made her refrain. Mouth dry, she took a sip from her glass of lemonade.

"How is your crop doing this year, David?" Mayor Hooper spoke to her father.

"We finished planting the wheat and hay. The carrots and other root vegetables have sprouted. I expect a good yield this year if we have more rainfall."

Mayor Hooper drank water. "It's looking like another hot summer's upon us."

Sophie took a bite of the oyster stuffing. The buttery crust melted in her mouth and gave way to flavors of garlic, bacon, and shallots permeating the oysters and cornbread. "This is very good, Mrs. Hooper."

The mayor's wife beamed brighter than the mounted lamp on the wall behind her. "Thank you, Sophie. It's my first time making that recipe."

Sophie could feel her mother's watchful gaze on what went into her mouth. She planned to eat the rest of the stuffing and nibble a few bites of the other items on her plate. Surely that would suffice.

"How is your petition coming along?" Mayor Hooper addressed her after she finished chewing. "I hear you've collected an interesting assortment of names." He glanced sideways at Chad, whose countenance took a dour turn.

Sophie twisted the edges of the napkin resting on her lap.

"I plan to have the petition completed within a week. There are several areas in town where I haven't yet spoken with the ladies." She withheld mentioning her intent to go to the rail station and ask for signatures. Her mother didn't need to choke on a pepper.

"I admire your diligence, Sophie. No doubt that is one of the many reasons why my son has chosen to court you."

She watched Chad cut into the tender venison as though it were tough buffalo hide. He commented to his father while resting his eyes on her. "I find Sophie's other qualities as engaging, if not more so, than her liberal notions." He kept his tone light, but Sophie heard the disapproval beneath his words. No one else appeared to notice.

"But you were kind nonetheless to humor me in my whims." She batted her eyelashes at him. "When other gentlemen see your name signed to the petition, I just know they'll follow in your example."

The mayor set his fork down. "You didn't tell us you also signed the petition, Chad." Unlike his son, he was more practiced in concealing his astonishment.

Chad stabbed the venison with his fork. "A gentleman should always do his best to honor a lady's wishes."

"How noble," Sophie's mother declared. "I thought the age of chivalry had long since passed, but you've proven me wrong."

Sophie thought the remark was a bit too flattering, but her mother had gotten away with worse. She took satisfaction in having stood up to Chad's disparaging comment. He may be her beau, but that didn't entitle him to show her up in front of her family.

"I intend to prove the same to your daughter, Mrs. Charlton, if she will allow me to."

Was this his typical demeanor, to sulk when people didn't respond to him in the way he thought they should?

Sophie washed down the oyster stuffing with more lemonade. Perhaps it was her teasing that made him so glum. Not every man could handle a woman's backtalk, good-natured or no. Not every man was Dusty.

She wondered what he was doing that evening. The night's warm weather was perfect for a stroll in town, where McIntyre's stayed open late for the rail passengers. While preparing for the Hoopers' dinner party, from her window she saw Dusty leave the farm. He may have gone to Claywalk instead. There were twice as many shops and restaurants in that town to occupy his time. Claywalk also had three saloons and a dancehall.

Her mother's notion of sweet-talking cowboys took up residence in her thoughts. Sophie pictured Dusty twirling some shapely little miss across a hardwood floor, hurdy-gurdy piano tinkling in the background. The image didn't sit well at all. Her stomach grumbled in protest.

"Who's ready for dessert?" Mrs. Hooper came into the dining room with a deep dish pie. Sophie didn't realize she had gotten up from the table. "I made it with elderberries."

"Sophie and I will have to decline," her mother declared. "The dinner was very satisfying."

The pie was sliced and served to all but the two of them. Chad declined a piece. "I thought Sophie and I would take a moment to sit outside and watch the sunset."

"That sounds like a wonderful idea. You would like some fresh air, wouldn't you, daughter?"

Sophie knew better than to say anything but yes. She excused herself and went to where Chad stood in the doorway. She walked with him through the hallway toward the front door.

"I see you're wearing the necklace I bought you. Do you like it?"

"Yes, it's lovely."

He held open the door for her. Crickets chirped and serenaded in the grass below the porch steps. Sophie seated herself on the red cedar swing in the corner. Feeling too full, she didn't care for the bench as it rocked. Her beau sat close to her, his trouser legs almost brushing her dress.

"Did you read the note I sent along with the necklace?"

"Of course I did. I know you're a busy man at the bank. You didn't have to tell me twice."

He looked down. "I guess it was my way of telling you that I was sorry for how I acted when you came by the bank. You may have gotten the impression that I didn't like you asking Sterling to sign your petition."

"I know you didn't."

"He's a hired hand. I still don't see how much clout his name carries, especially when the outcome of your cause won't directly affect anything he does."

"Your name is on the petition as well. Exactly how will women's votes affect you?"

"Sophie, don't be difficult when I'm trying to make sense of his participation in this."

"It's about more than clout. I needed many signatures." Sophie wrinkled her forehead. She had been granted a boon that her mother wasn't outside with them to hear Chad's speech. He concealed none of his jealousy. "But it wasn't just the petition that made me upset. You wanted me to kiss you while you sat in that chair and did nothing. You made me feel like I was obligated. Forced to, even."

Chad leaned forward to see into the house. "Don't say that. You know I would never force you to do anything," he retorted, sharp and curt.

Sophie moved away from him on the swing. An unpleasant sensation arose in her stomach again. She took in gulps of air, hoping to suppress the building queasiness.

He moved down with her. "We should let this matter go."

Face softening, he regained his temper. "Put it in the past along with the other mistakes."

The mistakes *she* made. Sophie didn't think he'd ever forget about the Claywalk festival blunder.

"It is a pleasant evening, isn't it?"

She looked toward the setting sun and saw the moon beginning to make its ascent. Nausea rolled over her as her stomach growled despite having just eaten. She clenched her teeth, mortified. "It really is." Sophie talked over the noise, praying that Chad couldn't hear it.

He put his arm over the back of the swing behind her. "It's not often that you get to see the sun and the moon at the same time. An instructor told me a story once about how the sun and moon were once man and woman, ill-fated lovers who died in each other's embrace. Out of mercy, they were placed in the sky so that they could be together forever, if only to meet during the short interlude transitioning from day to night."

"Your instructor was a romantic." Sophie draped her arm across her middle in attempts to ease her indigestion with a hug.

"He doctored in literature, actually. The story came from a Greek or Roman myth. I can't remember which one." Chad's hand came to rest on the sleeve of her dress. He walked his fingers down her arm in a tickling motion.

An overwhelming urge to retch came upon Sophie. She sprang from the swing and ran from the porch. Chad plodded after her.

"Sophie, what's wrong?"

Please, please not here. She reached the fence and swallowed air until it made her lightheaded. Fighting against the burning sensation in her chest, she whirled around and thrust her hand out to prevent Chad from coming any closer.

"You're pale." His eyes widened. "And you're perspiring."

"I don't feel well." She spoke in breathy syncopation as cramps constricted her abdomen.

Chad backed away from her. "I'll go get your parents." He stumbled as he turned to go inside the house.

Sophie made a beeline for her family's wagon. Using the back frame to hoist herself, she scrambled inside. Next to the rifle, her father kept a wooden crate in the corner containing hooks, canvas tarp, and a canteen. She threw back the lid and lifted the canteen out, hurrying to unscrew the top. Lukewarm water spilled over her hands. She tilted the canteen up to her mouth and poured it down her throat.

It tasted wretched, of salt, old leather, and bitter metal, but she drained the contents dry, until her stomach seemed to be temporarily appeased.

Her mother dashed out the door of the mayor's house, trailed by her father and Mayor Hooper. The three of them came to the side of the wagon. "Sophie, Chad said you were ill. What's happened?"

The nausea came in a small wave. Sophie's lips trembled in fear that it would escalate again. "I must go home. Now." She tolerated her mother laying a hand across her forehead.

"She's warm. I'll get the rest of the children and tell your wife that we have to leave, Mayor."

"I'll let her know. Stay out here with your daughter." Mayor Hooper returned inside the house.

Sophie's father untethered the horses and got onto the wagon. "What did you do?"

"I don't know, Daddy." Sophie sat on the wagon floor and dabbed her face with a handkerchief. "It came on all of a sudden. I think it was what I ate."

"Do not let Mrs. Hooper hear you say that." Her mother got in the wagon beside her and fanned her face.

Sophie kept her eyes closed until her siblings could be heard approaching the wagon. As they climbed in, she heard her parents speaking with the Hoopers. Everyone's voice faded in and out as she put all her focus on willing herself not to be sick in front of them.

The wagon began to move. Its jostling and bumping along the uneven dirt road put her in dangerous proximity to losing control. The water that she consumed to abate her illness now sloshed about inside like bilge within a ship's hull.

Her mother never ceased fanning her, though the air she moved with her hand was minimal. "Try to be at ease, Sophie. We'll be home soon."

CHAPTER 20

*D*USTY KNEW WHEN to count his blessings, and this evening he had another one to add to the list. He was Zephyr Ranch's newest cowhand.

After two hours of answering Mabrey's questions about his previous work and experience with cattle, along with several demonstrations of his ability to turn a herd, separate a bull from the nursing cows, and run down a calf to rope it, he walked away with a deep sense of accomplishment. The only thing left to do was notify Mr. Charlton of his pending departure.

"Take the time you need to tie up loose ends with your old boss," Mabrey said. "How long do you think it'll be?"

"No more than a few days. The plantin's all done for the spring." Work never ended where crops and livestock were involved, but Dusty took solace in that he completed the majority of the large tasks set out before him. "I just need to clear my effects from the bunkhouse and see if my employer needs me to do anything else."

"Be here by the middle of next week, then. It's almost time to separate the older calves from their mothers. We'll be branding after that."

Dusty left the ranch at a quarter past seven after Joe congratulated him and the other cowhands gave him a friendly welcome. He had just enough daylight to get through town and back to the farm. Along the way, he rehearsed how he was going to tell Mr. Charlton about his new job. No matter how he said it, it was going to look like he chose to leave because of what took place concerning his friendship with Sophie. He'd have a hard time explaining that wasn't the main reason for his actions when it was what finally drove him to do something.

"Can't be helped, can it, Gabe?" He patted the stallion's muscular shoulder. "A man's gotta make a livin'."

He hoped Mr. Charlton would understand. The worst thing a man could leave a job with was bad standing with his employer.

Dusty reached his destination after eight o'clock, allowing Gabe to stretch his legs and run from the edge of town to the farm. He spotted the Charlton wagon pulled up by the front of the house. Sophie's father and her brother David were busy unharnessing the horses. They were home awfully early from dining at the mayor's.

"How was the dinner, Mr. Charlton?"

Sophie's father had removed his jacket and draped it over the porch banister while he took the yoke apart. "Sophie fell ill. We had to leave early."

Tension took hold of Dusty and twisted his insides into a knot. Sophie didn't look sick when he last saw her. "Do you need me to run and get Dr. Gillings?"

"Not just yet. We'll see how she does in the morning. Her mother's with her now."

Dusty had a dozen questions about the specifics of her malady, how she had taken ill all of a sudden, but judging from Mr. Charlton's brief explanations, no answers were going to come tonight. "If there's anything I can do, let me know."

Sophie's father removed the pole straps from the horses' legs, not answering. His son kept quiet while he assisted.

Dusty rode into the barn and had Gabe unsaddled, rubbed down, and fed before Mr. Charlton talked again.

"Did you go into town tonight?" The two of them left the barn.

"I did. There's something I need to tell you, but it can wait until your daughter gets better." Dusty's anticipation about the new job and his anxiety about telling his boss ebbed away as he considered Sophie's questionable state of health. He'd promised Mabrey that he'd be back at the ranch in a few days, but now he wasn't so enthusiastic to leave.

Sophie spent the night in a fevered state. Between chills that drove her burrowing under the covers and vicious sweats that made her toss them over the foot of the bed just as easily, her stomach did things. Horrible, unspeakable things, so that when morning came, she vowed never to eat oysters again for the rest of her life.

Her mother slept in the room with her, leaving only to go downstairs to prepare breakfast. Sophie smelled the bacon grease that was used to fry the griddlecakes and whimpered as another bout of nausea roiled through her empty belly.

Her mother returned with a pot of weak tea and a bowl of watered-down porridge. Sophie waved them away. "If you can't stomach anything, I'll have to send for the physician."

Sophie rolled over on her side and stared listlessly at the wall. Her head pounded when she lifted it in order to push the damp cowl of hair off her neck.

"Very well." Her mother took the tea and porridge back downstairs.

She heard voices from the first floor just before falling into a light sleep. Only a minute or two seemed to have passed when she opened her eyes again to the din of louder voices coming from below. Her mother sounded agitated.

"What's this? I sent for your father, Dorothea."

"Yes, Mrs. Charlton, but my father had to remain in his office because of a patient who accidentally shot himself in the knee. He thought I could tend to Sophie by myself."

"My daughter is very ill, young lady. I won't tolerate any imitations of doctoring upon her."

"I can assure you, ma'am, that I have completed all of my training and am fully licensed to practice medicine in the state of Kansas."

Sophie drifted into an odd daze where she was neither asleep nor fully conscious. She regained lucidity to find both her mother and Dr. Dorothea Gillings standing over her.

"How are you feeling, Sophie? Mrs. Charlton tells me that you had something to eat for supper last night that didn't agree with you."

"I didn't say supper," her mother defended. "It had to have happened before the fact. Mrs. Hooper prepared a beautiful supper for us yesterday. No one else in this house has felt the unpleasant effects of what my daughter's experienced."

Sophie murmured, "Oysters."

Dr. Dorothea leaned over the bed to hear. "Was that oysters, you said?"

It was a great labor to open her eyes, let alone speak. "I had oyster stuffing for supper. I know that's what caused my suffering. I barely touched anything else on my plate."

"She's saying it was the oysters, Mrs. Charlton. I have to go by her word."

Her mother fussed at Dr. Dorothea again. She rested her eyelids while listening.

"Explain why the rest of us aren't sick then. We all tried the stuffing."

"She may possess a sensitivity to it. Such cases are documented."

"Nonsense. Sophie ate oysters all the time in Louisiana."

"Well, where did Mrs. Hooper get the oysters?"

She heard the door to the bedroom close. Her mother's voice was farther away. "She said they were brought in by train from St. Louis."

"How long were they on the train? How long ago had they been caught?" A small weight dropped onto the bed. A parcel or valise of some sort.

"Why would I think to ask such a question to my dinner hostess, young lady?"

"I ask because the food may have spoiled during the journey."

Sophie felt the weight of the bed shift again. She opened her eyes to find Dr. Dorothea seated on the edge beside her, going through the contents of a medical bag. The lady's face was set in a much-utilized mold of patience, although telltale lines of irritation lined her mouth. She put her back to Sophie's mother.

"How much of the oyster stuffing did you eat?"

Sophie illustrated using her hands. "Two palmfuls. It gave me a fever too."

The doctor turned to address her mother. "Maybe you didn't share in any of the symptoms because your portion of oysters wasn't as large."

Sophie wished she hadn't said that. Now her mother would blame the condition on gluttony.

"Mrs. Charlton, could I trouble you for some boiled water?" Dr. Dorothea asked as she withdrew a long-handled syringe from her bag.

Sophie thought she might faint. What was Dr. Dorothea planning on doing with that wicked-looking instrument? She almost cried out for her mother to remain in the bedroom, but the door had already closed.

"Relax, Sophie. You just had some tainted food last night. The worst consequences are probably over."

"Then why do you have that syringe?"

"This?" Dr. Dorothea grasped the instrument between her fingers as another woman would a delicate paper fan. "It isn't to administer you an injection. I'm going to give you a few doses of paregoric to take. I just have to extract it from one bottle to another. This syringe keeps me from spilling it." She demonstrated by removing a brown bottle from her bag and a smaller blue one.

"What do you need boiled water for?"

"I thought you might want some hot tea after you take this." Dr. Dorothea glanced at the door with a tiny smile. "And your mother needed something to occupy herself."

Sophie giggled. "She'd have a fit if she knew the real reason why you sent her downstairs."

"I understand she worries. What mother wouldn't for her child? But being female doesn't make me an incompetent doctor."

Sophie watched Dorothea transfer the paregoric. In the years that she lived in Assurance, she had known of Dr. and Mrs. Gillings' only daughter, but rarely had the chance to speak with her. Dorothea was a few years older than she, of a quiet disposition, sharp-minded and studious. Even before going to medical school, her nose was always in a textbook. Sophie never could find a subject to converse with her on without feeling intimidated or unknowledgeable.

"My mother meant no harm."

"She was expecting my father. Everyone does when they call for Dr. Gillings."

Sophie attempted to sound helpful. "You can change your name when you get married."

Dorothea glanced at her as though the suggestion was just too precious for words. "Bless your heart, but I worked hard to become a doctor. I won't have a man telling me that I must give up my practice in order to take his name."

"You mean you don't want a husband?"

"Not unless he accepts me for who I am."

"There aren't very many gentlemen whose wives are physicians."

With the blue bottle filled, Dorothea stuck a dropper into it and administered four drops of the medicine to Sophie. "Precisely, and I don't intend to devote the rest of my life to feeding a man's confidence, assuring him constantly that he's more intelligent than I am. Take another four drops of this in the afternoon. It might make you sleepy."

Sophie swallowed the peculiar-tasting medicine. It wasn't bitter or syrupy sweet, but it soothed her stomach going down. "Dr. Dorothea, how do you feel about women voting?"

"Besides the fact that almost every town allows it but ours?"

It was the answer she was looking for. "I have a petition that I want people to sign allowing for us to vote in this year's election. It's only for school ballots, but it's a start. Would you care to add your name to the list?"

Dorothea withdrew a slim case containing a thermometer from her bag. She swabbed it in a tube of alcohol before placing it under Sophie's tongue. "I'll sign. Where is it? Point. Don't try to speak while the mercury measures your temperature."

Sophie indicated for her to open the first drawer on the bedside table. Dorothea turned the first page. "My, my. Look at Mr. Hooper's signature. I thought I saw his name on our Constitution too, if I'm not mistaken."

The thermometer kept Sophie from laughing. After five minutes, the doctor read her temperature.

"You still have a fever. I'll leave some of the tea with willow bark extract that my father likes to treat his patients with."

"Thank you, Dr. Dorothea. For signing my petition too."

Dorothea returned all her medical equipment into the

bag. In the process of packing the thermometer case, she paused and studied Sophie. "I never thought for a moment that you would turn out to be a suffragist."

Sophie sank into the pillows, grateful for the medicine beginning to work its miracles on her queasiness. "I wouldn't call myself that. It all started when I needed a cause after winning the town belle contest."

"But you do think we ladies have the right to make our own choices?"

"I have, since I've become so involved. My mother and father tried to stop me at first."

Dorothea grasped the handle on her bag. "How old are you, Sophie?" Her question was a request for fact, but it sounded accusatory.

"Twenty-one."

At that, the doctor's brows went up. "Twenty-one is a good age to start making your own decisions."

Sophie defended herself and her parents. "I wasn't raised to be disrespectful. They didn't want me to be entangled in politics. They meant well."

"You can be respectful while still defending what you believe in. If you want to get more names on that petition, you're going to have to show people that you can do that."

She held back a response to Dorothea's comment. The doctor wasn't casting judgment upon her, but giving encouragement, even if it came in a dose that burned a little going down.

Dusty had a long drink at the water pump as Dr. Dorothea came walking out of the house. He released the lever and caught up with her as she got into her small horse cart. "Dr. Dorothea, how's Sophie?"

He caught her off guard by failing to offer a standard

formal greeting. "Hm? Oh, she'll be fine. She just had a stomachache."

"Must have been pretty drastic to have to send for a doctor."

"Sophie will live to get another petition signed." She smiled and bid him good day.

Dusty languished in the feeling of relief that Sophie had not fallen into some disastrous ailment. He still preferred to see how she was faring for himself, but he took what was offered. It remained for him to complete the task that left him uneasy.

After filling a canteen with water, he carried it to Sophie's father, who was busy seeding the carrot patch. "Mr. Charlton, sir, I need to talk to you."

Mr. Charlton reached into the faded canvas seed bag strapped across his torso and sprinkled a handful in a meticulous plot near his feet. "Yes?"

"It's about my employment."

He let the rest of the carrot seeds simply fall from his hand. Dusty prepared for a worse reaction to come. "No easy way of sayin' this. I thought about it for over two months now. I figure it's time for me to leave the farm, see what else there is to do."

Mr. Charlton moved slowly, stepping over the carrot plot. "I wasn't aware you were looking to go. You've been here for a long time."

"Yes, sir, and I appreciate you keeping me on and all, but it's time for me to start thinking about permanent work. I want to begin planting my own roots, maybe have a house and family like yours one day."

Sophie's father smiled at that. "This farm didn't shoot up overnight. It was twenty-four years in the making from the time I began working for hire at seventeen to the time I moved my family to Assurance."

"That's why I'd like to make my way. At seventeen, you had yourself more of a head start than I did."

"Are you going to stay in town?"

"Sort of. I applied for a position as cowhand at the Zephyr Ranch off the main road. The foreman's expecting me to report for work as soon as I get things settled here. That's what I was going to tell you yesterday evening before Sophie fell ill."

Mr. Charlton looked instinctively at the house, to his daughter's window. "Does your wanting to leave have anything to do with Sophie's recent arrangement?"

Dusty scuffed the ground with the toe of his boot. He was free to admit his discontent since he would be leaving the farm in short time, yet it wasn't good to part on bad terms. So far, Mr. Charlton was taking the news better than he expected. "This was on my mind well before last week."

Uh-oh. That didn't sound too good.

"Why didn't you say something?"

He scuffed the ground with his other boot. "It took me a long time to make my decision."

Mr. Charlton put his hands in the pockets of his overalls. "I'll have to find your replacement, but I won't obligate you to stay on until I do."

"I can stay till this Tuesday or Wednesday, finish up on arranging the tack in the barn."

"No, the boys will do that. You can leave as soon as you have the bunkhouse cleared. I'll write you a letter to verify your good standing as a worker here."

Dusty had the feeling that he was being dismissed, albeit courteously. "Thank you, Mr. Charlton. Before I leave, may I say good-bye to your family?"

"The boys are in the wheat field. The ladies are in the house. I think my wife has Rosemarie doing Sophie's chores." Mr. Charlton went back to sowing carrot seed in the soil.

Dusty made his rounds, tracking David and Bernard down to tell them first. David took no pains to hide his disapproval.

"You can't go and work for somebody else. You tended the farm this long."

Dusty didn't mind being scolded by a sixteen-year-old when he knew that the boy only said it because he would be missed. "I gave Mr. Mabrey my word. I won't be too far away from town. You and Bernard can ride out to the ranch and visit if your father allows."

David crossed his arms and lowered his head in an older version of a child's pout. "You still need to finish teaching me how to lasso and shoot."

"Who said anything about shooting?"

"A long time back you said you'd let me try the Winchester."

Dusty remembered no such thing. "Supposing I did, I'll let you fire the rifle another day. Maybe."

He went to the house next, hesitating at the front door. Mr. Charlton didn't say he couldn't enter when he asked to say good-bye to Mrs. Charlton and the daughters. He knocked on the door. Sophie's mother answered.

"Yes, Dusty?" She wiped her hands on a dishrag.

He removed his hat. "Ma'am, I just talked to Mr. Charlton and told him that I will be taking a new position at a ranch outside town. Today's my last day working for you."

"How unfortunate." She spoke the words, but they didn't sound like they rang true. She smiled with her lips but her eyes remained discerning. "We've certainly appreciated your hard work."

"Thank you, Mrs. Charlton. I wondered if I could say good-bye to Sophie and Rosemarie before I go."

She snapped the dishrag before folding it into a perfect square. "Rosemarie is helping me in the kitchen. Sophie is still not feeling well. The medicine the doctor gave her makes her sleep. She's unable to receive visitors."

Astonishment took control of his senses. Sophie's mother had always been strict, but he never thought that she would be harsh enough to keep him from saying good-bye to her daughter. It wasn't as though the ranch was next door to the farm where he could walk across the field and say howdy at any time of day.

"Ma'am, the ranch is outside of town. I won't be in Assurance much."

She offered him no pity. "If I see you in church, I may decide to let Sophie tell you a final good-bye."

A final good-bye? He thought she misunderstood him. "No, Mrs. Charlton. I won't be leaving Assurance to go across the state or anything like that. I just won't be close as I once was."

"I know very well what you meant, Dusty, but I may not have made myself clear. Sophie's father and I will decide when and if she will be permitted to speak to you again." Mrs. Charlton regarded him coolly. "When I watched you from that window, I saw the way you looked at my daughter. I was her age once. She may not recognize the signs, but it's obvious what you intend to do should you get her away from the protection of her family."

Dusty was rendered speechless, and for a moment, had a mere trace capacity to shake his head. "I'm not that kind of man. The wrong I did make was in not telling you sooner that I came to care for Sophie. For that, I'm regretful."

Sophie's mother twisted her lips in disgust. "She is my precious daughter, not some painted dancehall girl that you may hope to charm with empty words and fleeting promises."

She would have done better to strike him across the face. The shock would have been far less bracing than the vitriol of her accusations. "I've never treated Sophie in that manner,

Mrs. Charlton. You know because you've seen with your own eyes."

She took a step back inside the house, her hand on the door handle, ready to close it in his face. "I see that Chad Hooper is a more suitable match for my daughter, Dusty. Not you. Not a hired hand."

Her true opinion of him finally emerged, based on far more than him not being able to shower Sophie with riches. He was from the wrong station. No matter what he did to earn money and prove himself stable, Mrs. Charlton would always see him as a drifter for hire.

Dusty steeled his jaw as he looked down at her. "Well, ma'am, that's a true shame. I hope one day to raise your estimation of me."

With that, he proceeded to the bunkhouse to gather his things, to leave the farm that had been his livelihood for three years and the home of the woman he had come to love.

CHAPTER 21

THE RIDE TO the ranch softened Dusty's anger toward Mrs. Charlton, though it by no means lessened his resolve to prove her wrong. Such measures took time and he prayed that in his absence she would not be able to persuade Sophie to view him the way that she did. It tore him up that he was forced to leave without being able to tell Sophie where he was going or why. Her mother could pick and choose how to explain his departure, and if he were a gambling man he could bet his horse that the explanation would put him in a bad light.

Please, Lord, give Sophie discernment.

Dusty arrived at the ranch where Mr. Mabrey greeted him with a clap on the back and told him to see Joe about getting settled in one of the bunkhouses.

Joe joked with him. "It's much easier to share quarters with a wife than it is a bunch of workers that don't wash regularly. You ought to try it sometime."

"I plan to. Soon as I get a wife." Dusty set his few belongings on the floor of his new living space in the ranch bunkhouse. He was spoiled for so long having an entire structure to himself at the Charlton farm. He had to get used to sharing a bunkhouse with other cowhands all over again.

He viewed the newspaper clippings and old calendar pictures that were posted along the walls as decoration. A

French portrait was displayed prominently in the middle of the two sets of bunk beds, featuring an attractive young brunette who left very little to the imagination.

Joe averted his gaze from the provocative art. "Can't do nothin' about that. The other boys all banded together to get that picture tacked up on the wall."

"It's alright. I tend to sleep with my eyes shut."

The assistant foreman chuckled. "What happened to that gal you said you had your eye on?"

"She's still in town. It's gonna be harder to visit her now that I'm out here." Under no circumstances could Dusty mention Sophie's exact whereabouts to anyone on the Zephyr Ranch. After having just left the Charlton farm, it looked quite the scandal to declare that he was sweet on the daughter of his former boss.

"If you're keen on stayin' 'round long enough, you might want to see about building a house nearby. There's still enough land to be sold at a good price. That's what I did."

Joe's suggestion sounded like a good one. "How much is the land going for?"

"Ten dollars an acre. If you put away a little less than half of what you earn each month, you could have yourself a homestead by this winter."

The idea appealed to Dusty. He could purchase twenty or thirty acres of land at that moment with part of his bank savings. The cost of timber to build a house would be more, but he could make the purchases in increments. "I'll have to see. I'm still looking to get into ranching myself one day, and Mr. Mabrey wouldn't take kindly to having another man's cattle grazing so close to his."

"He'll let you buy cattle off of the ranch as long as you agree to give him a share of the sale price. No competition that way."

Joe left him to get situated. As Dusty was the newest man

hired he had to settle for a pallet on the floor until a new bed could be put in for him. It was the tiniest inconvenience in light of the higher wages he would make and the satisfaction of rising every day to do the work he loved.

He arranged his spare pair of boots and extra clothes near the pallet, all the while thinking of the opportunities Joe described. Land. A chance to build a house, to raise his own cattle. His dream was getting closer to his reach day by day.

Only one exclusion to that dream persisted to taunt him. The choice shouldn't have had to come between remaining at the farm with no chance of bettering himself or leaving Sophie behind.

He peeled back a dark heavy tarp that hung over one of the bunkhouse windows. Staring at the road leading back to Assurance, he wondered if she had already been given the news.

Sophie felt better enough on Sunday morning to eat a small bowl of oatmeal, but not quite steady enough to attend church. Her mother stayed home with her.

"I think I've been sleeping for the past two days," she said, after having a bath and putting on a clean dress. "What's happened since then?"

Her mother helped her change the bed linens. She folded the corners of the laundered sheet and tucked it under the mattress. Her lips remained silent.

"Mother?" Sophie stopped manipulating the sheet on the opposite side of the bed. "What's going on?"

"It's over, Sophie. There's no need to tell."

"Tell me what? Did one of my brothers or Rosemarie also get sick?"

"No." Her mother pulled the sheet up to the head of the mattress. "Dusty left. He's taken another job at a ranch."

Sophie sat down on the half-made bed. In her weakened state, she had to repeat what she had just heard for clarity. "Dusty left us? Why?"

"Not us, the farm. I suppose he left for reasons why any worker for hire should. More pay."

Sunlight made reflections on the glass window, casting little lights across the wall. Sophie stared at them without blinking until they all merged into a cluttered mural. "Didn't Daddy offer to increase his wages?"

"We can't afford to maintain our wealth by giving our employees more money than they deserve. Your father plans to go into town tomorrow to look for a new worker. It shouldn't be difficult. Young men come off the trains all the time seeking a new start."

Sophie was long used to her mother's intentional deflections of the actual matter at hand but this time she was unable to let her get away with it. "I'm not worried about Daddy finding another worker. Why didn't Dusty say good-bye?"

"Given his rough-and-tumble background, you must make allowances for his slip in manners."

"No, he would have said good-bye to me. Why didn't he?"

Her mother let out a deep breath. "He came to the house just before going to gather his belongings. He asked to see you one last time. I told him you were asleep."

Sophie looked at her, aghast. "You could have woken me."

"I didn't feel it was necessary to drag you from your bed."

"But I don't know when or if I'll see him again." The possibility brought tears to Sophie's eyes, threatening to spill over the brims.

Her mother frowned at that. "Don't you dare cry over that cowboy. He's not part of our family."

Two fat tears rolled down, anyway. "Yet he's supped at our table and accompanied us to church. Most hired hands leave when the day's work is done."

"That's where we made our mistake." Her mother turned to rearranging the contents of the bedside table since the task of making the bed halted. "We've always dealt liberally with Dusty when he showed himself trustworthy. This time he's overstepped his boundaries."

"Please don't talk about him that way. You make him sound like an outlaw."

Lucretia put the empty medicine bottle on the vanity table to remove from the room later. "He's worse than that. He has feelings for you, Sophie. I know because he stood on the porch bold and told me without a bit of shame."

So he finally admitted the truth to her family. It was a brave act; one that could bring him trouble depending on how her mother and father decided to use the information. Sophie turned away from her mother's astute gaze, fearing that her face would give her away. How could her family go from having respect for Dusty to despising him on the small reason that he fancied her?

"You're not saying anything. Am I to assume you feel the same way toward that drifter?"

Sophie resumed making the bed. "I just wanted to have a chance to say good-bye to Dusty."

"Remember what I told you. Your place isn't to associate with the help."

That teaching made sense to Sophie for so long but it was beginning to unravel. Her place wasn't to associate with anyone her family didn't approve of, let alone Dusty. She murmured as she picked up the bed coverlet.

"What did you say, daughter?"

She forced herself to be brave. Dusty risked destroying his future in the town by confessing how he felt about her. She could risk a tongue-lashing from her mother in comparison. "Dusty didn't deserve the way we treated him but he was too respectful to say so. We owe him an apology."

"We owe him nothing. I'm surprised how freely you speak these days." Her mother took the other end of the coverlet and pulled it taut with extra force. "It's that voting business and petition peddling. I'm telling your father that you need to stay at home until you remember how you've been brought up."

Sophie's shoulders drooped in frustration. With each day that passed, the little freedoms she was granted slipped away. She had no purpose, no cause to which to devote her time and energy, and now, no Dusty.

Her mother continued doling out the punishment. "Until I see fit, you will leave only to attend church and when Chad calls upon you."

Her beau was the last person on her mind. "Mayor Hooper is expecting the petition. How am I supposed to get it completed if I remain at the farm?" Or to find Dusty, she dared not utter.

"We're done talking about this." Her mother finished making the bed and gathered the bottle on the vanity table. "If you insist upon forgetting yourself, I'll keep reminding you."

Sophie counted her mother's footsteps until they reached the downstairs floorboards. She ran to the window, threw the catch, and hoisted it open. A brisk wind swept in and blew one of the small porcelain figurines off the vanity table. It fell to the floor, one of the limbs shattering.

She returned her attention to the path leading to the main road that resided twenty feet below. There was no stealing away from that height. She was certain to get caught if she tried to sneak out from the front or kitchen door.

Her stomach felt uneasy again. Sophie continued to study the fields below opening to vast prairie in the distance. She didn't want to disobey her parents or cause them to be angry at her, yet neither did she want to continue being treated like a child.

Dr. Dorothea was correct in her assessment. Twenty-one was a very good age to start making her own decisions. Sophie just wished it were that easy.

A full six weeks passed before Sophie was granted permission to resume her usual activities within the town. During the month and a half that she was forced to remain at home, she found little reprieve in visits from Linda and the ladies of her mother's weekly tea gathering. No word was spoken of her punishment to them, but Sophie surmised that the entire circle of her family's friends and associates knew that something was amiss on the farm. Everyone was simply too polite to raise questions.

Chad called upon her twice weekly, having dinner with her family on Tuesday evenings and taking her strolling upon the promenade by the lake on Saturday afternoons. Without her saying anything he took prompt notice of Dusty's absence, and the timing of it couldn't have made him happier.

He remarked upon it again one Tuesday in mid-July after he arrived at her house and had to tether his own horse to the fence. "I don't mind that he's gone. I was always dubious of Sterling."

Sophie stood by as he put his coat on the rack beside the door. He always wore a coat no matter the weather. Cautious and predictable.

"Sterling's quick and sudden departure confirms he was up to no good," he prattled on. "I'm surprised he didn't try to take anything of value with him."

"Not every man of modest means is born to be a thief," she replied, goaded into defending Dusty yet again. She thought by now she would be used to his carrying on about Dusty. But nothing she said ever assuaged his jealousy of the cowboy.

"I don't refer to valuables only as jewels and trinkets. Sterling had another treasure in mind, one that he failed to win." Chad took one hand from the coat rack and stroked her cheek. Sophie moved his hand away.

"Regardless of what you believed about Dusty wishing to court me, his absence doesn't give you liberties with my person."

Chad pressed his lips together until they formed a ring of white. "You keep talking as though the man stood a chance of rivaling with me for your affections."

"He doesn't. *Didn't.*" Sophie shifted, uncomfortable speaking about Dusty when her parents were just down the hallway. "I keep talking because you insist on bringing this subject up time and time again."

"Let's change the subject, then. The food in the dining room smells good. How are you and your family this evening, my darling?" He took to giving her endearing names now. In another time she would have thrilled at them. Today they just sounded tired and uninspired.

The table was set and Sophie's family awaited them in the dining room. Chad conversed in more amiable fashion once the food was passed around.

"My father's giving his annual party next month before the elections. He'd like for you and your family to be the guests of honor, Sophie."

She put her fork down. "Why?"

Her mother gasped. "I think what my daughter means is, to what do we owe this honor?"

Chad wiped his mouth on a napkin. "For your continued support of his campaign. It really has been one of the reasons for his success. He wishes to honor that."

"Tell your father thank you and that we will surely honor his invitation." Sophie's father spoke for all of them.

"Yes, Mr. Charlton. The party will be on the first Saturday of August. I have the formal invitation with me. My father would have told you himself, but he figured that Sophie would enjoy hearing it more from me."

Sophie closed her eyes so she could roll them. It wasn't Chad's father who reasoned that way.

"You removed your necklace."

She opened her eyes again to Chad's observant gaze. She put her fingers to her bare neck. "I didn't wear it this evening."

"I can see that you don't have it on. Is anything the matter?"

In truth, Sophie had removed it before helping to prepare the evening meal, at her mother's insistence that the necklace was too precious to wear while doing housework. "No, Chad. I didn't want it to fall into the batter while I was baking."

"Yet you forgot to put it back on."

"I did forget."

Her simple answer made him raise an eyebrow, but he abandoned the subject and talked with her mother about the last pre-election party.

What was wrong with her? She shouldn't feel so short of temper around Chad when she was willing to overlook his jealousies before, even consider them to be a form of flattery. Dusty's departure had caused her to change, to be impatient with the things that previously brought amusement. Sophie didn't want to sit through the evening meal and listen to Chad talk of another company he planned to acquire, another trip that would take him to Missouri for two weeks.

She waited and waited until dinner was finished and the plates were washed and stacked in the cupboard. It was no longer good to let Chad court her. Sophie considered how she stopped accepting gifts and invitations from that lawyer's son in Claywalk after he insisted on attending every picnic, dance, and supper party with her. Her father hadn't been too pleased with her decision to dismiss the young man after he gave him permission to court her, but he eventually let the matter subside, saying she was only eighteen, after all. Would he do so again if she called an end to Chad courting her? Her parents were probably eager to have her settled very soon.

She sat through a round of checkers that her father and Chad played while her mother and siblings watched. The ticking of the grandfather clock in the sitting room made her foot tap anxiously in time. She excused herself and went to her bedroom to retrieve the necklace Chad had given her. Heart pumping fast, she began thinking of words to say when the time came to return the gift.

The clock chimed half past seven when Sophie's family allowed her to have a few moments alone outside with Chad before he left. Sophie listened to the sounds of evening on the farm, though none of the usual cricket chirps brought that familiar sense of comfort. She looked to the bunkhouse that appeared devoid of life now that it was no longer occupied by Dusty, but by Mr. Kent, a new worker that Daddy spared no time in hiring.

Chad strode alongside her, carrying his coat under one arm. "You'll enjoy the party this year, Sophie. My mother will be trying several new recipes. We've also hired a band of musicians from Chanute to play throughout the evening."

She dug into her skirt pocket and unfolded the handkerchief. The cool chain of the necklace brushed the back of her hand. "Chad, I think the time has come for me to tell you something."

"If you're embarrassed about falling ill the last time you

supped at my family's home, not to worry. My mother says it happened to her when she was being courted by my father. A woman's delicate nerves is all it is."

Was he aware of his habit of interrupting people and presuming to finish what they had to say? "No, it isn't about that. It's about our courtship. I haven't been forthcoming with you." As he drew his brows together, she produced the necklace from her pocket, dangling it by the toggle clasp. She took a fortifying breath. "I don't think we should continue to see each other."

He stared at the gold rosebud that swung on the chain like a miniature pendulum. As though mesmerized by its movements, he met Sophie's eyes only when it stopped. "What do you mean that we shouldn't see each other?" He made no effort to reach for the necklace.

She dropped her hand to her side. "My feelings have changed over the past weeks. I realize that when you asked my father for permission to court me, your intentions were to establish a...." Her mind fished for a different word for marriage. "...a degree of permanence. But I'm afraid that I'm no longer in agreement. Therefore, I cannot knowingly accept this token of your affection."

He glanced at the hand where she held the necklace. "Stop trying to be formal with me and explain why you suddenly want our arrangement to end."

Sophie's spine grew rigid. He called their courtship an arrangement, making their time together sound as dry and procedural as one of his bank transactions. "I don't see anything that's arranged here. This necklace was a gift, not surety."

He took hold of the dangling flower bud, but didn't pull it from her. "Why won't you let me show affection with gifts or with embraces? I've been courting you for almost two months. People would think you didn't care for me."

Chad was right about the timing of their courtship. Here it was the middle of July, and after her father approved of their pairing, not one kiss had she allowed Chad, save the occasional peck on the cheek. She was unable to explain the way she felt, but the thought of kissing him didn't stir any notions of romance.

"It isn't that I don't care for you. One cannot rush these things. Love and affection take time to blossom." Sophie wished she could believe her own words. She willed herself to relive the heady rush of excitement that came at the spring festival when Chad bid on her food basket. It was an adventure to flirt with him, then.

He dropped the necklace charm. "You keep that. Once again, you parry and deflect from what's being asked of you. A year ago you knew that I wanted to court you. There's no point in pretending that we need to start all over again." He crossed the front yard to untie his horse from the fence. "You needn't flirt with me anymore by playing coy."

Sophie huffed at his audacity. "That is an awful thing to say. You know better than to speak that way to me."

He gave a wearied reply. "I'm beginning to think you speak to me only for the enjoyment of sparring."

"Be well assured that I do no such thing." If only she could find the man she did enjoy bantering with. No one in her family had seen or heard from Dusty since he left. "Chad, please don't make this more difficult than it has to be." She marched up to him and the horse, prepared to drop the necklace into Chad's coat pocket if necessary.

"You're upset, Sophie. It's my fault. I've made you feel rushed and I promise not to do it again. I'll see you at the party." He gave her hand a final squeeze before getting onto the horse.

Sophie had one last chance. "This is hard for me to express, but I don't think I—"

"Say no more. I won't pressure you. You'll kiss me when you're ready." He gave her a formal smile, one that she'd seen him give his bank clientele, and turned his horse toward the road.

Why couldn't she speak fast enough? Chad rode away and she went into the house, promising herself to confront him again the next time they met.

CHAPTER 22

THE FOLLOWING DAY Sophie put her frustrations with Chad aside as she prepared to go into town. She finally had the chance to resume getting her petition signed and sent to the mayor before the party. While David readied the wagon, she made sure she was dressed appropriately to stand at the train station for a long period of time, choosing a white blouse with full sleeves and a plaid skirt.

"This time, don't forget to wear the necklace Chad gave you." Sophie's mother fastened the chain around her neck before helping to tie her hair up in a green ribbon. She did not share in her daughter's anticipation of obtaining names for the petition. "Whether you get two signatures or two hundred today, I want that list out of your hands by tomorrow."

"I will give it to Mayor Hooper by morning," Sophie promised. As soon as the ribbon was tied she wasted no time in leaving the house.

Outside she passed the new hired hand as he stood at the fence, giving it a fresh coat of varnish. Short in stature, with a stocky frame and hair that was beginning to thin at the temples, he appeared to be at least fifteen years older than Dusty.

"Good afternoon," Sophie said. He looked about as though he couldn't determine the direction of her voice. When he eventually recognized her, he jabbed his full-bearded chin down in a terse nod and went back to painting.

Her brother saw it from the wagon. "I don't like Mr. Kent too well. He's about as curmudgeonly as one of those traveling orators that come to town."

"At least the orators engage in conversation." Sophie didn't like how unsociable the new worker was, either. No doubt that was her father's reason for hiring him. He spoke solely to her father, hid in the bunkhouse after all the chores were finished, and had a habit of spitting tobacco on the ground where everyone could see. She sidestepped a wad of it near the wagon's front right wheel.

"Farm work's been more tiresome than ever with Dusty gone," David voiced when they were down the path and well out of earshot of Mr. Kent.

"Is that why you readily agreed to accompany me to the train station?" Sophie teased rather than admit that she also missed Dusty. It took his leaving to make her realize how much she did speak to him on a given day. She found herself missing the warm smile and affection he'd shown her, even when she sought to irritate or rebuff him. Would she experience that again or did her family's harsh treatment convince him to stay well away from her for good?

"We should go see him."

The sun got in her eyes. She squinted to look at David. "Excuse me?"

"You heard me. He's at the Zephyr Ranch. Mr. Hastings the blacksmith said so the last time Pa and me went into town. He only told me when Pa wasn't listening."

Sophie leaned over the side of the wagon to see if they were out of earshot. "You know we can't do that."

"Why not?"

"Because Mother and Daddy expect us to be at the train station. We can't lie to them."

"We can go to the station now and go to the ranch afterwards. They won't know."

Sophie took the tempting idea into contemplation. Guilt at deceiving her parents won out. "No, that would be wrong."

David made a face at her. "You're just as stodgy as Mr. Kent."

"Just drive the wagon and I'll never ask you to help me get another petition signed." She quieted her brother but kept thinking about visiting the ranch. How would Dusty take to seeing her after leaving the farm under cold circumstances, all of them her fault?

The Assurance train station was a mile and a half outside town. Built upon the connecting tracks from the Claywalk line, the little depot provided a marker of civilization amid the wind-worn shrubs and the grass that turned brown under the hot sun. Weeds sprouted along the border of the tracks, threatening to creep through the gravel and into the ballasts.

Sophie and David made their way to the building. The simple structure of wood and brick was built on the same level as the train platform, still in the process of being made larger to accommodate increased passengers and freight. Sophie glanced at the clock mounted on the side of the building.

"The train should be arriving in seventeen minutes." She read the schedule posted below the clock.

"You should ask those folks to sign." David referred to the people gathering beside the platform. One middle-aged man and his wife sat waiting on the long bench. A woman traveling with two small children walked to the platform, carrying a carpetbag. After inquiring as to their town residency, Sophie got a signature from the woman. The older couple declined.

As Sophie waited for the approaching train in the

distance, she saw movement to her left. Turning, she discovered five of the new black settlers, two young men and three women. She recognized two of the women, a mother and her daughter, from having seen them seated in the same pew near Dusty in church.

The daughter spotted her and held eye contact. She broke away from her party and came forward. Her mother appeared to call out to her, but Sophie couldn't hear the words over the train's shrill whistle. Sophie froze until the young woman stopped five feet away.

What should she do or say? She had never spoken to any of the new settlers before.

"Excuse me, miss," the young settler addressed her when the train whistle died. "You don't know me, but my name is Violet Emmers."

Sophie found her voice again. "I've seen you in church. You and your family sat next to a friend of mine. Uh, what brings you to the station?"

"My mother and I are helping Mrs. Willis and her sons welcome Mr. Willis back home." Violet glanced over her shoulder at them. "I heard Mrs. Willis and Mama talking about your petition. That's a brave step you're taking to get women the right to vote."

Sophie fidgeted with the string securing her pencil to the petition. "I'm not fighting for the full right to vote. Not yet, I should say. This is just for school elections."

"I'd like to sign your petition."

"You would?" Sophie's surprise made her question sound more like an outburst. She winced, hoping Violet would not take offense.

Violet offered a polite nod. "If it's fine with you."

Sophie saw her brother watching them from the depot with rapt interest. The older couple and the lady with her two small children pretended to be more concerned with the train as it rolled its way closer to the station.

An emotion prodded Sophie. The country had changed since the war, since she was a little girl. People like Violet were able to live their lives as she did. Freely. In the past years since Sophie matured and grew closer to the Lord, the more she realized that this was the way it always should have been.

She extended the petition to Violet. "I'd be pleased to have your signature, Miss Emmers."

Violet's face glowed when she smiled. She looked back at her mother, who nodded her approval. She took the petition and wrote her name. "And I'm pleased to support this worthy cause."

Now it was Sophie's turn to smile. To Violet, the simple right to vote in school elections meant another freedom secured. Her boldness in approaching and asking to sign the petition made Sophie think. What would happen if she also dared to embolden herself just a little more?

Violet and the other settlers moved on to wait near the edge of the platform. David came to Sophie when they left. "I can't believe you did that," he said with equal parts surprise and admiration. A familiar persistence returned to David's face. "I bet we can get more signatures if we went to the ranch."

"I don't think the ranch workers are concerned about the goings-on in the town, least of all ladies voting."

"Dusty signed it. He'll be able to get them to sign the petition too."

The train whistled again. Sophie observed two plumes of smoke billowing on the horizon. "I doubt it. Besides, I imagine the owner of that ranch would not be pleased to see two strangers trespassing on his property."

"We're not trespassin'. We're askin' 'em to show their support, and they'd be right nice to you because you're a lady."

Sophie hid her amusement at David's perfect display of the Charlton stubbornness. He was going to find a way onto that ranch no matter what he had to do to get there. His point was valid. Gathering signatures for a petition was an acceptable, even if slightly far-reaching reason for her to visit a cattle ranch. No more or less outlandish than handing out the petition at a train station.

And didn't she just think about exercising a new degree of boldness?

She weighed the matter once more. Dusty's place of work was considered to be well on the outskirts of town, yet still part of it. A portion of the workers had to be residents.

"I'll think about it," she told her brother, but her mind was made up. The road to the ranch lay wide open before them, free from manmade obstructions and, more importantly, people. With their parents well behind on the farm, Sophie and David were free to roam without observation or objection.

Sophie reminded herself to stop thinking like a child and feeling guilty. She was grown, and no one could stop her from doing what she pleased. Wasn't that what Dr. Dorothea implied?

David raised his voice as another train whistle sounded. "You stay here if you want to. I'll go by myself."

"You can't leave when you're supposed to be chaperoning me. I'm the eldest, so I will decide where we go." She let him make a show of his irritation before she finished her statement. "And the ranch it is."

He bounded to the wagon with renewed vitality. She followed after David, but didn't bother to keep up with his hurried steps. Dusty might be happy to see her brother, but he might not take pleasure in seeing the woman who had a part in making the last days of his employment difficult and degrading.

Sophie and David stopped the wagon under the sign of the Zephyr Ranch. Wooly red cattle lowed in the distance, but no workers were to be seen near the entrance. Sophie eyed the sign as it creaked back and forth above their heads. "We may have come too late. The day appears to be done for them."

"We left the station at three. It ain't even close to supper-time yet."

Reflexively, she started to correct his grammar when a gunshot sounded. Sophie shrieked and lowered herself onto the footboard of the bench. "David, get down!"

Gunshots fired again. One sounded like it came from the north, the second from the east. The cattle ceased lowing until a third shot made one the bovine creatures produce a sound of alarm.

Sophie covered her head. "I knew they'd think we were trespassers. Turn this wagon around now before we get killed."

"Sophie, I don't think anyone's shooting at us."

"I know the sound of a shotgun when I hear it."

"No, I mean we're not the targets. Listen. The shots are coming from behind that house over yonder."

Sophie took her hands from her head and rose up on her arms. She saw the house David referred to, across from the two smaller bunkhouses. Two consecutive shots fired, this time from a smaller gun. "It does sound like someone's shooting on the opposite side."

Her brother reached around her and pulled the rifle from the back of the wagon. "Grab a few of those cartridges from that crate. I'll see what's going on."

"Are you insane, David? Don't you dare leave this wagon." Sophie made a grab for his shirt collar but he jumped down from the driver's bench out of her reach. "I'll drive back to Assurance by myself and leave you here."

Her brother kept walking. He went past the gate, treading a path in the grass toward the house.

"Hardheaded child." Sophie grabbed her skirt hem and jumped down after him. The horse neighed. Not wanting to lose sight of her brother, she seized the reins and tied them in a haphazard knot to the gate. The horse could break free if it wanted to. She hoped their means of transport would be there when—if—they made it back.

She broke into a light run to catch up with David. The ten head of cattle she'd seen as the shooting commenced had since gone farther down to pasture. She leapt over a scattering of dung to where David stood in the grass like a wild boy of the woods, holding the rifle and staring down at the main house.

"This is surpassing foolish. We should go back before we're caught."

David put a finger to his lips. "I hear laughing. I think they're playing a game."

Sophie listened and soon she could also decipher the sound of men's coarse laughter. One of them made a statement that was followed with more of the same. "What they're laughing about doesn't sound funny, David. Let's go."

A door slammed. The sound cracked the air as good as any gunfire. Sophie jumped and moved behind her brother. She watched a man come out from one of the bunkhouses, brawny, bull-shouldered, and carrying a rifle that looked as though it could have given birth to the one David was holding. He fired a warning shot in the sky.

"What are you children doing? This is private property." The man growled at them from the under shade of the bunkhouse's slanted roof. Despite him calling them children, he didn't lower the rifle. It remained aimed in their vicinity.

Sophie raised her hands, unable to control their tremors.

"Sir, we're sorry for coming onto the land like this. We're looking for a man who works here. He's a friend of ours."

"Dusty Sterling," David supplied.

The man lowered the rifle, but just slightly. "Who's lookin' for 'im?"

Sophie stepped partly out from her brother's shadow. "I'm Sophie and this is my brother David. Mr. Sterling used to work in the same trade as our father." She deliberately withheld the information that Dusty was a former employee. Enough trouble had already commenced with their trespassing.

The wind blew at the man's red neckerchief. "What you want with Sterling?"

"Only to visit. We came all the way from town to see him. We mean you or him no harm."

"Then tell your brother to stop pointing that gun like he means to make the sun shine through my gullet. 'Cause he won't get a chance, I can tell you that right now."

Sophie saw what her brother was doing. "Gracious, David, lower that rifle before you get us both shot."

"I don't trust him."

"We don't have much of a choice. Everyone has a gun on this property."

David did what she said. Sophie repeated to the cowhand, "My apologies. I told you we meant no harm."

Finally, the man lowered his rifle to a neutral position and came from the bunkhouse. Sophie planted her feet in the ground as he approached, so as not to take off like a frightened rabbit. She smelled him before he got to her. His scent was a mixture of unwashed skin and horse sweat.

"You're no child. Just a tiny woman." He chuckled at his observation. "You two go around the house. The men are target practicing. Helps keep us sharp in case cattle rustlers come along at night."

Sophie and David walked in front of the cowhand. She glanced behind her every few seconds to make sure that cowhand's rifle stayed lowered.

Target practicing. What were the men shooting?

None of them were shooting anything when she and David reached the back of the house. The gunfire ceased for the moment as five men, Dusty included, stood waiting amidst a field of painted bull's-eyes placed in strategic locations. Stacks of empty cans, bean brand labels still attached to them, also decorated the grass and the limbs of nearby trees.

"What's this, Freeman?" the man on the far right asked. Sophie guessed him to be the owner of the ranch. Standing at medium height, with curling dark hair and broad mustache, his clothes were cleaner and of a higher quality than the other workers. The other men also seemed to defer to him, immediately quieting when he spoke and making way for him as he moved to the front.

Freeman spit a wad of yellow phlegm. "Some visitors here to see Sterling, Mr. Mabrey. Said their father and him used to work together. Looked to me like they were trespassin'."

A tall Negro man on the left stood with his hands on his hips. Violet's father. Sophie recalled seeing him in church with Violet and her mother. "We've had enough of those in the past two months."

Sophie felt some of the tension leave as Dusty's eyes locked onto hers. He came forward. She saw the revolver in his hand before he returned it to a holster at his hip. "I know them, Mr. Mabrey. They're the children of my former boss, Mr. Charlton."

Sophie didn't like Dusty mentioning her as a child, even though she knew that he said it in reference to her being her father's progeny.

"They were telling the truth, then?" The ranch owner's

face was nowhere near as frightening as Freeman's, but it harbored suspicion.

"David and Sophie come from a well-provided household. They wouldn't be out here up to no good."

Freeman harrumphed. "Then they should have called out from the gate instead of creepin' through like they did."

With Dusty vouching for them, Sophie deemed it safe to speak freely. "We would have, but we didn't see anyone. You were all back here shooting. I told my brother not to go onto the property."

"You could have stayed in the wagon," David countered.

"And let you get killed?"

"I had the gun in case I needed it. What did you have?"

"The good sense to stay behind."

"Well, you didn't use it. And you didn't even bring the rifle cartridges like I told you to."

She shot him a cool glance, irritated that the cowhands were being entertained by their bickering. At least it made their hard expressions melt into more agreeable countenances.

Mr. Mabrey addressed her. "You and your brother seem harmless enough, Miss Sophie, ma'am. Most trespassers come from competing ranches and farms. My name is Eli Mabrey, and I'm the owner of the ranch here."

"You have my word that we're not in any competition with you, Mr. Mabrey. We harvest wheat and vegetables on our farm, not livestock. We came because my brother wanted to see Dusty."

"Just him?" A roguish smile spread across Dusty's lips. "You could've waited in the wagon if you didn't want to be bothered with a visit, Miss Sophie. I know how the ranch is no place for a lady." He was rewarded with chortles from the surrounding men.

Sophie didn't know whether to berate him for teasing her in front of the other cowhands or be grateful that he still had words for her after what she and her parents put him through. She unfurled her hands after realizing she had made them into fists. "As a matter of fact, there's a second reason for why we came here. I wanted to know if any employees of this ranch would be interested in signing a petition."

Dusty turned back to the men. "Any of you want to help enable this lady to vote in school elections?"

One of the two cowhands that didn't speak previously sought to voice his opinion. "Vote? What for? She seems outspoken enough already."

Sophie decided not to take offense, remembering that her audience did not consist of the mild-mannered merchants and familiar residents of Assurance that she normally approached with the petition. "It wouldn't be just me you're helping. The other ladies of Assurance would be most grateful to know that you support them in the right to vote in school elections."

"Name's Wilcox." A lustful smirk appeared on his face. "I'd have to see just how grateful those ladies would be."

"I'll sign it," Mr. Mabrey volunteered. "Might as well make an impression in the town. Who better to start with than the ladies?"

Freeman quipped to his boss. "You may find yourself a woman that way. All of us can, 'cept Emmers, 'cause he's already got one."

The dark-skinned man replied proudly, "And won't ever need or want to look for another."

"Where's the petition, Sophie?" Standing before her, Dusty was lean and handsome in his rawboned way. Being in his preferred milieu of cattle, horses, and apparently, sixshooters, seemed to make him more attractive.

She commanded herself to focus on what he asked as opposed to how tall and tanned he was. "I left it in the wagon. I'll have to go get it."

"I'll come with you." Dusty withdrew the gun from his holster belt and presented it handle-first to her brother. "David, practice on the targets while I'm gone."

"A Colt revolver." David accepted the smaller, more expensive firearm and let the rifle clatter at his feet.

Sophie began to protest when Dusty stopped her. "Don't worry. The men won't let him get hurt."

"It's not the gun that I worry about hurting him."

"They won't, either. Mabrey and Emmers will see to that. They'll teach him how to better hold a firearm." He put a hand on her shoulder to steer her away.

CHAPTER 23

 T'S NOT ABOUT how well he can hold a firearm.
That rifle was strictly for defense, Dusty. You're
encouraging my brother to be a gunslinger." Sophie continued to worry about leaving David behind the ranch house
with those rowdy men, especially the trigger-happy one with
the surname Freeman. "I thought ranching involved tending
livestock. I hadn't the slightest inkling that you took time to
practice sharpshooting painted targets and old bean cans."

"You'd be surprised how many men want to steal cattle.
Much easier and more profitable to take a calf than to run
off with an armload of crops." Dusty dropped his hand from
Sophie's shoulder once they were clear of the house.

"This is why my father doesn't want him to be a rancher.
It's dangerous."

"He's turning seventeen. If your brother doesn't want to
be a farmer, there's nothing your father can do to change his
mind. You have to let a person be who they are."

As they walked the range, Sophie noticed that several
members of the cattle herd had returned from further afield.
They would go back once the cowhands and her brother
resumed shooting. "Are you happy with who you are at this
ranch?"

"I've always been the man I am, no matter where I
worked." He gave a passing glance to the Herefords. "But

yeah, the work here's good. The foreman and the other cow-hands respect me."

Sophie latched onto the word *respect*. "Dusty, I can't say how sorry I am and how terrible I feel about what happened on the farm. It wasn't right of my family to ban you from our house and supper table."

She knew when the tic in his jaw resumed that he was careful in choosing his words. "Your mother and father did what they thought was best to protect you. No one can argue with that."

"But they weren't protecting me because I wasn't in any danger. Not from you." She walked around the horse and stopped by the side of the wagon. Dusty moved her way. The gold flecks in his eyes held her attention.

"Sophie, I can't fault them. I cared for you. It wasn't getting easier to hide it."

Her heart quickened until she thought he could also hear it pound. "Do you still care about me?"

"Yes." His voice became husky. He didn't try to hide the inflection. "What they did doesn't change that."

A longing crept over her to go closer to him. Carried by the sensation, she stepped closer and allowed herself to utter words that she kept in secret. "It doesn't change the way I feel, either."

He encircled his arm about her waist, closing the gap between them. The heat of his embrace was warmer than the summer air. Rising on her toes, Sophie reached to put her arms around his neck. She closed her eyes as he kissed her long and slow.

For minutes, hours, she didn't know or care, her consciousness drifted from her surroundings until all she could sense was the tactile heat of his skin, the strength of his arms, and the taste of his lips. When he pulled back, she was disappointed that it couldn't go on forever.

"This is what your parents were afraid of." He played with the hair that curled behind her ears. "Their sweet daughter being taken in by some careless cowboy."

She felt the green ribbon which her mother had so meticulously tied begin to loosen. "You're not careless. You're very attentive."

To her delight, he demonstrated skillfully with another kiss that started at her lips before descending into a warm trail that ended at the base of her throat. "I should stop before I'm tempted to give you more attention," he murmured, pulling back.

Sophie heard noises in the background and remembered that they left her brother and Dusty's fellow cowhands engaged in shooting practice. "I don't think they'll notice how long we've been gone." What was she doing? Inviting him to continue?

His eyes closed down. "We should head back." He gave her the ribbon that had fallen across her shoulder.

Sophie turned away from him while she attempted to refashion her coif. Without a mirror and comb, the best she could do was make a simple bow at the nape of her neck. She hoped the others behind the ranch house didn't study the way she wore her hair when she first came onto the property.

"Is Chad still courtin' you?"

Her elated mood came back to the cold, hard ground and turned into guilt. She had told Dusty that he wasn't careless, but she had certainly let her own restraint fly the coop. The gold necklace Chad gave her burned a ring at the base of her neck, just below the place where Dusty had kissed. She wished her answer could be in the negative, that she and Chad were no longer considered a pair, but she was the only one privy to that truth. "I told him that I wanted to end it, but he wouldn't listen. I'm going to tell him again that I no longer wish to be the subject of his attentions."

Dusty groaned. "Sophie, you led me to think that he wasn't pursuing you anymore. Why didn't you say something before you let me kiss you?"

Sophie felt shame in not telling him sooner, but instead of apologizing, she grew defensive. "He courts me only with words. I don't feel any affection from him."

"He's still courtin' you."

Sometimes Dusty's simplicity could be one of his most engaging qualities. At that moment, Sophie considered it to be his most irksome. "You're the one who said that the rules of courtship didn't make anything final until a lady was spoken for. Chad hasn't asked for my hand."

"That's not how I meant it. Don't you see?" His drawl thickened as he took her hands in his rope-calloused ones. "I thought you fancied Chad a bit at first, and I was gonna do my best to make you look my way. Now you're tellin' me that you don't care for him, yet you still let him court you. That's gettin' to be dishonest." He weighed her with a serious face.

Sophie hated being accused, but not as much as she hated not being firm enough in response to Chad's insistence at continuing to see her. Her mind spun in search of a reply to Dusty. "But I don't play coy or coax him anymore. I don't love him."

"Then end the courtship. You can't have it both ways where you're visitin' me in secret and steppin' out in public with him." He let her hands fall. "That may enliven you, but I'm not a pair of boots you can put on and kick off whenever you please."

She winced at his strong words, knowing that he had a right to say how he felt. It all started as a game when she first told him about Chad paying her notice at the Founders Day Festival. She didn't stop to think that Dusty could truly be hurt if she continued to goad him. "Chad went to Missouri for one of his family's companies. He won't be back until the first week in August. I'll tell him again when I attend a party his father's having."

"Make sure you do." He touched her temple and let his fingers glide down her cheek. "'Cause this is turning into a lie that I'll have no part of."

She nodded. There was nothing else to say on the matter until she had her conversation with Chad.

Dusty waited for her to get the petition from the back of the wagon. Gunfire was in full force as they walked toward the ranch house again.

"I wasn't lying when I wanted you to kiss me, though," she stated to lighten the mood.

He turned up a smile. "I've known for three years that you wanted to kiss me."

"How so?"

"Please, Sophie, you're not slick enough to fool me. Maybe you can pass one over on Chad Hooper, but not me."

"I don't know if I should be offended by that."

"What, that you can't fool me?"

"No, that you called me slick."

He gave her hair a tug. "I beg your pardon, ma'am. I'll be pleased to make up for it and call you something more winsome after you tell that mayor's boy to stop comin' around the farm."

"You made yourself clear the first time, Dustin Sterling."

They went around to the back of the ranch house after the gunfire settled.

Dusty knew Joe and the other cowhands were sitting on pins and needles, waiting to ask him about Sophie. After she and her brother left the ranch, taking five new signatures on the petition with them, he arose to saddle up his horse for an evening run.

Joe, Freeman, and Wilcox beat him to the stables. "Pretty little lady you got that showed up today." Freeman grinned, showcasing the gold fillings in his teeth. "All dainty with eyes blue as cornflower. No wonder you ain't told nobody about her."

Dusty carried his saddle over to Gabe's stall. They followed him. "I figured that French picture you have on the bunkhouse wall was enough woman to tide you over, Freeman."

"She's not flesh and blood."

Being new to the ranch, Dusty debated over the proper time when he could talk to Wilcox and Freeman about being more respectful of women. "Nope, that she is not. You ought to tear it down and go find yourself a real woman in town to court properly. Leave Miss Charlton be, of course."

Joe snickered as Freeman wandered away. "Is Miss Charlton the lady you intend to build that house for?"

Dusty made sure the saddle straps were snug around the horse's withers. "No house built yet."

Wilcox went ahead and said his piece. "You went and bought the land, though. You tell her while she was here?"

Dusty felt like he was toting a lead weight on his back. In the past month, he often pictured how he would tell Sophie about the twenty-five acres of land he purchased. All his, with room to buy more when he wanted. When he first saw her on the ranch today, he even imagined her riding out there with him to see where the house was going to be built. She'd sit behind him in the saddle, her small hands wrapped tight around his waist, the wind kicking at her long blonde hair.

He well-aimed to do just that after they shared that first kiss behind the wagon. After several kisses. Then she had to go and mention that Chad was still courting her. What a fool he was to ask in the first place. Sophie always kept the interest of town bachelors, whether she intended to or not.

"No, I didn't say anything." He placed a bit in Gabe's mouth, wishing he could do the same for the three men that followed him around the stables. "Don't y'all have things to do? Joe, I know your wife's waiting for you to get on home, especially now you have a new baby boy. And Wilcox, you said you were fixin' to go into town."

"I'll go in a few minutes to get my drink." Wilcox leaned against the wall as though he had no plans of leaving so long as talk of women continued.

"Better head out before it gets too dark. You'll have to stay in town overnight."

"Oh, I plan to." The cowhand gave a coarse grin, hinting at his less-than-honorable intentions. "You should join me. I got a girl meetin' me. She might have a friend."

"Go on now with that," Joe admonished him. "You know Sterling doesn't carouse."

Wilcox laughed and shrugged. "Sorry, Emmers, I forget you two find your women in the church. See you in the mornin'."

Dusty led his horse out of the stables after Wilcox departed. Joe was still shaking his head. "I'm gonna have to hide my daughter in the house once she comes of age. Somebody like Wilcox come near Violet or my wife, I might have to be escorted to the sheriff's when all's said and done."

"You can always teach your wife and daughter how to shoot."

"Say, what about your Miss Sophie? I hope she can stand the coarse-talkin' workers out here."

Dusty got in the saddle. "She's tougher than she looks. She can put a man in his place if she's a mind to. But Joe, Sophie's not my woman. At least, not official."

"But she's gonna be. She kept lookin' at you sweet-eyed."

Should he tell Joe? The assistant foreman wouldn't air his business out to the other cowhands, but it was still embarrassing to admit that he was waiting on her to quit some other man. He didn't want to bring disgrace to her reputation, either. "She comes from a well-to-do family. They got certain expectations of the people she associates with."

"Is that why you left her family's employ? You got caught together?"

"Not the way you think." Dusty hurried to explain further. "I did nothing that would taint her honor, but her folks did get wind that I fancied her. Look, Joe, that's why I didn't say anything before. I don't need gossip circlin' around me when I'm tryin' to do my job."

"What you say to me won't reach another ear."

"Thanks." He pressed his heels into the horse's flanks to make the stallion walk.

"Dusty," Joe called.

"Yeah?"

"It sure takes a lot of gumption and bold steppin' out to build a house for a woman that ain't yours yet. I know you're gonna live in it too, but still."

All Dusty could do was agree. "Yeah, I reckon I'm crazy that way."

"Men have done worse. I s'pose you got a bit of hope. She came out to see you. Maybe she is willing to let go of where she came from."

"Maybe." Dusty turned his horse into the setting sun. "That's a decision she has to make for herself."

"Guess so, but she better not take too long."

"I'll agree." Dusty made himself sound tough as old rawhide, but on the inside it ate at him that he couldn't do anything to help Sophie along. He was unsure if she really wanted to take such brave measures. The choice to follow her mind instead of that of her parents, to end the courtship with

Chad and accept his attentions, and ultimately to choose a rough ranching life instead of a refined town life—it was all in her hands.

Thursday morning Sophie put the petition in Mr. Shaw's hands. "Will you please see that Mayor Hooper gets this?"

The mayor's assistant took the envelope that held the three pages of signatures that she had collected over the summer. "He's in his office as we speak, Miss Charlton. I will take it to him now. Can I get you a glass of water to drink while you're here?"

"No, thank you." Sophie declined in spite of the humid morning air that made her hair swell into a nest of undefined curls and her dress sleeves cling to her arms. "I should get back to the farm. Good day to you, Mr. Shaw."

She left the house to return to her father awaiting her in the wagon. He offered his hand to assist her onto the bench. "Your mother will dance for joy, glad you and that petition have parted."

Sophie studied her fingernails. Her mother wouldn't be in a good mood for too long once she found out that her daughter and Chad Hooper would also be parting. "Thank you for letting me see it through to completion, Daddy. Mother would never have allowed me to."

"Your mother just needed to see that you could devote yourself to a cause while still being a dutiful daughter."

Dutiful. She touched her lips where they were still sensitive from kissing Dusty yesterday. Her father waved to one of his friends in the town square on the way back home. "Now, if only we can teach your brother to be obedient."

"David's obedient to you and Mother."

"He does his chores, but on the inside, he's willful as an ox. All these notions of cattle herding and gun-slinging. I'm ready to give him more work to drive those ludicrous whims out of his head."

Sophie took it upon herself to keep David out of trouble. "He is young, Daddy. Mother said that boys his age are easily excitable."

"I think that boy intends to become a cowhand. The other day I found a lasso in the barn. I thought Dusty had left it, but your brother told me that it was his. He bought it at the general store with the money I gave him. A waste of funds."

Sophie turned her head so she could smile. Once able to control her show of mirth, she spoke. "What if David does find work involving cattle herding when he gets older?"

The red heat rash on her father's face darkened. "I won't allow it. Ranchers and cowhands don't do honest work. They steal from each other, pass money under the table when they think no one is looking. Then they participate in things that I won't mention to you because you are my daughter. Things involving strong drink and weak-willed women."

No alcohol was involved when Sophie let Dusty take her into his arms. She wondered if her father would consider her worse than weak-willed. "There must be men of that trade who have their scruples."

"Point one out to me."

You hired one but then you drove him off. Sophie kept her lips sealed.

"See? There isn't one. Read the papers and you'll see how they come up to Abilene and Dodge City, tearing up those towns like the devil's minions themselves. Most of them probably do have horns under those Stetsons."

Sophie's laugh came out in a high-pitched squeak. She put her hand over her mouth promptly as her father turned to glare.

"It's no laughing matter, Sophie. I won't have my son,

who was brought up in a God-fearing home, earning money in a saddle and throwing it away in a saloon."

"David wouldn't do those things if he became a rancher or a cowhand. Can't you let him prove that to you?"

"He won't have to prove it to me because he will be a farmer." Her father squared his broad, thick shoulders and sat with his back straight.

Sophie cast her eyes downward, dejected. If her father was willing to force her brother into being like him, how was he going to react when she refused to be courted by the man he gave leave to pursue her?

She touched the necklace at her throat. The humidity of the morning was going to be nothing compared to the unbearable evening of the mayor's pre-election party.

Chapter 24

The first Saturday of August arrived with all of the town's well-to-do flurrying to appear at the mayor's residence in their finest evening attire. Sophie spent the afternoon in preparation with her mother and sister, starching petticoats, polishing shoes, and heating tongs over the stove to turn Rosemarie's straight hair into a bevy of sausage curls. She coaxed her little sister to remain still for the hour-long process.

"Mother says we can stay at the party later now that I'm older." Rosemarie beamed. "Last year we had to leave before the cake was served."

Sophie tried to match her sister's enthusiasm, if only for appearance's sake in front of their mother. "I think it had buttercream frosting. We'll see what Mrs. Hooper decides to do with it this year."

"No cake, Sophie," her mother declared from across the table as she ironed the boys' suit trousers. "Remember what I said about paying attention to what's on your plate."

Her mother would not have to worry. Sophie didn't possess an appetite, knowing that she had to succeed in breaking off with Chad that evening.

She finished arranging Rosemarie's hair before readying herself. She wore a blush-rose gown that her mother had chosen for the event.

"I have the notion that this will be a most memorable night." Her mother gave her ensemble a final once-over before the family left.

They reached the mayor's residence at five that evening when most of the guests had arrived. The mayor and his wife greeted people at the door. Sophie counted off the familiar list of town notables as she walked with her family through the house entrance. The Gillings family was present, with Dr. Dorothea choosing to wear a simple but tasteful gown. Linda and her family were there. Sophie's friend looked bored, likely on account of her gentleman caller Wes Browman not being extended an invitation.

"You look beautiful as always, Sophie." Linda greeted her with a hug. "I told you rose suited your complexion."

Margaret joined them from the sitting room. "It goes especially with the rosebud necklace you're wearing."

Sophie touched the pendant at her neck and murmured a thank-you. She heard strains of music filling the house. "Where is that music coming from?"

"From outside, in the back. Your beau is there."

Sure enough, Sophie saw him come from that direction, looking like the personification of Lady Whitecastle's lover. Chad wore a dinner jacket and pinstriped trousers. A dandyish yellow carnation decorated the front of his lapel. White spats peeked over the gleaming tops of his shoes. He saw her and a smile eased across his face. Sweeping a hand over the top of his precisely parted hair, he came forward.

"Good evening, my dear Sophie. You are a lovely sight." He gave her a chaste peck on the left cheek. The gesture sent Linda and Margaret into giggles before they excused themselves and flitted elsewhere.

She smelled his expensive French cologne. "How are you this evening, Chad?"

"Now that you're here, superb." He placed her hand on his arm and made sure she kept it there for the next hour.

Dusty watched the town of Assurance get smaller in the distance as the train rolled away from the station. He never thought much of the combustible steam engines that clicked and clacked along the rails each day. Now he was forced to ride inside one all the way to northern Nebraska. The noise coming from the engine was about to drive him mad.

Joe sat beside him on the bench in third class, appearing less harrowed by the discomfort. "Mighty nice of Mabrey to get us tickets up to this shorthorn ranch. Saves us two or three weeks of ridin' there and then drivin' the cattle back down to Kansas."

But it would keep him away from Sophie for one week. A lot could happen in seven days. "I'll be happy to get there and back in one piece."

"Your first time on a train, Sterling? Better get used to it if you want to have your own ranch. This'll soon be the only way to transport the herds."

"I'll send someone in my stead." He watched the scenery blur around the edges of the window as the train picked up speed after clearing the station. Right now Sophie was at that party at the mayor's house. Would she do what was needed and set Chad straight about leaving her alone?

"I asked Mabrey for you to accompany me. I didn't want to go two hundred miles worrying about Wilcox or Freeman chasing down women in each car."

He turned to Joe. "Thanks for giving me the chance to show the boss I can be responsible to purchase cattle for him."

"It's not just for him. Buy several for yourself. I promised Violet I'd see about getting a yearling for her. She wants to be the first lady rancher in the state."

"Must get her ambition from you."

"Yep, I moved my family from Georgia when the war ended so we'd have a chance to earn a real livin', be part of a town. Say, did you see that Violet signed Miss Sophie's petition too? I'm proud she stood up for her beliefs."

There was bravery on Sophie's part, too. That gave Dusty some thought as he tapped his boot heel on the train floor. Would she be brave enough at that party to tell Chad and her own family that she didn't want to become Mrs. Hooper?

Assurance disappeared from view, swallowed by the plains. Dusty wished he could have gone to that party with Sophie to make sure that Chad understood the word no, but his kind would never be invited to such an event.

Fidgeting nervously, Sophie stood by Chad as the guests gathered outside the house after dinner. Not once did she get the chance to be alone with him to reiterate that she was through being courted. The band from Chanute played while people enjoyed the cool evening breeze. Mayor Hooper was preparing to give a speech and thank everyone for attending.

Chad drank from an expensive crystal glass. "You'll be pleased to know that your petition had enough signatures to warrant a school election. My father said it will be on the ballots this September."

"Wonderful." Sophie welcomed the bit of good news. At least she could celebrate in doing one thing right that summer. She may not have entered her project in the most auspicious manner but she'd managed to conclude it to her satisfaction.

"That isn't the only surprise I have for you." He handed her his glass and slipped away amongst the guests.

The band stopped playing. Sophie caught sight of her parents speaking to the mayor as he ambled to the front of the crowd. Her father gave her a warm nod before ceasing to look at her again. What was going on?

Mayor Hooper called everyone to attention. "Ladies and gentlemen, my family and I thank you once again for coming to our annual dinner. But this year, we also thank you for showing your support in the upcoming September election. I have no worries about the outcome, because I know we will have another two years of progress...."

Sophie shut out the political speech as she pondered Chad's whereabouts and kept glancing at the house. She swirled the stem of Chad's glass between her fingers while she waited for the mayor to finish talking.

"...and now my son would like to make an announcement."

Sophie turned with the other guests as Chad came from the house. In passing, his glance her way contained a hint of secrecy.

"Are you running for deputy mayor?" Mr. Euell called out from among the guests, making a few of them chuckle.

"Sorry to disappoint, Mr. Euell." Chad stood before them with his head held high. "However, I do have something else that you might see fit to print in this week's newspaper." He paused with dramatic effect, waiting for everyone to be quiet. "Tonight, I am officially announcing my engagement to Miss Sophie Charlton."

Sophie heard her name and thought there had been a mistake. Surely he had not said the word *engagement* in reference to her. She searched the faces around her for confirmation of her belief, but all the guests looked her way with smiles and murmurs of surprise.

"Congratulations." An elderly matron touched her shoulder with a silk-gloved hand. "You'll make a lovely bride."

The world slowed as though Sophie were in a dream. She moved her head to look past the swirling sea of faces to behold Chad standing in the center of them all. Her breath caught in her chest. She struggled in vain to force down more air. Little pinpricks of light clouded her vision.

"…so happy she's speechless…" Chad's voice was drowned out by a sudden ringing in her ears. She gasped, but the tight lacing of her corset only permitted a tiny pocket of air to be drawn into her lungs.

Why were they all laughing? This was wrong, so wrong. Her hands tingled. She couldn't feel the nose on her face. Her skin crawled with a thousand ants biting to get inside. She swayed on her feet as she tried to hold herself upright, her head heavy as a bowl filled with punch.

Was she holding a glass? Sophie heard it shatter just before she felt the weight of her body tumble backwards.

"Would all of you please move away? She needs air."

Sophie could hear Dr. Dorothea's voice among what sounded like dozens of flies buzzing around her ears. Where was she? The atmosphere felt hot, cloying.

A sharp, pungent odor filled the air and burned Sophie's nostrils. She opened her eyes to Dorothea looming over her, holding a bottle of smelling salts. Chad peered over her shoulder.

"You fainted, Sophie." Dorothea waved a fan. "It was due to all of the excitement."

"What excitement?" Sophie's voice croaked as she moved her head to view her surroundings. She was outside. It was nighttime. The dozens of flies buzzing were actually dozens of people standing around her, whispering. She recognized their faces, seeing those of her mother, father, and siblings among them.

Then she remembered why they were all there.

"I announced that we were engaged, my dear." Chad moved in closer until his face was bigger than everyone else's.

"I wanted the surprise to take your breath away, but not to this extent."

"How could you?" Her voice came in a ragged whisper.

"I beg your pardon? I didn't quite hear what you said."

She narrowed her eyes at him when her voice failed to produce the desired effect. "You heard me just fine, Chad Hooper."

He moved back from her and looked to the people standing over them. "I think my fiancée needs a few minutes to gather herself."

"Take her into my study," Mayor Hooper voiced from Sophie's left.

A pair of arms came to support her back and legs. As Chad lifted her from the ground, she twisted to peer over his shoulder. Why weren't her mother and father doing anything? Why were they letting him take her away?

How could they let him say he was going to marry her?

Her family followed behind Chad and Dr. Dorothea, who was giving more instructions. "Open a window in the study, Chad. She may faint again. I think you and your wife should wait in the sitting room, Mr. Charlton. We can't have too many people crowding Sophie."

"I will stay with her until she's fully recovered." Chad carried Sophie into his father's study and set her down onto the settee. "You can wait outside too, Dorothea. I'll call for you if need be."

Sophie watched the doctor give him a vexed look before being forced to offer a compliant nod. *No, Dorothea, don't go away. Don't leave me with him.*

The door of the study closed. Chad locked it behind Dorothea. "You'll need to fortify yourself before attempting the trip home."

He crossed the small room and opened the lower panes of the window. The breeze offered Sophie little relief from the tension that built inside her. Fury began to replace her former disorientation.

Chad went to a small table behind the desk and opened a decanter of amber brown liquid. He poured some into a snifter glass and offered it to her. "Brandy?"

"Not unless you want it tossed in your face."

"Is that any way to speak to your betrothed?" He set the snifter on the desk and leaned against the edge of the furniture. "You're going to be a married woman soon and I just gave your father more status by bringing our two families together. You should be the happiest girl in Assurance."

"Chad, you knew I didn't want our courtship to go on. How could you make that false announcement to all those people?"

He crossed one spat-covered boot over the other. "It wasn't false. My intentions to marry you were clear from the day I asked your father permission to call upon you. He gave me his blessing yesterday when I asked if I could propose."

"You didn't propose to me so much as told a lie to your guests. You knew I couldn't have said anything in front of them without causing a scandal. I told you two weeks ago that I didn't want to go through with this anymore."

"You didn't know what you were saying."

Sophie rose up on her elbows, ignoring the residual lightheadedness that made her want to shut her eyes. "I told you that my feelings have changed."

"How can your feelings change when you agreed to let me court you? I've taken you about town, given you flowers and jewelry. I even helped you with that ridiculous petition. What are you saying, exactly?"

She clenched her stomach muscles as he pelted her with rebukes that left her guilt-ridden and insulted. "I don't have any affection for you that warrants me to call you my beau or my fiancé. Your rudeness and the way you've taken liberties tonight seals it."

Chad huffed a sound of disbelief, laughing once. "You
vain and frivolous little girl, always leading men along by
the nose. You led me on once before and I won't be foolish
enough to let that happen again."

She bolstered her courage with a lungful of air. "At that
time I was wrong. I intentionally misled you into escorting
me to that fair because I didn't want to be seen without a
gentleman. I apologize again for that, but this time it's different. There is someone else."

"Not this foolishness with Sterling again." He took to
pacing the room. "Who has sold you these nickel notions
that you can take up with him? What is it you intend to do,
live in a sod house with rats crawling over your bare feet
while you wait for him to come back from the range?"

"I'm getting tired of you casting aspersions upon Dusty
and me. Is it any wonder that I don't wish to become your
wife?"

"Your father will never let you marry his former employee."
He marched over to the couch and dropped beside her. "Let
me remind you that your family is one of the wealthiest
in this town, second only to mine. How well do you think
you'll be received for wanting to be with another man, one
who dirties his feet in cow dung and works with Negroes
and whoremongers?"

Sophie was speechless at the lengths Chad went to
express himself.

He taunted her. "You thought I didn't know? The owner
Mabrey took out a loan for that ranch. I personally went out
there to make an account of the property's value. I saw the
caliber of men he hires."

"They may be a rough lot, but they work hard. And I met

Mr. Emmers. He's as diligent and upright in character as any man."

"You have become quite liberal." Chad assessed her with a sneer. "It's unfortunate for you that the influentials of the town don't see things your way." He dug into his coat pocket and pulled out a small item. "Put that on." He tossed it into her lap.

Sophie picked up the ring. The gold band and inlay of large diamonds lay heavy in her hand. "Take it back. I won't wear it."

"I will not take it back. You're going to wear that ring and you're going to marry me after the September elections. Snub me again, and I'll ruin you and your family." His smooth tone belied his abrasive words. "I'll make sure the whole town knows the type of lady Miss Charlton is. One who lusts after yokels and sympathizes with former slaves."

The blood in Sophie's veins became ice and fire as she watched Chad leave the study. She expected him to be angry about her not wanting to marry him, but not so vindictive that he'd personally see that her family's good name was dragged into the streets.

She closed her fist tighter around the ring until the edges of the diamond cut her skin. She failed to think things through when she expressed her feelings for Dusty. Chad was accurate in that a lady of her status couldn't just up and do what she wanted without bringing disgrace to her parents.

The door opened and in walked her mother. "Sophie, how are you feeling? Better enough to go home?"

She blurted. "He didn't propose to me, Mother. Chad never asked me if I wanted to marry him."

Her mother stooped down and felt her brow. "No fever."

Sophie moved away. "How could you and Daddy allow him to stand before all those people and claim me like I was some prize to be handed out at a carnival?"

"How dare you take that tone with me, young lady?"

"Mother, please, tell me why."

Her mother sighed. "I was not happy with the way Chad announced the engagement. Your father and I thought he would ask you first before he told the guests. But is that not a small disappointment that you can get past, in light of the fact that you did want to marry him?" She smiled with genuine tenderness. "You'll still have a wedding."

Sophie cringed, the full weight of her situation finally sinking in. Chad didn't have to say anything to ruin her family. If she didn't keep quiet and put on that wedding veil, she could do it all by herself.

CHAPTER 25

𝓕OR THE FIRST time in her life Sophie dreaded going to church that Sunday morning. She dreaded witnessing word of her engagement to Chad Hooper spread like prairie fire in the town, dreaded seeing people that her family knew, and hated standing still for her friends as they cooed over the gaudy ring on her finger.

Chad sat with her family. Throughout the service, he kept one arm draped possessively over her shoulders. Between hymns being sung and Reverend Winford delivering the sermon, pairs of eyes would look her way, until finally she hid her face.

She looked in vain for Dusty. Since moving out to the ranch, he had not appeared in church. She knew he was a faithful believer and churchgoer, so she suspected he had stayed away on her account.

"I'll see you Tuesday evening." Chad kissed her hand before leaving church with his family.

Sophie wiped it on her skirt when no one watched. She felt like a Jezebel, having let two men show her affection, one of whom didn't even know that she was now engaged to be married. A frightening thought took over as she settled into the wagon with her family. What if Dusty had heard about her engagement?

She needed to talk to him. She had to tell him why it

was necessary to go through with the wedding. A sharp pain struck her chest and resided into a dull ache across her body when she imagined his reaction.

At the farm, David pulled her aside before she could go into the house. He scratched at the first dark sprouting of hair that formed on his chin. "When are you gonna tell Ma and Pa that you're sweet on Dusty?"

Sophie played down her awkwardness at being asked such a question by her younger brother. "Why do you ask?"

"I know you like him more than you do Chad. You never snuck off to see him at the bank the way you did for Dusty at the ranch."

She realized that David was no longer of the age where she could give him a pat answer and send him on his way. "I'm never going to say anything to our parents about Dusty. You saw how the town responded last year when Reverend Winford started courting Marissa. It was a scandal."

"Most people don't talk about her being a saloon girl now that she's his wife."

"That's because he's a minister, and she being his wife has put her into a more respectable position. We're Charltons. We can't get away with doing as we please. You see that now with Daddy not wanting you to be a cowhand."

"I'll be a man soon, and Pa can't say anything to me."

Sophie refrained from scolding him for thinking of falling out with the family when she had been doing outrageous things herself as of late. "You may find yourself disinherited."

"I'm not spending my days tending the land. I don't care if he gives the farm to Bernard."

"You may think different once you're trapped in a bunkhouse, penniless."

"Better to be poor doing something you love than rich hating every minute of your life." David stomped off.

She tamped down the unrest that grew in her as she considered her upcoming wedding date. Thirty-four more days before she had to call the Hooper house her home. Maybe it was the bad oysters, or maybe something entirely different, but suddenly the Hooper's glittering china, sumptuous furnishings, and rich food had lost their appeal. Unlike her brother, she'd take as much time on the farm as she could get.

Sophie pursed her lips in thought.

But perhaps not. Maybe life on a ranch could work just as well.

The week passed slowly as Sophie waited for an opportunity to visit the Zephyr Ranch. She went to town with her family on Saturday and visited Linda at the seamstress shop, where her friend could not stop talking about Wes Browman.

"Do you think I should let him court me? If my father gives him permission, I mean?" she asked with a wistful look in her eyes.

"If he treats you kindly and you enjoy his company."

"Oh, I do. He's very sweet, which is unexpected for a tanner. I suppose a seamstress can be courted by a tanner."

Sophie forced a smile. Linda had finally found a beau. She told herself that she should be happy for her friend, even if her own circumstances weren't so cheerful. "You can stitch embroidery on the leather he finishes treating."

Linda giggled. "We can combine our trades." She went to attend a customer that came through the door.

Sophie wished she did not feel envy at her friend's position. Linda had a bit more freedom when it came to choosing bachelors. No one would fault her much if she didn't pick the most eligible man in town.

"I have the skirt finished on your wedding dress." Linda

resumed when the woman left with a newly altered blouse. "It looks just like the one in *Godey's Ladies Book*. Do you want to see it?"

"Maybe when my mother comes in from the Arthurs' shoe store."

"Sophie, you're getting married in one month. Less than that. Twenty-eight days." Linda pushed back the hair that always seemed to droop forward when she was working. "You don't seem yourself. Is it because Chad's away on business again?"

Sophie took to examining the dress forms in front of the shop. "No."

"Well, what is it? I'm sure it can't be so awful."

Sophie adjusted the dress form's measurements to that of her own. "Linda, I told Chad before he announced the engagement that I no longer wished to be courted."

Linda's gasp resounded in the shop. "What on earth has gotten into you? You like Chad, don't you?"

She expected such a reaction. "I thought I did once, but I don't anymore. I'm not sure I ever have."

"But you've been courting for over two months and he's given you flowers and a necklace. And before he went away to school you used to flirt with him all the time."

"Chad is different from what you think, Linda. He changes when he isn't in front of people. You should have heard the way he spoke to me in the study after the mayor's party." Shivers ran down her spine thinking about it. "His behavior was horrible."

"But I saw him carry you there in his arms. He was so gentle with you, like Lord Haverston."

Sophie lost her restraint. "Stop painting him as gallant and dashing. This isn't *The Adventures of Lady Whitecastle*."

Linda's eyes widened as she stood dumbstruck, as though

Sophie had taken her by the shoulders and given her a good shake.

"I'm sorry, Linda. I didn't mean it. You and Wes can certainly have that kind of romance. It will not be that way for Chad and me."

She came to stand between Sophie and the dress form. "If you spoke to Chad the way you just spoke to me, then what reaction did you expect of him? I can't see any man taking kindly to that."

Sophie felt so alone. Her closest friend didn't understand. "Chad was demanding before I confronted him. It's part of the reason I did it."

"What are the other reasons?"

She chewed her cheek and gazed out the shop window. Linda's reflection showed realization dawning on her face.

"Don't tell me this is about Dusty."

Sophie continued to watch the passersby in the streets.

"I was just teasing you about him when I said those things a month ago. I didn't think you really fancied him, that you would actually want to...oh, Sophie, this is a terrible jumble." Linda put distance between them. "You can't have feelings for your hired help."

She had heard similar words from her mother, but listening to her friend say them brought a different kind of condemnation. "No one knows that I acted upon them."

"You sinned with him too?"

"We shared a kiss." Sophie couldn't look at Linda. "It was wrong, but I thought you would understand."

"Why, because I'm being called upon by a tanner and not a rich man like Chad? It's not the same as you amusing yourself with the attentions of two men. That's deceitful."

Sophie gulped hard as tears started to burn behind her eyes. Was everyone set on making her seem like a scheming shrew? "I said I was wrong and I've been trying to make it right since. I'll come back later to try on my wedding dress."

"Sophie, wait. Don't get mad. Just put everything in order before it gets worse. Tell Chad you were remiss in saying you didn't want to marry him. All of this will be forgotten."

"He's not thinking about it anymore. You saw him sit with me in church. We're considered a definite pair." A perfectly matched set on the outside, but an unsightly motley work on the inside.

Her friend sighed with relief. "Oh, thank goodness he's so forgiving. How can you not fall in love with a man like that?"

"I'll see you in church tomorrow." She left the shop before Linda could say more. A spirit of heaviness hung over her as she dealt with the new knowledge that her friend was never going to comprehend the depths of what she was experiencing. Linda just couldn't see Chad any other way except for the polished, ambitious person that he showed himself to be. Even Sophie's family didn't know of the jealousy that sparked in his eyes whenever he spoke of Dusty, or the insecurity that he kept well hidden.

Searching for her mother, Sophie hurried across the street to get to the shoe store before a horse and rider came down the road. Stopping on the sidewalk, she saw that the rider was Wilcox from the Zephyr Ranch. He tied his horse to the post outside of McIntyre's before going inside the restaurant. She reversed course and followed.

The restaurant smelled of smoked meat and giblet gravy. She heard it sizzling on the stove as a server came from behind the kitchen door. Her eyes took in the patrons at each table as she looked for Wilcox among them. If he was back in Assurance, then Dusty had to be too. A roar of laughter from the back of the restaurant made her lift her head. Joe, Freeman, Wilcox, and Dusty shared a table, partially blocked by a wooden support beam that reached from floor to ceiling. Wilcox made a remark that sent the other men into uproarious laughs again.

"You need a table, Miss Charlton?" A server at the front approached her side. "Or are you looking for your brother David?"

Another server came by the cowhands' table to remove the empty plates. Once the clutter was gone, she spotted her brother seated amongst them at the far end. "I came for my brother. Thank you."

Heart pounding like it did at the mayor's party, she walked to the back of the restaurant, feeling the eyes of the patrons following her. It didn't slip her mind that what she was doing could be potential gossip fodder, a lone woman going to have a seat with the cowboys of Zephyr Ranch. She hoped that her brother's presence along with Chad's engagement ring would be enough to quiet tongues and ease assumptions that she was up to no good.

Or the ring could serve to make the situation much worse. She hoped not to faint again.

David's welcome was an annoyed stare. "I thought you were visiting Linda."

"I was. Now I'm here." She greeted the cowhands. "Hello, gentlemen."

Wilcox and Freeman gave her cold stares. Joe lowered his head. Dusty looked puzzled by their reaction. He ran his hand through his hair, a light brown in the restaurant's dim interior.

"Let your sister have a seat." He ushered her brother from his chair. David rolled his eyes and went to the opposite end of the table.

"They didn't say nothing to him," David whispered in her ear.

Freeman left. Joe and Wilcox went too, until only Sophie

and Dusty remained at the table. She took the now empty seat beside him, darting a glance at David, who kept his head studiously away, appearing to read one of Mayor Hooper's political tracts nailed to the wood beam.

"They're not being uncivil," Dusty explained. "They think you just want to talk to me alone."

She wished he had heard something about her engagement. The announcement was proclaimed in Monday's paper. She rationalized that the ranch was far enough from town where news couldn't get to them on time. "I didn't know my actions were considered predictable."

"Isn't that why you're here?"

She liked the way his eyes twinkled when he was flirting. "I can't talk to you this way anymore, Dusty. I went to Chad and attempted to have a word. You're not going to like what happened but I had no choice."

She stretched her left hand before him.

CHAPTER 26

USTY STARED AT the sparkling monstrosity on Sophie's tiny little finger. If she raised her hand and struck him with it, he would have been no less shocked. Or mad. "You got engaged?"

She pulled her hand back. "Chad announced that we were engaged last Saturday at the mayor's party. It's been in the paper since Monday."

"I've been in Nebraska buying shorthorns. I'm gone for a little over eight days and you get yourself spoken for by another man?" He cast his eyes about the restaurant, where several people were looking at him and Sophie, no doubt putting a tale together. "That's why the men were all actin' strange at the ranch when Joe and me got back this morning."

Sophie lowered her lashes until they made golden fans across each cheek. "I didn't know you went away. I was waiting all week until I had a chance to tell you."

Was she being charming again, or were her intentions true? Sometimes it was hard to tell. Dusty felt like the wind got knocked out of him. "How could you do this, Sophie? I thought you were going to tell Chad to leave you alone."

She pushed her chair closer to his so that the other patrons of the restaurant wouldn't hear them. He wished she didn't. He smelled her clean, powdery scent and wanted to hold her in his arms. But he couldn't do that anymore. She was truly spoken for this time, symbolized by a ring that he could never in his life afford to give her.

The server came to the table. "Can I bring you something to eat or drink, Miss Charlton?"

"No, thank you. I won't be here long."

The server looked at her funny, but went away. Dusty waited for her to resume as he wrestled thoughts of everything men in town had warned him about Sophie Charlton. Vain. Indecisive. Collects admirers like other women collect tea sets. He wanted for none of it to be true, but if Taylor Hastings or Wes Browman were at the table, they'd tell him the proof was staring him in the face with a pair of big blue eyes.

"Chad refused to end the courtship when I asked him."

"That doesn't sound right. If you don't want him, you don't want him."

"It's not that simple. He promised to slander me and my family's name all over town if I refused to marry him."

"He threatened you?" Dusty pushed his chair back to stand.

Sophie grabbed his hat before he could reach it. "No, you don't."

"Sophie, give me my hat."

"I'm not going to let you run into that bank. He's out of town again, anyway." She put the Stetson on her lap. "Please, Dusty. Sit down. That way isn't going to solve anything."

He obliged after a long pause. "You folks have the strangest ways of doing things up here. Where I come from, if a man refuses to let a woman alone, she is well within her rights to get someone to act on her behalf."

"This isn't Texas."

"I know it's not Texas. A man like Hooper would not be able to get away with those things if he were down there. Sophie, you don't have to put up with him."

She played with the brim of his hat. "Yes, I do. He has money and influence just like my family. Those things can be very powerful."

"You'd let him court you just to keep him from raisin' a fit?" Dusty shook his head. "What'll happen to you?"

"Nothing. He's not a violent man, if that's what you mean."

"Maybe he's not, but he is mighty spiteful. You'll be prancin' on eggshells."

She covered her ring with her right hand. "I have no choice."

"Don't repeat that. You do." Dusty leaned across to her. "I didn't say a word when you first came to the ranch, but I bought twenty-five acres of land out there. I'll have the foundation of a house built by the end of autumn."

A bit of hope built in her eyes. "You did talk of wanting to own land."

He reached for her, and then, remembering that they were in public, made no further effort to touch her hand. "I did it for you."

Her small shoulders trembled. "Me? Dusty, you shouldn't have done that. I mean, I can't just leave my family's house."

"I'm not asking you to just leave. We can get married. I'll take you away from this."

"It's not that simple."

Her words wrenched painfully at his heart. "It is, if you let it be. I kid and joke all the time about bein' sweet on you, but it's more than that. I love you." He wanted her to say something back. She stared at him. What was going through her mind? "It took me three years to say those words without feeling like I'd scare you off."

She spoke. "Dusty, it is more complicated than you think. Our differences in social standing, for instance. You may not care about those things, but they are important to my family, to the town. The choices I make affect not just me."

"But you were willing to quit Chad before he put that ring on your finger. What changed?"

"I didn't expect you to say you could marry me."

"You mean you didn't think I was serious?"

She gave a small nod. "Maybe."

"You thought I was just toying with you?" Disbelief colored his voice. "I know you heard about the ways of some cowboys, how they have a girl in every town, but I don't play games. What did I tell you at the Rev'ren's wedding last year? One day I intended to make you mine."

"That day can't come now, whether I love you or not." She stood.

"Some people say you've just been flirting with me. So I ask you, do you love me, Sophie?" He reached for her hand, not caring now if people saw. Better they were present, to keep him from being tempted to kiss her one last time. She was slipping from him each minute and there was little he could do to stop her if she was intent on making that decision.

"It doesn't matter." She bit her lower lip until it turned red.

"It does to me."

She pulled her hand from his. The ring scratched him. "Yes, I love you, but I can't do any more than say that." She laid his hat on the table and departed.

Sophie left a part of herself back in that restaurant with Dusty. She had, in a sense, left the truth of her heart with him.

No grown man ever told her that he loved her before. When she was a child, boys teased and pulled her hair to show affection. When those boys became young men, they flattered and attempted to get permission to court her, but it wasn't the same as this.

Dusty loved her. Chad did not. He may have enjoyed her company and admired her appearance, but he wouldn't sacrifice himself for her. Dusty was willing to leave the farm peacefully after her family accused him of being dishonorable, rather than damage her reputation.

She couldn't picture Chad taking the blame for anything.

"Sophie, do smile. No one wants to look at a dour-faced bride."

She obeyed her mother as she stood before the dress mirror in the seamstress shop. Linda continued to pin and tuck the train of the dress behind her.

"How do you like the fit, Mrs. Charlton? I can always adjust."

Sophie remained unperturbed under her mother's critical eye. She was going to be the dutiful daughter and marry whom her parents wanted. What more was there to say?

"I really don't like how small the flare of the skirt is. Can we add more tulle?"

"Yes, ma'am." Linda went into the back room of the store to find the fabric.

Sophie watched her mother's face alight as her requests were granted. "I wish I had been able to afford such a gown at my wedding, Sophie. I told you about your grandparents, how I came from a family of sharecroppers. We couldn't afford to put bread on the table each night, much less buy me a new dress to wear when I married your father."

"Is that why you make sure Rosemarie and I are impeccably dressed?"

"I want my daughters to have what I couldn't."

"But you married Daddy, anyway. Out of love."

"Yes, of course I love your father. We were fortunate enough to surpass those lean years because of our persistence. But Sophie, a marriage can't be built on love alone. It needs a foundation of security. The man you marry must be willing to work hard to provide for you and your future children, the same as your father did for me."

Sophie thought of Dusty and his twenty-five acres of land. The whole summer he had been acquiring property and planning for a house and she didn't know anything about it. All for her.

"Consider yourself blessed to enjoy the fruits of your family's labor. Chad will be able to give you even more."

What could he give her more of? For the moment, he wouldn't give her so much as the respect to let her say yes or no to marrying him. She wondered what the future would hold for her and her soon-to-be husband. Would he exert the same degree of control upon any children God chose to bless them with?

And what about Dusty? She knew it was going to be impossible to look upon him again without caring, without feeling any sort of affection for him. His face would forever serve to remind her of what could never be.

For the first few days after their meeting, Dusty had hope. Hope Sophie would come to her senses. Hope she would change her mind. But as the weeks passed he struggled to keep that hope from dimming.

Dusty worked on building his house over the course of August. When work on the ranch wasn't enough to keep the ache from his heart, he took to adding more to the house's structural foundation. The other cowhands helped him when they had nothing more pressing or entertaining to do in their spare time. By the end of the month, he had two rooms put in, and space for a stove in what would be the kitchen.

He planned to put the roof on by November, but there was no need to rush so long as he got it completed by the first winter's snow.

After all, he often heard the wind rasp between the foundations of the house, *she won't be here when it's finished.*

The men never asked him if he planned on attending Sophie's wedding. Dusty never told them. The Saturday arrived one cool September morning when he went out to the stables to saddle his horse.

"Where are you going?" Mr. Mabrey was there, cleaning out the hooves of a young gelding.

"Not much work to be done until this afternoon, sir. I thought I'd head out this morning."

"You wouldn't be thinking of heading into town to see that girl get married, would you?"

"I might be."

The ranch owner scraped at the crevices of the gelding's front hoof. "Don't take your guns to town."

Dusty understood Mabrey's concern. "They're locked in a chest in the bunkhouse."

Mabrey looked at him to be certain. "Just make sure they stay there. I'm not looking to hire another worker because one got thrown into jail for shooting a bridegroom. Don't raise your fists, neither."

As much as he wanted to teach Chad a thing or two about coercing Sophie, he wasn't about to ruin her day by engaging in a fistfight. "Rest easy, Mr. Mabrey. I don't intend on getting myself into a fix over a woman today."

"Then what do you plan on visiting the church for?"

Dusty grabbed his saddle off the rack. He wanted his will to have as much bravado as his words. Folks said he could never quit Sophie. "To see if she actually goes through with it."

"And if she does?"

"I'll let her be."

"You sure about that?"

"Don't have much choice." He readied his horse and rode from the stables.

On the way to town, Dusty noted the starkness of the

landscape. Wide open, as empty as his soul felt at that moment. Dirt blew off the road and into his face in grainy pebbles that stung his eyes.

Today was the last day he'd see Sophie Charlton as an unmarried woman. Let the town laugh at him a final time as he watched her give her hand over to another man. In a few hours, he'd be back at the ranch and on his way to forgetting about her for good. He hoped.

"Do you, Sophie, take Chad to be your lawfully wedded husband, to honor and cherish, for as long as you both shall live?"

Sophie turned away from Reverend Winford to glance at the wedding guests seated in the decorated pews behind her. Almost every citizen of Assurance was present to attend what should have been the happiest day of her life. Instead, uncertainty and dread filled the spaces in her mind where elation was supposed to be.

She suppressed a cough in her dry throat as she caught the eyes of the groom's parents. Newly reelected Mayor Hooper and his wife sat across from her own mother and father. All of them looked at her with gazes fixed and expectant.

An arranged marriage. That's all it was, and she knew it.

Reverend Winford cleared his throat. Chad squeezed her white-gloved hand to bring her attention back to the altar. But just then she spotted him. At the rear of church, standing in the open doorway, was someone that Sophie thought would never show.

Dusty leaned his long and lanky frame against the door. He hadn't bothered to change out of his scuffed boots and faded work shirt that had more or less been his uniform since she had first met him. His hair was uncombed. More blond today than brown.

"Dusty," Sophie whispered beneath her veil.

He didn't hear her. She didn't expect him to, but he could see her. He stared as though she were the only living being in the sanctuary. Sophie became locked in the target point of his eyes.

Reverend Winford repeated the question louder. "Sophie, do you take Chad to be your lawfully wedded husband, to honor and cherish, for as long as you both shall live?"

Dusty's look challenged her. He didn't move any further into the church. Crossing his arms in front of his chest, he awaited her response to the question that would seal her to Chad Hooper forever.

One day.

She remembered Dusty's words to her a year ago at the wedding of Reverend Winford and Marissa Pierce. A promise that she would be his at a future time. *One day you'll see, Miss Sophie.* He followed that promise with an assured, almost rakish smile and continued to pursue her, no matter how many times she turned him down.

Sophie scoffed at Dusty then, but a peculiar sensation washed over her now as she stared at him. She could have been more insistent that he leave her alone, but even in those earlier times, somewhere deep inside, she didn't want him to. Her skin tingled and warmed as though he'd touched her. Her breathing sped as it did when she tried to keep from laughing at his antics.

That boyish charm would no longer be reserved for her if she became Mrs. Chad Hooper today.

"No!" She turned back to her groom, voice and hands trembling. "I'm sorry, Chad…but I can't!" Sophie pulled away from his grasp and ran down the aisle.

She felt a tug on the train of her dress as it ripped from the hands of Linda, her maid of honor. Linda's squeal reached high up to the church rafters. Commotion ensued as Sophie hiked up the full skirt to her ankles and dashed after

Dusty. Outside the prairie wind wrenched the veil from her face and tore her hair loose from its pins. "Dusty!"

His long legs took one stride for her every three as he walked away from the church. In one fluid motion, he swung into the saddle of his horse. "You went and did your choosing, Sophie. It wasn't me in that church standin' beside you."

"But I'm not going to marry Chad. Didn't you hear?"

He pulled on the reins as she ran toward the horse. "I heard, but that has nothing to do with me."

The horse's tail flicked across her dress when he turned the stallion in a different direction. Sophie tried to speak, but the words stuck like glue to the roof of her mouth. Dusty never turned her down before. Never. Finally, she was able to call out. "I know who I want. It's you."

"You'd better talk to your parents about that. They might change your mind."

"Dusty, I'm sorry. You believe me, don't you?"

"I'll be seein' you, Miss Sophie." Dusty rode away without so much as a second glance.

Chapter 27

Sophie choked on the dirt and debris that Dusty's horse kicked up as he rode in the direction out of town. Panic welled inside her as he left her behind, the last thing she expected him to do after she chose him.

You deserve it, vain and frivolous little girl. The elements left her bare and exposed, as if the whole world could see her folly and laugh.

She would not go back inside that church. All those people, her friends, family, Chad. She couldn't face them. It was all over.

She ran down the path leading to the farm. Behind her, people scuffled out of the church, calling her name. Someone would come after her soon, but there could be no stopping. No turning back.

Sophie carried an armful of tulle as she ran through the forested area and past the lake shore. Mud splattered on her legs. The weight of her train dragged as it collected stagnant water and silt. She continued to pull it along. The strength of her legs waned as the path sloped upward.

She was halfway to the farm when she heard her father yell behind her. The wagon wheels creaked and the axles groaned as he drove the wagon hard through the path strewn with ruts and uneven terrain.

"Get in this wagon now," he thundered, exertion and anger turning his face a deep shade of red.

Sophie's legs quaked beneath her layers of petticoats and bustle. She had to be strong and stand up to him. "I'm not going back to that wedding. I will not marry Chad."

"I didn't say you were going back to church. I said get into this wagon."

She looked down at her dress and realized just how ruined it was. Beads torn from the bodice, seams torn all along the skirt. Linda's work had completely gone to waste. "I want to go home."

He extended his arm to aid her onto the bench. With effort she pulled her straggling train up after her and climbed back to the floor of the wagon where she could keep the train from getting caught in the wheels. The canvas cloaked her from the world as her father drove her the rest of the way home.

"Go into the house," he told her once he helped her from the wagon. He and Mr. Kent set to unharnessing the horses. The new hired hand spared her and her bedraggled attire a curious glance, but kept his mouth shut.

Sophie looked up the road and saw another wagon coming. Her mother and siblings rode with Linda's family. As they got closer, she could see that her mother was livid.

"I said to get into the house." Her father lost patience and shouted again.

She made haste for the door, shutting it behind her. Outside she heard him talking, thanking Mr. Walsh for taking the family home. She walked through the hallway to get to the stairs before they came in.

The door opened and shut. "Sophie, where are you?" Her mother's voice rang.

She walked back to the front of the house. David and her younger siblings passed her to go up to the second floor, hardly daring to look at her. Her father was the last to come inside. Sophie braced herself for the storm that was about to ensue.

"What were you thinking?" he roared. "Chad Hooper is the mayor's son. You've humiliated yourself, the Hoopers, and this family in front of the whole town!"

"I'm sorry I embarrassed you, Daddy, but I couldn't go through with it."

Her mother grabbed her arm, fingers pinching, and led her into the sitting room. Sophie noticed her trousseau trunk and valises set in the corner, still waiting to be taken to the mayor's residence. They would have a long wait.

"This is a disgrace, you rejecting Assurance's most eligible bachelor. Anyone can get a man, Sophie, but you have to *earn* someone who has high status." Her mother turned her loose in the middle of the room. "Don't you realize the odds are slim for a young lady to marry up in this town? Have you forgotten our struggles in Louisiana?"

Her mother's constant reminders of their lean years hit Sophie like rotten fruit at a county fair dunking booth. Ever since they arrived in Kansas, her parents groomed her to rise above her humble beginnings to a life of privilege, even at the expense of happiness. She couldn't tolerate the idea any longer. "I don't love Chad."

"What did you say?"

Sophie tore off her gloves and kicked off her white silk wedding slippers on the elaborate woven rug of the sitting room. Little remained of them after her race past the lake, humiliated and heartbroken. "I won't be trapped in a loveless marriage just so I can be *comfortable.*"

Both parents scoffed. "Be seated," her father directed.

She plopped onto her mother's white fainting couch, barely able to hold down the dirty mass of lace and tulle that fanned over her lap. Why did she choose such an ornate wedding dress, as tiny as she was? The frock may have looked good on the girl in *Godey's Ladies Book*, but it made her feel like the cream filling in a pastry puff.

"You don't know what makes a good marriage," her father rumbled on. "You could have had one today instead of running after that cowboy."

"He was your hired hand, Daddy, and you used to think highly of him."

"That was before he went to great lengths to entice you to throw your life away and to turn my own son against me. You and David were never so disobedient. Sterling's ruined this family."

"Dusty didn't do those things." She got up. Her father made her return to her seat.

"If I see him near you again, if he comes upon this land, I will take action with the full force of the law behind me."

Sophie almost put the fainting couch to its intended use as her head swam with the realization that her father intended to have Dusty shot or thrown into jail. "Please don't hurt him."

Her mother threw her hands in the air. "I can't believe you persist in defending that scoundrel. If he is without fault as you claim, then why did he leave you calling after him outside the church?"

Sophie's heart broke again as she relived the moment that he turned his back on her for good. "I made my choice too late."

"You made the wrong choice. Now no eligible man in this town will have you. I don't see how you will ever get past this scandal."

She didn't argue with her mother. Scandal was not the most pressing matter. With Dusty gone, she couldn't see how she would get past the following days and weeks without despairing of what she truly lost.

The *clop-clop* of Gabe's hooves did little to drown the pitch of Sophie's cries that still echoed in Dusty's ears. A part of him had wanted to turn his horse around and lift Sophie into the saddle with him. However, a voice in his head had kept him riding for the horizon.

How can you be sure she will actually leave her family and the comforts of wealth behind for you?

For years he waited for Sophie to choose him, but the events of the past summer and seeing her today, about to marry someone else, succeeded in tearing him up and sowing doubt in his mind. *Even if she doesn't want Chad, ultimately her loyalty lies with her folks. Not you.*

That's what made him turn so cold. That's why he left her at the church. Her parents would never accept him, never respect him. Even if Sophie did marry him, could she handle living without the blessing and support of her parents? Could he? And after all the comforts she had grown used to, could she be happy living with the hardships of ranch living?

Dusty blinked and the entrance to the Zephyr Ranch was before him. Now he'd never know the answer to those questions. Maybe Sophie's father had already smoothed things over and got her to marry Chad. She had her life. Now he had to make his.

You could never make her happy. The wind made the sign creak on its hinges like an old door closing. That same force attempted to press on Dusty's heart to close it to Sophie for good.

Sophie spent a sleepless night in bed that evening and stayed home from church Sunday morning. She gave her father the engagement ring to return to Chad's family, glad to be rid of it but remorseful that she allowed events to culminate to such a point.

Reverend Winford paid her family a visit in the afternoon. She was drying dishes in the kitchen when she heard him talking to her mother in the hallway.

"If it's possible, Mrs. Charlton, I would like to have a word alone with your daughter. Is she able to receive visitors?"

"Just a moment, Reverend. I'll see."

Sophie dried her hands on her apron. Why couldn't he have given her time to bear her shame in private before coming over to lecture her on how sinfully she behaved the day before? She considered telling her mother not to allow Reverend Winford to come in, but knew it would be of no use. Her parents were still irate and thin of patience with her, and would be for some time to come.

Her mother stuck her head in the kitchen doorway. "Reverend Winford is here to see you. Straighten your appearance and go into the sitting room." She left without waiting for a reply.

Sophie removed her apron and smoothed down her hair. She walked into the sitting room where her mother offered the Reverend a slice of pumpkin pie, a dessert that was originally intended for the wedding reception.

"No, thank you, Mrs. Charlton. I don't intend to stay long." He sat down in her father's chair across from the couch.

Sophie greeted him after her mother left. "I'm told you wanted to speak to me."

"I've come to see how you were feeling since yesterday. Can we talk?"

She remembered the old pastor Reverend Thomas coming to the house years before he left town with his family. Sophie couldn't see herself being counseled by Reverend Winford, a man not so much older than she, and one who witnessed her snub Chad at a dance last year. A new flood of embarrassment carried over her. "If you don't mind, Reverend, I've been admonished many times since I ran from what would have been my wedding yesterday. My mother and father will no doubt continue to reprove me for months to come."

"I didn't come to scold you, Sophie. Since yesterday, I've been praying for you to have strength to carry through your decision."

Startled, she dropped onto the couch. "Why would you do that? Everyone else wishes I had married Chad."

"It's not what other people want that matters here. Marriage is a union between man, woman, and God. How can you honor God in your marriage if you can't love the person you're with? Yes, a wedding is meant to be a celebration of the whole community when a couple is joined together, but without love between man and wife that celebration is a sham and a lie."

She realized that he was sensing the pressures that had led to her decision, perhaps even blaming her parents for the botched wedding. But she knew she'd played a part too. She looked at the pattern on the rug. "I was wrong for leading Chad on in the beginning. I let him court me because I thought he was dashing. He seemed quite the catch after he came back from college. He was successful at the bank and had a good name."

"Money and status don't always ensure a happy marriage, Sophie. I know that's not the popular view but it's the truth."

Sophie hoped her parents were somewhere listening. "No one would ever have approved if I confessed to caring for Dusty."

The Reverend smiled sympathetically. "But you did confess it."

"Yes, and it didn't matter. I waited so long and did so many things to make him fed up with me." She looked into the Reverend's discerning gaze. "You don't have to be kind. I know you remember some of the ways that I've treated him. It's no wonder that man despises me."

"I don't think Dusty despises you. He may be hurt or angry, but he's been smitten with you for a long time."

"You didn't hear the words he had for me yesterday. He's not coming back this time."

Reverend Winford was silent as the clock ticked through half a minute. "What are you prepared to do if he does come back?"

The possibility of such an idea brought light to Sophie's gloom. "I'd ask him to forgive me, and tell him that I'd never be so callous with him again."

"And if he doesn't come back?"

The gloom returned. "I don't think there's much I can do in that circumstance, now is there?"

"You can do something. Dusty may not be here today for you to talk to, but God is. You can pray to Him for forgiveness and healing."

Sophie bit her lip in trepidation. "If my earthly parents are cross with me I know that I've displeased my Father in heaven even more so."

"The Lord's ways aren't your family's ways, Sophie. He's always patient and ready to listen. You can't drive Him away." Reverend Winford stood. "If you like, we can pray before I leave."

Sophie got to her feet. "You may be standing awhile. I have quite a bit of forgiveness I need to ask for."

CHAPTER 28

One month later

$\mathcal{D}$USTY DROVE THE last nail into the wood shingle. There. The roof to his house was complete, with time to spare before the first hard frost. He climbed down from the ladder and stood back to admire his handiwork. Footsteps came from behind.

"Got another letter for you, Sterling."

Dusty caught the envelope Joe tossed his way. He didn't need to glance at the lacy handwriting on the front to know who sent it. "Thanks." He pocketed the letter without opening it.

"You know, I should start chargin' a fee for bein' a messenger. This is the fourth letter in three weeks."

"Where'd she leave it this time?"

"Her brother followed me into the general store and handed the letter to me. He knows I go into town each Saturday. Guess some folks are too particular to use the post office."

"She doesn't want people to know she's writing to me." *Especially her parents.* Dusty reflected on the bitter edge of his thoughts and made himself focus on something other than Sophie. Despite not writing back to her and staying away from town, thinking about her was one old habit that refused to lie down and die. "Got the roof on."

Joe looked from him to the new roof over the house. "You're 'bout to have that house completed by winter."

"Looks like it." Dusty gathered the box of nails and tools beneath the ladder to take back to the ranch. He carried it over to the supply wagon used to transport the wood to his land.

"You ever read those letters Miss Sophie sends you?" Joe grabbed the ladder and followed him.

"Yeah." He recalled the words from the last three he kept in his saddlebag. Words of apology, asking for forgiveness. He already forgave her, but that did nothing to solve the other obstacles in their path.

"She must have something important to say. You ever think of writin' back?"

"Got nothing to say to her, Joe. Not with her folks dead set against me." He dropped the hammer and box of nails on the wagon floor.

"They may have changed their minds. Go see about her."

Dusty sighed. "I'm not playing that fool anymore."

Joe placed the ladder inside the wagon. "It sounds like you're playin' a different one."

The severity of Joe's declaration made Dusty pay attention. The man wasn't normally harsh. "You haven't been in this town as long as I have. You don't know how her folks value wealth and status over all else."

"Is that what's botherin' you, not being rich? It seems to worry you more than it does Miss Sophie. You said she apologized when she ran after you at the wedding. Instead of acceptin' it, you rejected her in front of the whole town."

"It wasn't like that."

"It sounds like an eye for an eye to me."

"I didn't do it for revenge." Dusty kicked at a wagon wheel. One thing he didn't want to hear from his friend was a church sermon. "Her father will never accept me, and without his blessing I doubt she'd be happy."

"Have you even asked?" Joe shrugged his heavy shoulders. "How long are you gonna keep playin' the hired hand, doing what you think Mr. Charlton wants? You gotta step up, speak up, if you want his respect."

Dusty stared at him. What if Joe was right?

Joe put an encouraging hand on his shoulder. "It just ain't like you to hang back. Becoming your own man ain't easy, but the Lord knows you've proven yourself. You got a house and some land to offer now. You deserve some respect. Now all you have to do is ask for it." He slapped Dusty on the shoulder. "Come on. Let's get this wagon back in case Mabrey needs it later."

Before leaving, Dusty glanced again at the newly built house. Proof. Yes, maybe that's what he'd needed. And now he had some. Would it be enough?

One month, and no word from Dusty. Sophie wondered if her letters reached him. David told her he gave the letters to Joe to deliver each time he saw the assistant foreman in town. Mr. Emmers struck her as an honest man, so he wasn't a likely cause for Dusty not responding.

Maybe Dusty just didn't open her letters. She remembered how cold he was at the wedding, and so completely unmoved when she ran after him to declare her love. How could she blame him for wanting to leave her standing in the road outside the church? She had treated him as a plaything for so long that he just grew tired of her games.

It looked like she was going to have to start thinking of life without him. Each time she considered the prospect, her stomach gave her such a sick feeling as Mrs. Hooper's oyster stuffing never could.

She went to town with her family on the second Saturday of October, carrying the fifth letter to Dusty in the pocket of her wool coat. Winter was coming. The sky was gray and the grass had since dried into a brown crust, signaling the end of warm, vibrant life.

Sophie felt just as withered as she walked along the sidewalk past Linda's seamstress shop and the general store. People treated her differently since the wedding scandal. Thankfully, Chad had taken a job at a bank in Philadelphia, leaving Assurance for good. Still, citizens gave her odd looks from across the street, knowing glances when they thought she couldn't see. Not only that, the fact that her petition gained women the right to vote in school elections further contributed to her tarnished reputation. After all, fewer people had signed the petition than not.

She pretended not to hear a boy snicker at her when she walked past.

At the far end of the square, Sophie caught sight of a tall, thin man going into the Arthurs' shoe store. Not being able to distinguish his face, she saw the hat he wore. It looked similar to Dusty's.

Her steps faltered. Could she go inside the store and talk to him? Once he saw her, would he walk away and leave her standing speechless again? More risk was in not finding out. She didn't know when the chance would come again where the two of them would be in town at the same time.

She quickened her pace until she arrived at the door's threshold. He stood at the counter while the Reverend's wife, Marissa, wrote something down in a ledger book. Sophie strained to see his profile under the broad brim of his hat. The long nose didn't belong to Dusty.

The man turned and she saw that it was just someone else wearing a tan Stetson. He excused himself as he left the store as quickly as he arrived.

"Hello, Sophie," Marissa greeted her from the counter. "Can I help you?"

It occurred to her that she was blocking the doorway, but Sophie was uneasy about entering the store. "Actually, I thought I recognized that man, but I was wrong."

"Mr. Fontaine was here to check on an order he placed earlier. Who were you looking for?"

"It doesn't matter. I shouldn't have come in." Sophie pivoted to leave when a question pressed at the forefront of her mind. She stopped, hand on the door. "How did you stand it, Marissa?"

"Stand what?" Marissa came from behind the register to go to the window. She adjusted a sign.

"Being an…an outcast. Before you married Reverend Winford, people treated you bad." Sophie couldn't look at her when she talked, knowing full well that she was one of those people.

Marissa finished straightening the sign. "I still get looks and whispers, even from a few church members. Eventually you come to accept that some people will never change their minds about you."

"Marissa, I'm sorry for the things I said to you before when you worked at the saloon."

The Reverend's wife studied her. "That was more than a year ago. I've since forgiven you. Why are you bringing it up now?"

Sophie's voice broke. "I know now what it feels like. To be shunned, I mean. Everyone knows what happened at the botched wedding, but I just couldn't go through with it." A hot tear trickled down her cheek. "I hurt so many people that day when I waited too long to choose Dusty. Now he's not here, either."

Marissa continued to listen, her face calm and without judgment. Embarrassed at the emotions she could barely keep under control, Sophie wiped the tear from her face before she could break into sobs. "I'm not asking for words of comfort."

"It's alright, Sophie. You can talk to me."

"You're the only one that understands."

"I don't know about that." Marissa pointed up the street. "I think I see Dusty going into the bank."

Sophie came closer to the window and stood on tiptoe to see over a shoe display. This time it was Dusty. She recognized his easy gait as he strolled inside the building.

"You'd better hurry before he can leave."

She almost ran into two customers on her way out of the store. "Thank you, Marissa."

"Sophie." Marissa gave her a smile. "I'm glad that you're following your heart."

"I hope I can make Dusty appreciate it too."

She squeezed around the customers and darted through the street. With coat flapping behind her, crocheted bonnet slipping back from her head, she made a spectacle as she reached the doors of the bank. A bearded man arrived at the same time as she. Sophie collided into his arm. "I beg your pardon, sir."

"You sure are in some hurry, little lady. You'd think the money in the bank was going to run off and leave ya."

She stood back and noticed the dirty stains on his coat and the unkempt appearance of his facial hair. He must have been traveling for a long time. The suede finish of the satchel he carried was worn to the grain. "I should have watched where I was going."

"No worries, ma'am. Here you go." He held the door open for her. He kept the other hand in his pocket.

She rushed inside the bank and looked about for Dusty. He stood behind four men waiting for the teller. "Dusty?"

He looked over his shoulder. Sophie froze in wait for his response. Suddenly his face went from neutral to alarm.

"Look out." He pulled her to him just as a gunshot rang through the bank.

She lost her balance and fell to the hard floor. Shouts sounded from all around. Pairs of feet scuffled in her line of vision. Sophie raised her head to see the man in the filthy coat behind her, now brandishing a pistol, aimed at the stunned teller behind the counter. The first bullet struck the wood paneling of the teller's window.

"Everybody stay where you are and there won't be no trouble." He strode to the front. "You, sir, put the money in here." He pulled the satchel from his shoulder and tossed it on the counter. The teller's hands trembled as he reached for it.

Sophie felt Dusty's protective arm around her. She heard the bank door swing open. Another man came in with a gun and remained standing at the entrance.

"It's the Lubbett Brothers," the customer in front of Dusty said. He was rewarded with a kick to the face from the first bank robber.

"You know who we are, son? Then you know to keep your yap shut."

The teller put four stacks of bills into the satchel, along with a bag of coins. "That's all we keep up front."

The bank robber blocking the door called to his accomplice. "Cordell, tell him to go in the back for some more money. I know they keep it somewhere around here."

Sophie could hear the teller's teeth chatter in his head as he spoke. "The safe is in the back. I'll get the money out of it. Please don't harm anybody."

Cordell kept his gun on the teller. "Hurry up."

The frightened teller scrambled to one of the back offices and jangled the door knob. "It's locked. I can't get in."

Cordell swore. "Get on the ground. Now." He swiveled the pistol on the remaining bank customers. "When the bag comes your way, put your valuables in."

Sophie watched as he thrust the satchel in the first customer's face. The man, with blood trickling from his nose, reached into his pocket and tossed his wallet into the bag.

"The chain watch too," Cordell ordered.

The man dispensed of his timepiece before proceeding to put his head back down on the floor. The next man, wearing a navy coat, threw his money clip and a ring into the bag. The next two followed suit until the bag came to Dusty. He gave Cordell his billfold.

"Your turn, sweetheart." The bank robber pushed the satchel Sophie's way. "Let's see what moneybags you got under that dress."

"I'm not carrying any money. I came to town with my family."

Cordell lowered the pistol under her chin. The cold metal bit into the soft flesh of her lower palate. "Pretty faces don't fool me. You just don't walk into a bank with no money on you."

"Please." She choked as he pressed the tip of the barrel hard against her throat. "I'm telling the truth."

"She's not lying to you," Dusty spoke. "She came in here because she saw me."

Cordell looked at the two of them and smiled broken teeth. "Well, ain't that just the sweetest thing? You hear 'im, Harrison? Got us a pair of lovers in here. Think I should put one in him or her first?"

Cordell's brother glanced outside. "We better move. People know somethin's goin' on at the bank."

"In a minute. One last time, little lady. Your valuables."

Sophie shut her eyes as he cocked the gun.

"Cordell, they're coming!"

Sophie heard a commotion at the door. She opened her eyes to see it burst open with several men shouting and grabbing at Harrison. Cordell uttered another expletive and seized her up by the hair.

"Touch my brother and I will make this blond heifer's hair blood red." He moved the pistol to her skull. "Turn him loose."

Sophie heard Cordell grunt before feeling the butt of the pistol slam her shoulder and clatter to the floor. She fell again as a force behind her sent her plunging forward. Dusty dove for the man's legs and brought him down. The two struggled in a tangle of fists.

"Sophie, the gun," Dusty yelled.

The firearm lay inches from her foot. As she squirmed to kick it to Dusty, Harrison pulled away from the men holding him at the door. He raised his gun at her. Dusty let go of Cordell and dropped in front of Sophie as Harrison opened fire. The sound of the shot reverberated off the walls of the bank.

The men regained control of Harrison, wrenching the gun from his hands and beating him to the ground. Sophie looked down at Dusty as blood streamed from his left arm. He pushed to his knees.

"No, stay down." As she said the words, a hand grabbed her coat collar. She clawed at Cordell, screaming. Dusty twisted, made for Cordell's dropped pistol with his right hand, grabbed it, aimed, and squeezed the trigger.

The bullet fired so close that Sophie could hear the air crackle with heat. Cordell's body jerked and fell away from her, not to move again. She scrambled from him and crawled over to Dusty.

A pool of blood welled under him, continuing to spread as he sank to the floor. She put her arm beneath his head and discovered that the blood was not flowing from his arm but from a wound in his chest. His hazel eyes glazed over.

"Get the doctor!" She screamed at the bank customers that remained to ogle them. The man in the navy coat ran out, followed by the teller. She touched Dusty's face as it began to pale over. "You're going to be alright, Dusty. Do you hear me?"

"The Lubbett Brothers?" he mumbled.

"They've been caught. You shot one."

A spasm racked his body. "I think one got me too."

Sophie grew dizzy as his blood trickled warm through her fingers. "That bullet wasn't meant for you. You jumped in front of me."

The corners of his mouth lifted. "I reckon I'm crazy that way."

He slipped into unconsciousness.

CHAPTER 29

USTY WOKE UP in a room that smelled strongly of carbolic acid and chloroform. His eyes adjusted to a spectacled man seated beside him. As the fog lifted from his head, he recognized the man as Dr. Gillings.

"Good. You're awake. We were worried about you, Dusty." The doctor stood and pulled the curtains back from a window. Sunlight burst through in a stream of painful, yellow light.

"Draw the curtains again." Dusty groaned and tried to turn on his side. Sharp pain ran through his chest and down his arm. He pulled back the bedsheet and saw that his torso was bandaged to the waist.

"Careful. You've been shot and lost a lot of blood. That wound's going to take a long time to heal."

"How long have I been out?"

Dr. Gillings appeared again at the bedside. "You were unconscious for several hours after the incident, and have been sleeping for two days. You're lucky that bullet missed your heart by two inches."

Dusty remembered the robbery at the bank. His mind shot to Sophie and he tried to sit up. The skin pulled where the bullet struck him in the chest.

"I told you to be careful. Don't rip those stitches."

"Sorry, Doctor. I need to see Sophie. She was at the bank with me when the Lubbett Brothers tried to rob it."

"No one has to worry about those men now. The one, you shot in the lung, and the other's sitting in jail waiting for the hanging judge. The sheriff says you're to get the reward for shooting Cordell, whether he lives or meets his Maker."

Dusty didn't care about the money. "Is Sophie alright?"

"Miss Charlton and her father are outside waiting. I'll send them in."

While Dusty waited, he saw his clothes folded on the table in front of the room, his boots on the floor. He looked at a cabinet that held swabs and physician's instruments.

The door opened and Sophie's father entered. "How are you feeling, Dusty?"

"Like the time I felt when your plow mule kicked me, Mr. Charlton. Only worse. How's Sophie?"

"She's fine. I had her wait because I wanted to speak to you first." Mr. Charlton sat in the chair by the bed. "Thank you for protecting my daughter from those bank robbers. She told me that you shielded her from a bullet and shot the man who attacked her."

"I love your daughter, sir. I would've died for her."

"You almost did." Sophie's father steepled his fingers as he looked at the physician's instruments in the cabinet. "And Sophie seems to feel the same way about you."

The wound over Dusty's heart produced a constant dull ache. "I'd like to prove to you and Mrs. Charlton that I can provide for Sophie."

"Dusty, if I step away and allow my daughter to make her own decisions, I don't want her getting hurt. Do you understand?"

"Yes, sir."

Mr. Charlton got up from the chair. "I'll get Sophie to come in. You make sure to heal, son."

Dusty couldn't believe Mr. Charlton's gracious act of extending the olive branch. It must have taken a heaping dose of restraint for him not to want to shelter his daughter in the house forever after the bank incident. Dusty would make sure not to alter Mr. Charlton's new and fledgling trust.

That's if Sophie still had the heart to forgive him for distancing himself this past month.

She came into the room, a little tired, dark circles under her eyes, but no less than beautiful to him. He wanted to reach out to her, but his newly minted badge of courage made even the thought of raising his arm a foolish fancy.

Sophie approached the bed where Dusty rested. She was used to seeing him outside moving, full of masculine energy. The small confines of a doctor's office was no place for him.

"Hello, angel." He welcomed her with the drawl she enjoyed hearing, but she was taken aback by what he called her.

"I'm no angel."

"You're about the closest thing I've seen to one. I haven't treated you like so."

She didn't take the chair, but stood at the head of the bed. "No one could blame you after the foolish things I've done."

"We've both done wrong to each other. I was wrong for turning my back on you when you ran out of the church."

She looked at the bandages wrapping his chest and arm. "You had a right to. I cared more about what other people thought than I cared about you."

"You changed your mind later than I would have liked, but you still didn't go through with the wedding. I'm sorry I let my hurt turn into a grudge. I hope you can forgive me."

Sophie let her fingers roam through his sandy hair that tousled and bent into a cowlick at the crown. How could she ever prefer controlled, lacquered locks to this? "I forgive you, Dusty. Did you receive my letters?"

"Each one. I'm sorry I didn't write back. I hope you forgive me that, as well."

"I had another letter to give you that day I went into the bank. Do you still want it?"

"Not unless you wrote sayin' you want to marry me before Christmas."

Sophie's stomach fluttered. "You mean that?"

He pushed himself up on the bed with his uninjured arm. The action still made him wince. "I can't offer what you're used to, Sophie, but I can give you everything I do have. A house with room to grow, land to call your own, and more love than you know what to do with."

Joy and warmth spread through her. God had answered her prayers and given her a second chance. "I don't deserve how good you are to me."

"You deserve more, and one day I plan to give you that. So, Miss Sophie, you think you can live on a ranch surrounded by Herefords, shorthorns, and surly cowhands?"

She laughed. "I can, if you can live in a house filled with stacks of *Godey's Ladies Books* and serials of *The Adventures of Lady Whitecastle*."

He grinned. "We'll have our own adventures."

"Is that a promise, Dustin Sterling? Because if it is, there's only one way to seal it."

Sophie leaned in for a kiss.

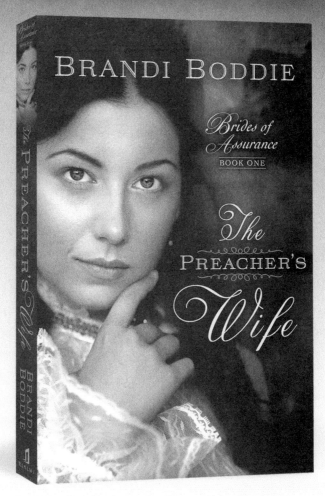